The Tattered Quilt

Return of the
Half-Stitched *Amish* Quilting Club

Wanda E. Brunstetter

Print ISBN 978-1-61626-086-6

eBook Editions:
Adobe Digital Edition (.epub) 978-1-62416-447-7
Kindle and MobiPocket Edition (.prc) 978-1-62416-446-0

All Scripture quotations are taken from the King James Version of the Bible.

All German-Dutch words are taken from the *Revised Pennsylvania German Dictionary* found in Lancaster County, Pennsylvania.

This book is a work of fiction. Names, characters, places, and incidents are either products of the author's imagination or used fictitiously. Any similarity to actual people, organizations, and/or events is purely coincidental.

Cover photography: Brandon Hill Photos

For more information about Wanda E. Brunstetter, please access the author's website at the following Internet address: www.wandabrunstetter.com

Published by Barbour Publishing, Inc., P.O. Box 719, Uhrichsville, Ohio 44683, www.barbourbooks.com

Our mission is to publish and distribute inspirational products offering exceptional value and biblical encouragement to the masses.

ecpa Member of the Evangelical Christian Publishers Association

Printed in Canada.

Dedication

In memory of my mother, Thelma Cumby,
who many years ago gave me her mother's tattered quilt.

If we love one another, God dwelleth in us,
and his love is perfected in us.
1 John 4:12

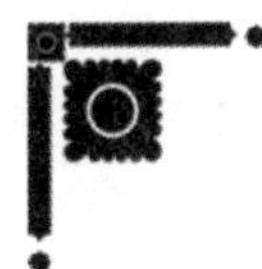

Prologue

Shipshewana, Indiana

Emma Miller's husband, Lamar, plunked a bottle of suntan lotion on the kitchen table in front of her and said, "How'd you like to take a little *feierdaag* and get away from these chilly days we've been having this fall?"

Her eyes widened. "You want us to go on a holiday?"

"That's right. I was thinking we could go down to Florida for a while. We can rent a place in Pinecraft." Lamar's green eyes sparkled as he drew his fingers through the ends of his full gray beard. "Just think how nice it would be to spend a little time on the beach."

Emma patted Lamar's hand affectionately. "That's a nice idea, but have you forgotten that I recently placed an ad for another six-week quilting class?"

"*Jah*, I know, but no one's answered the ad yet, so maybe you won't have any students this time."

Emma took a sip of hot tea. "I suppose that's a possibility, but I was looking forward to us teaching another class together. Weren't you, Lamar?"

"Of course; all the classes we've taught for the past year and a half have been great." Lamar leaned closer to Emma and touched her arm. "If no one signs up by the end of the week, will you go to Florida with me?"

Emma mulled things over, then finally nodded. "I suppose it would be nice to get a little sunshine and take some long walks on the beach, but we can't go until we get our roof fixed," she quickly added. "With all the rain we've had so far this fall, it could start to leak at any time if we don't get a new roof put on."

Plink! Plunk! Plink! Three drops of water landed in Emma's cup. She looked up at the ceiling and groaned. "Oh dear, I spoke too soon. I'm afraid it's already leaking."

"Not to worry." Lamar gave Emma a wide smile. "I called your roofer friend, Jan Sweet, and he and his coworker will start in on it next week."

Emma reached for her husband's calloused hand and gave his long fingers a tender squeeze. "Is it any wonder I said jah when you asked me to marry you? You're such a *schmaert* man."

"And you, Emma dear, are the best wife any man could want." Lamar leaned over and kissed Emma, causing her cheeks to warm. Even after more than a year of marriage, he could still make her blush.

Chapter 1

Middlebury, Indiana

Anna Lambright wanted her freedom. She'd turned eighteen a week ago, but her parents were holding her back. Most of the young people she knew had at least started their *rumschpringe*, but not Anna. Her folks held a tight rein and had forbidden Anna to do any of the things other kids did during their running-around years.

"What are they worried about? Do they think I'll get into trouble?" Anna mumbled as she tromped through the damp grass toward the barn to feed the cats. It wasn't fair that she couldn't have the freedom most of her friends had to experience some of the things English teenagers did.

When Anna entered the barn, the pungent odor of hay mixed with horse manure made her sneeze. *If I weren't Amish, what would I be doing right now?* she wondered, rubbing her eyes as they began to itch and water.

To make matters worse, Anna's mother thought Anna should do everything expected of an Amish woman. Anna didn't enjoy cooking, and sewing. They just weren't her thing. She'd tried sewing a dress and had made a mess of it. She couldn't even manage to sew something as simple as a pair of pillowcases without making stupid mistakes. Mom had tried teaching Anna to quilt, but Anna was all thumbs. Her stitches were uneven and much too big.

Anna felt like a misfit. She hadn't been baptized or joined the church yet, so she was free to leave if she wanted to. Only trouble was, where would she go, and how would she support herself? If she left, she'd have to stop working at Dad's window shop, because she was sure he wouldn't let her stay on.

Inside the barn, Anna spotted three cats—one white, one black, and one gray with white paws, sleeping on a bale of straw. As soon as they sensed her presence, they leaped off the bale and zipped across the room to their empty dishes.

"Are you *hungerich*?" Anna asked, reaching for the bag of cat food on a shelf near the door.

Meow! Fluffy, the all-white cat, stuck her nose in one of the empty dishes. The other two cats pawed at Anna's legs.

"Okay, okay, don't be in such a hurry." Anna filled the dishes and then set the food back on the shelf.

While the cats ate, Anna wandered over to the horses' stalls and stopped to watch Cindy, Mom's honey-colored horse, eat the oats Anna's fourteen-year-old brother, Dan, had given the mare a short time ago.

Anna didn't have a horse of her own. She borrowed Mom's whenever she had somewhere to go that was too far to walk or ride her bike. Anna actually preferred riding her bike. It was easier than trying to manage the horse. Even a horse as gentle and easygoing as Cindy could be unpredictable.

One time when Anna had gone to Shipshewana to run some errands for Mom, a motorcycle had spooked Cindy, and Anna had struggled to get the horse back under control. Her mouth went dry just thinking about what could have happened if she hadn't been able to get Cindy settled down. The nervous horse could have crossed into the other lane of traffic, run off the road into someone's fence, or taken off down the road.

Just last month a woman from their community had died in a buggy accident that happened between Middlebury and Shipshewana. Anna figured she'd be safer in a car, although even then there were no guarantees.

"Do you ever feel like breaking out of here and running away?" Anna murmured as the horse finished up with her oats.

Cindy's ears twitched as though in response; then she ambled across the stall and stuck her head over the gate.

Anna scratched behind the mare's ears. "What do you say, girl? Should we escape together?"

"Who are you talking to?" Dan asked, surprising Anna when he came out of nowhere.

"I was talking to Mom's *gaul*, and you shouldn't sneak up on me like that. Where were you anyway?" she asked, turning to look at her blond-haired brother.

"I was up in the hayloft." Dan's blue eyes twinkled, and he grinned at Anna like he'd been doing something special. "I like to go up there to think."

"What were you thinking about?"

He shrugged his broad shoulders. "Nothing really. Just pondering a few things."

Anna tipped her head. "Such as?"

"Wondering what I'll be doing next year, when I graduate from eighth grade."

"I thought you were gonna work for Dad in the window shop."

"I might, but I'm not sure yet. There could be something else I'd enjoy doing more."

Anna could certainly relate to that. Mom and Dad expected her to help out in the shop, answering the phone and taking orders from customers. The only part of the job she enjoyed was being able to use the computer. Because they had to order a lot of things online, they'd been given permission from the church leaders to have a computer in their shop. Of course, they'd never have one in their home. That was against the rules of their Amish church, and Mom and Dad were not about to knowingly break any rules. Anna enjoyed having access to the Internet. When things were slow at the shop, she would take a few moments to explore different websites showing places to visit. She knew without a doubt that spending a good deal of the day on the computer would have been no problem for her, if it were allowed. Anna couldn't believe all the information out there, available by just the click of a mouse.

"Have you ever thought about what it would be like if you didn't join the Amish church?" Anna asked her brother.

Dan shook his head vigorously. "No way! Where would I go? What would I do?" He reached out and stroked Cindy's neck. "Don't think I could be happy if I left our way of life."

Anna didn't say anything. If she told Dan the way she felt, he'd probably blab it to their folks. It was better if she kept her thoughts to herself, at least until she'd made a decision.

"I'd better get back in the house and help Mom with breakfast," Anna said.

"Okay, see ya inside. I've still got a couple of chores I need to do." Dan ambled away.

Anna shook her head. If her brother had chores to do, what was he doing up in the hayloft, thinking about his future? She gave Cindy a good-bye pat and hurried out of the barn.

When Anna stepped into the kitchen, she found Mom in front of their propane stove, stirring a pot of oatmeal. Anna wrinkled her nose. Oatmeal was not one of her favorite breakfast foods.

Anna studied her mother. She was only forty-seven years old but seemed to be aging fast. Maybe it was the fine wrinkles across her forehead, or it could be the dark circles beneath her pale blue eyes. Mom's hair was a mousy brown, and some telltale gray was showing through. Anna hoped she wouldn't look as haggard as Mom when she was in her forties. She hoped her light brown eyes wouldn't lose their sparkle, and that her auburn hair would keep the depth of its color well into her senior years.

"Did you get the cats fed?" Mom asked, breaking into Anna's musings.

Anna nodded. "They were as desperate as usual." She removed her jacket and the woolen scarf she'd worn over her stiff white covering. After hanging them on a wall peg, Anna picked off some cat hairs she noticed clinging to her dress and threw them in the garbage can under the kitchen sink.

"Did you notice how chilly our *wedder* is getting?" Mom questioned.

"Jah, and I don't like cold weather," Anna mumbled as she began setting the table. "Summer doesn't last long enough for me."

"Some chilly or rainy days are what we can expect during the fall. Winter will be here before we know it." Mom flashed Anna a smile. "Before you start setting the table, there's something I want to tell you."

"Oh? What's that?"

"Emma Miller will be starting another six-week quilting class next Saturday, and I signed you up." Mom's smile widened.

Anna's mouth dropped open. "What? Why would you do that? You know I don't sew."

"That's true, and since I haven't been successful at teaching you, I thought maybe Emma would have better luck."

Anna frowned. "But Mom. . ."

"No arguments, now. Your *daed* and I talked this over last night, and we think it's what you need. I went out to the phone shack earlier this morning and left Emma a message, letting her know that you'll be taking part in her next class." Mom patted Anna's shoulder. "If you give yourself a chance, I'm sure you'll learn a lot from Emma. From what I hear, she's a very good teacher. And who knows? You may even enjoy the class."

"Right," Anna muttered under her breath. She'd heard about Emma's quilting classes, and the last thing she wanted to do was sit in a room with a bunch of strangers.

Los Angeles, California

Carmen Lopez had only been out of bed a few minutes, when her telephone rang. She glanced at the clock on her bedside table, wondering who would be calling her at 5:00 a.m. The only reason she was up this early was because she had a story to cover in Santa Monica and wanted to get an early start before the freeway traffic reached its peak during rush hour. There was nothing worse than sitting in a traffic jam with irritated drivers honking their horns and hollering at each other. Carmen always wondered why they did that. Did those people think it would make the vehicles miraculously start moving? Being a reporter, she'd learned very quickly that people liked making statements in any way, shape, or form. Truth was, being engulfed in traffic made her nervous, bringing back the memory of the tragic way her precious sister, Lorinda, had died.

The phone rang a few more times, and Carmen finally picked up the receiver. "Hello," she said, stifling a yawn.

"Carmen, are you awake?"

"Oh, Mr. Lawrence. Yes, I'm up. I'll be heading to Santa Monica soon to cover that story about the recently opened homeless shelter."

"Forget about that. I put Eddie Simpson on it."

Carmen's brows lifted. "You gave my story away?"

"That's right. You don't have time to go to Santa Monica today."

"Yes, I do. I got up plenty early, and—"

"I just booked a flight for you to South Bend, Indiana, and you need to pack. Your plane leaves in four hours."

Carmen frowned. Andrew Lawrence could be a difficult boss at times, and he was a little overbearing, but he'd never pulled her off an assignment and sent another reporter in her place. And he'd never expected her to fly somewhere without giving her advanced notice. "Why are you sending me to Indiana?" she questioned.

"There's been a lot of media hype about the Amish lately, especially with some of the reality shows on TV about Amish kids who've left their families and gone wild," he said. "Since you have connections in Indiana, I figured you'd be the best person to get the lowdown on this. You know—find out why these kids go wild and why their folks look the other way."

"Get the lowdown?" Carmen's eyebrows puckered. "I have no connections in Indiana, sir. And what makes you think I can learn anything firsthand about Amish kids going wild?"

"Your brother-in-law lives there, doesn't he?"

"Well, yes, Paul lives in Elkhart, but—"

"Didn't you mention once that he knew some Amish people?"

"Not in Elkhart, but in Shipshewana," she explained. "Paul took some quilting classes from an Amish woman, but that was over a year ago."

"That's perfect! You can pick the man's brain, nose around the place, ask a lot of questions, and maybe get into a few Amish homes. I'm expecting you to write a good story that'll shed some light on why all Amish kids go wild during their days of running-around. . . ." His voice trailed off. "What is the Pennsylvania Dutch word for it. . .*rumschpringe*?"

"I think that's it, but I'm not sure if Paul has stayed in contact with the Amish woman who taught him to quilt. Also it could take some time to get that kind of information."

"No problem. Take all the time you need."

Carmen blew out her breath. "Mr. Lawrence, I really don't think. . . ."

"It's all set, Carmen. Your flight leaves at nine, so you'd better get packed and hustle yourself to the airport. Give me a call when you get there. Oh, and keep me posted as you gather information. I think this will be a great story. It could even win you a promotion if it's done well, so you'd better not let me down." Mr. Lawrence hung up before Carmen could say anything more.

Carmen sank to the edge of her bed and groaned. She had to admit she was intrigued by this assignment, and if a promotion came from doing it, that would be great. There was just one problem: Even if Paul was still friends with the Amish woman who'd taught him to quilt, there were no guarantees that he would tell Carmen anything. Things had been strained between her and Paul since Lorinda had been killed. For several months after the accident, Carmen had blamed Paul, thinking he could have done something to prevent it. And even though she'd gone to Elkhart once since Lorinda's funeral to see Paul's daughter, Sophia, she and Paul had never really resolved the issue.

It was ironic that Carmen had been thinking about Paul lately. In fact, she couldn't seem to get him out of her mind, no matter how hard she tried. Even before her boss called with this new assignment, her conscience had been bothering her about the strained relationship. Was it right to blame Paul for her sister's death? Was she using him in order to have someone to blame? Could her anger against him just be a cover-up for her own grief? Maybe the best thing to do was apologize to Paul for having blamed him and then ease into the request for him to introduce her to his Amish friend.

Dark brown eyes stared back at Carmen as she smiled at her twenty-four-year-old reflection in the mirror above her dresser. Her hair looked pretty good, even in its tangled state. Just like her sister, Carmen had long black, lustrous hair she could style any way she wanted. As she pulled her thick locks into a ponytail, her plans seemed to fall right into place. She would apologize to Paul. This trip might work right in with the new assignment she'd been given and ease her guilt at the same time. At least it was a step in the right direction.

Chapter 2

Mishawaka, Indiana

Blaine Vickers hated his job. Well, maybe not all of it—just when he was asked to do something he didn't feel comfortable with. Like only moments ago when his boss, Stuart Johnston, had asked Blaine to give a demonstration on fly-fishing to a group of wannabe fishermen who'd be visiting the sporting goods store tomorrow afternoon.

"Can't someone else do it?" Blaine asked as he and Stuart entered the break room together.

Stuart shook his head. "None of the other employees knows fly-fishing as well as you, my friend."

Blaine grunted. "But you know I'm not comfortable talking to people."

Stuart gave Blaine's shoulder a quick thump. "What are you talking about? You're a salesman, right? You talk to people every day."

"That's different. I talk to people one-on-one, not in a group setting where all eyes are on me." Blaine had never mentioned it to Stuart, but he hoped to someday own his own fishing tackle store. It wouldn't be a big place like the sporting goods store—just a small place where he'd sell only things fishermen needed. It was probably nothing but a pipe dream, but it was nice to have a goal and something to focus on rather than thinking he'd be stuck working here for the rest of his life. Not that working for Stuart was bad; Blaine just wanted to do his own thing.

Stuart raked his fingers through the back of his curly dark hair. "You'll do fine talking to those people. Don't sell yourself short."

Blaine meandered over to the coffeepot. What choice did he have? Stuart was his boss, and even though they were friends, if he wanted to keep his job he'd have to do what he was told, like it or not.

"Say, Blaine," Stuart said, joining him at the coffeepot, "I'm going fishing at Lake Shipshewana on Saturday. Since you're not scheduled to work that day, why don't you go with me? Unless you're gonna be busy doing something with your lady friend, that is."

Blaine shook his head. "Sue and I broke up a few weeks ago. I thought I'd mentioned it."

"If you did, I must've forgotten. Between staying busy here at the store, going to my kids' games, and trying to keep Pam happy, I can only focus on one thing at a time." Stuart added a spoonful of sugar to his coffee and took a sip. "How come you and Sue broke up? I mean, you've been going out for a few years now, right?"

Blaine sighed. "It's complicated."

"It or Sue?"

"Both." Blaine pulled out a chair and took a seat at the table. He was glad he and Stuart were the only ones in the room, because he wasn't about to spill his guts in front of anyone else. "It's like this—I'm ready to get married, but Sue says she's not. I made the mistake of pushing the issue, and she broke up with me." As Blaine recalled the painful conversation, he rubbed his finger over the small scar on his chin, which had been there since he'd fallen off his bike as a child. "Things were going along fine between Sue and me, but I guess she thought it would mess up our relationship if we made a more serious commitment. For some reason, I think she's afraid of marriage."

"You're right about marriage being a commitment. It takes a lot of work to keep the fires burning." Stuart rubbed the side of his head. "Just ask me. It took months of marital counseling, not to mention six weeks in Emma's quilting classes, for Pam and me to get our act together and put our marriage back on track. But it was worth the effort. Our relationship is a lot stronger now than it was before all that, and we're communicating in a more civilized way."

"You two do seem to be getting along pretty well these days. Maybe it's for the best that Sue and I have gone our separate ways, since we don't see eye to eye on the merits of marriage."

"Yeah, it's better to break things off now than have her decide to bail after you're married."

Blaine sat quietly, drinking his coffee. He was thirty years old and still single. It wasn't that he didn't want to get married, because he did. What really bothered him was when his family got together for holidays and other special events. His two brothers were both married and living in Canada. Seeing how happy Darin and Steve were and watching how their wives looked at them with love and respect, made Blaine envious. He wished he had a wife who'd look at him that way. His sister-in-law, Sandy, adored her husband, not to mention her and Stephen's little boy, Chad, who was four years old, and a miniature replica of his daddy. Even at his young age, Chad seemed to idolize his father, often looking at him like there was no other man on earth. The last time Blaine's family got together for Easter, Darin and his wife,

Michelle, had announced that they were expecting their first child.

Blaine was happy for his brothers, but he couldn't help wondering what it would be like to meet the right person and know she was the one for him. That was what he thought he'd found in Sue, but he'd obviously been wrong. Since their breakup, Blaine had spent a lot of time asking himself if he and Sue had ever been right for each other, or if he had so wanted what his brothers had that he'd been trying to force the relationship to work. Maybe it was best that he'd found out now how Sue felt about marriage. If Sue had agreed to marry him, they might have ended up needing counseling like Stuart and Pam. One thing was for sure: Blaine was tired of going home every night to an empty condo and having a one-way conversation with the fish in his aquarium.

"You know, Stuart," Blaine said, shaking off his thoughts, "I think a day of fishing sounds pretty nice, so if the offer's still open, then yeah, I'd be happy to go with you this Saturday."

"That's great." Stuart thumped Blaine's back. "Say, how about we have a contest to see who can catch the biggest fish?"

"Sure, why not," Blaine said with a shrug. He'd always had good luck fishing, so he was confident that he would catch the biggest fish. "Is there a prize for the winner of this bet?"

"I don't know. Guess there could be. Better yet, let's make the loser pay a consequence."

"What kind of consequence?"

Stuart snapped his fingers. "I've got it! If you catch the biggest fish, I have to buy you a new fishing pole."

Blaine grinned. "That sounds good to me."

"But if I catch the biggest fish, you have to take Emma's next six-week quilting class."

Blaine's mouth opened wide. "You're kidding, right?"

"Nope. You gave me a hard time when Pam forced me to take that class, so it'll be your turn to eat crow."

Blaine chuckled. "I'm not gonna be eating any crow, 'cause I'll catch the biggest fish."

"Does that mean you're agreeing to the bet?"

"Sure, why not?" Blaine smiled to himself. *After all, I'll never have to take those quilting classes.*

Goshen, Indiana

Cheryl Halverson glanced at the calendar on her desk. In two months her grandmother would be celebrating her eighty-eighth birthday, and Cheryl wanted to give Grandma something special. But she couldn't decide what. Grandma didn't need much, not since Cheryl's mother had put her in a nursing home. When Cheryl asked Mom why Grandma couldn't live with her and Dad, Mom said due to the demands of her bank manager job, there was no way she could take care of her aging mother, who needed 'round-the-clock care. Cheryl's mother, Katherine, was fifty-five years old and wasn't ready to give up her job. Cheryl couldn't blame her for that. She didn't know what she'd do without her job as a secretary for an attorney in town. When Cheryl and her boyfriend, Lance, broke up six months ago, moving to Indiana to take this position was what had kept Cheryl going.

"Lance is a creep," she mumbled under her breath. "Wish I'd never met him!" Cheryl and Lance had dated two years, and just when she was sure he would ask her to marry him, she caught him cheating—with her best friend, April Roberts. To add insult to injury, since their breakup, Lance had called Cheryl several times to talk about April and ask her advice about a few things. *Talk about weird*, Cheryl thought, tapping her newly manicured fingernails on her desk. *Who but Lance would be unfeeling enough to call his ex-girlfriend and ask stuff like that? If I ever get involved with another man, I'll need to know I can trust him.*

Glancing once more at the calendar, Cheryl thought about Grandma's birthday. She remembered that her pastor's wife, Ruby Lee Williams, had taken some quilting classes awhile back. *Maybe I could take Grandma's tattered old quilt to Ruby Lee's Amish friend and have it repaired.* For as long as Cheryl could remember, that quilt had been as much a part of her grandmother as the warm smiles and comforting hugs Grandma had always given her.

When Cheryl moved to Indiana, Grandma had given her the quilt to remind her of all the fun times they'd had together. The more Cheryl thought about it, the more she realized it might offer Grandma some comfort to have the quilt now that she was doing so poorly.

Shipshewana

"Where we headed next?" Terry Cooley asked his boss, Jan Sweet. They'd finished tearing the roof off a house in LaGrange that morning and had just entered Shipshewana.

"We need to get started tearing off Emma and Lamar Miller's old roof," Jan replied. "After talking to Lamar the other day, I think he'd like to have it done soon, because if no one signs up for their next quilting class, he's taking Emma on a vacation."

"Where they going?"

"Florida, I think."

"Sounds like a good place to be. Nice, warm sunny beaches. . . Wouldn't mind going there myself for a few weeks." Terry took a drag on his cigarette and flicked the ashes out the driver-side window of his truck.

Jan grunted. "Sure wish you'd give up that nasty habit. It ain't good for your health, ya know."

Terry gripped the steering wheel tightly and kept his focus straight ahead. Jan was not only his boss, but they were good friends, even though Terry was twenty-nine and Jan forty-one. Terry supposed for that reason, Jan thought he could lecture him about his smoking habit, but he wished he'd quit bugging him. Terry was surprised that Jan didn't smoke, too. He had other bad habits, though. He used to drink, not to mention riding his motorcycle too fast. Of course, those days were behind him now. Ever since Jan had been reunited with his daughter, Star, he'd cleaned up his act. That, plus being around Lamar and Emma Miller, had turned Jan into a different man. He was still a bit rough around the edges, but there was a softness to him that hadn't been there before his quilting days. Terry still couldn't get over the fact that Jan had actually made a quilted wall hanging and proudly hung it in his living room. *You'd never catch me at no quilting class*, he thought.

"How are things with Star these days?" Terry asked, offering a change of subject.

Jan turned his head to look at Terry and grinned. "Good. Real good. Whenever we both have a free day, we spend it together."

Terry nodded. "Yeah, I know. That's why you hardly ever go bowling with me anymore."

"What are ya talking about, man? Me and Star went bowling with you and Dottie two weeks ago."

"I don't think taking your daughter bowling hardly counts as a double date."

Jan lifted his broad shoulders. "Never said it did."

"If you'll recall, when I invited you to go bowling, I said you oughta find a date, since I'd be bringing one."

"And I did." Jan smiled. "I don't need to explain that I have a lot of catching up to do with Star."

Terry took another puff from his cigarette. "You got that right."

"You know," Jan said, "I waited over twenty years to find my girl, and now that I have, I plan to spend as much time with her as I can."

"That's fine, but you need a social life, too. I'm sure your daughter has one."

"Humph! What would you know about a social life? All you ever do on your day off is bowl, play pool, and ride your Harley."

"For your information I took Dottie out to see a movie last weekend."

"Speaking of your girlfriend, how much longer are you gonna string her along before you pop the big question?"

Terry's brows furrowed. "I ain't stringing Dottie along. I'm not the marrying kind, and Dottie knows that, so things are just fine the way they are between us. Besides, Dottie and I are just good friends, same as you and me—except that she happens to be a female."

Jan shrugged his shoulders. "Whatever."

"Hey, isn't that your nosey old neighbor over there?" Terry said, pointing out the front window at an elderly woman walking along the shoulder of the road, wearing a lime green jacket and floppy beige-colored hat.

Jan nodded. "That's Selma Nash, all right. I see she's picking up aluminum cans, which is better than her running around our neighborhood, making a nuisance of herself."

"Has she been hollering at you about Brutus again?"

"Nope. Not since I started keeping the dog penned up while I'm at work. She likes to tromp around the neighborhood, telling others what she thinks." Jan grunted. "That woman is nothing but a busybody. She needs to get a life that don't involve telling other people what to do."

"Selma's jacket reminds me of that spicy green apple juice Dottie had me drinking the other night. Ugh, that was some nasty stuff!" Terry wrinkled his nose and coughed several times. After he cleared his throat to get the spastic cough under control, he asked, "Why don't you put Selma in her place if she bugs you so much?"

"I've tried, but it hasn't done any good. She can't seem to keep her big nose outta other people's business." Jan paused a moment, rubbing his tattooed arm. "It's sorta like me telling you to quit smoking."

"Yeah, I hear you," Terry retorted. "Maybe Selma has too much time on her hands. Could be if she had something to do, she wouldn't have time to stick her nose where it don't belong."

Just as Terry pulled into Emma and Lamar's yard, Jan slapped his knee. "I've got it! I'll enroll Selma in Emma's next quilting class. It'll occupy her time and give her something to do besides snooping on everyone in the neighborhood and telling 'em what to do."

Chapter 3

Selma Nash groaned as she bent to pick up a rubber ball she'd found on her lawn. She'd been out collecting cans all morning, like she did most weeks, and every bone in her sixty-eight-year-old body ached. She shouldn't have to come home and pick up the neighbor children's toys! "What's wrong with their parents?" she mumbled. "Those kids ought to be taught to keep things in their own yard."

Between the dogs and kids on her block, it seemed her yard always had something that shouldn't be in it. Thankfully, Jan Sweet, the burly biker who lived next door, had been keeping his German shepherd penned up when he wasn't at home. The big brute of an animal used to run all over the neighborhood, taking things that weren't his and digging up people's flowers. Of course Jan had replaced the flowers Brutus dug up in Selma's yard, and he'd been compliant when she asked him to keep the mutt at home. But other dogs lived in the neighborhood, and their owners hadn't been as willing to listen.

Selma marched over to the Bennetts' house, which was on the other side of her place, and knocked on the door. When no one answered, she knocked again. Still no response. She'd thought her days of cleaning up after someone had ended when her husband, John, passed away from a heart attack five years ago.

Selma scoffed, remembering how all the complaining in the world hadn't changed her husband's bad habits over the course of their forty-year marriage. All her grumblings hadn't made one iota of a difference, and in hindsight, it had caused a sense of sadness in her every time she thought about how things stood between her and John before he died. It was hard to admit, but she sometimes missed picking up after her husband.

Selma's thoughts went to her daughter, Cora, who'd left home when she turned eighteen.

The last time Selma had seen Cora was when she'd come home for John's funeral, but of course, Cora hadn't stuck around very long. Hadn't even said good-bye to her own mother, for goodness' sake! The spiteful young woman had tossed a rose on her father's casket, jumped in her car, and headed off down the road. It was probably for the best that Cora came back only for the funeral. Selma was so mad at her that any more time spent together would have deteriorated into a series of arguments. Selma tried not to think about it, but many times she asked herself how things would be now if John were still alive.

Heaving a sigh, Selma set the ball on the porch and pulled a notebook and pen from her pocket. She scribbled a quick note and left it with the ball, letting the kid's parents know that if she found any more of his toys in her yard, she'd throw them away. "Guess that's probably a bit harsh," Selma muttered, "but maybe they'll get the point."

She headed back to her house, as a gust of wind blew a cluster of fallen leaves across the grass. She grabbed hold of her hat, fearing it would be blown away. Fall was definitely here, and soon the frigid days of winter would swoop in. When the weather got too cold, it would put an end to her walks, so she'd need to find something else to occupy her time.

Selma stopped at the end of her driveway to check for mail. Yesterday was her birthday, and she hadn't received a single card. Not even from Cora. Of course Selma doubted that she'd hear from her daughter again, yet she kept hoping for a phone call, or at least a letter or card. Maybe it was just as well. If Cora was still part of her life, they'd probably argue all the time. The girl was stubborn and wouldn't listen to anything Selma said. Despite the lack of a close relationship and years that had passed since then, there were moments like this when Selma missed having her daughter around. Of course, she'd never admitted that to anyone, or even talked about Cora. As far as Selma's few friends and neighbors were concerned, she lived alone and had no family.

Shaking her troubling thoughts aside, Selma stepped onto her porch. She was about to open the door, when Jan ambled into the yard and hollered, "Can I talk to you a minute, Selma?"

Selma slowly nodded. She wasn't in the mood to talk to Jan about anything right now—she just wanted to get into the house and fix herself a bowl of soup for lunch.

"What'd you want to talk to me about?" she asked when Jan joined her on the porch.

"Came to give you this." Jan handed Selma an envelope.

Her heart fluttered. Could it be a belated birthday card? Did Jan know that yesterday was her birthday? But how could he know? She'd never mentioned it to him.

With trembling fingers Selma tore the envelope open. What she discovered inside was not a birthday card at all. It was a piece of paper with a woman's name and address written on it.

"Who's Emma Miller, and why are you giving me this?" Selma asked, looking up at Jan through squinted eyes.

"She's the Amish lady I took some quilting classes from a year and a half ago. Only her name was Emma Yoder then. She's married to Lamar Miller now, and they—"

"What's this have to do with me?" Selma couldn't keep the irritation she felt out of her voice. Why was Jan wasting her time? Didn't he realize she had better things to do than stand on the porch and shiver while she stared at a piece of paper with an address of a woman she'd never met?

"I signed you up for Emma's next class." Jan grinned and pointed to the envelope. "So, what do you think about that?"

She pursed her thin lips. "Why would you think I'd want to take a quilting class? I've never said I did, you know."

He lifted his broad shoulders in a brief shrug. "Just thought it might be something you'd enjoy—especially since winter will be here soon, and your work in the yard will come to an end."

Selma stared at the envelope a few seconds more, trying to piece things together. "How much do the quilting lessons cost?"

Jan flapped his big calloused hand. "No need to worry about that. I've got it covered."

"You—you paid for my spot in the class?" she sputtered.

He nodded.

"Why would you do that?"

"Like I said, I thought it'd be something you'd enjoy. The class starts next Saturday. Will you be free to go?"

Selma tapped her chin, thoughtfully mulling things over. "I believe so."

Jan brought his hands together in a clap so loud it caused Selma to jump. "Great! I'm sure you'll enjoy the class as much as I did. Probably more, since you're a woman who likes nice things."

Selma couldn't deny it. Her flower garden was proof enough. Besides, she'd always prided herself on being able to sew, although she'd never made a quilt before. *I'm sure it can't be that hard,* she thought. *I'll bet my quilt will turn out better than anyone else's in the class.*

While Jan's gift wasn't actually a birthday present, it was the best thing that had happened to Selma all week. "Thank you, Jan," she said with a smile she hoped looked sincere. "I think I might enjoy that class, and it'll give me something to look forward to."

Elkhart, Indiana

As Paul Ramirez left his second-grade classroom that afternoon, he thought about the phone call he'd received from his sister-in-law, Carmen, last night. He'd been pleased when she'd said she was in town and wanted to come by Paul's place this evening to visit him and his two-year-old daughter, Sophia. That in itself was a surprise, since things had become strained between Paul and Carmen after Paul's wife died almost two years ago. Paul figured the reason Carmen had only visited once since then was because she hadn't completely forgiven him for not being able to prevent the accident that took Lorinda's life. The other thing that had taken Paul by surprise when Carmen called was that she'd asked if he still visited with the Amish woman who'd taught him how to quilt.

"Yes, I do," Paul had said. "I stop by to see Emma and her husband, Lamar, as often as I can."

There'd been a pause, and then Carmen said, "Could I meet her? I mean, would you be willing to introduce me to Emma?"

Paul had said yes, but he was confused by Carmen's request. Why would she be interested in meeting Emma? And how long would she be in the area? He wished now that he'd thought to ask. Well, she'd be coming by this evening, and he could ask Carmen for details then.

As Paul slid into the driver's seat of his minivan, his thoughts went to Sophia. It would be good for his little girl to spend some time with her aunt. Paul was grateful that his folks as well as his sister, Maria, and her family lived close by. Everyone, including Maria's three girls, doted on Sophia, and of course she loved all the attention. When Lorinda died, it had been difficult for Paul to cope, but with the help of his family and friends, he'd learned to deal with the pain of losing his beloved wife. Of course attending Emma's quilting classes and sharing his feelings with Emma and the other students had been a big help, too.

As Paul drove closer to the Loving Hands Daycare Center, where he dropped Sophia off each morning, he couldn't believe how quickly the leaves had turned color and fallen from the trees lining the street. The only leaves left were from some of the oaks.

Taking his foot off the gas pedal in time to let a squirrel run across the road, he smiled when he noticed that the bushy-tailed critter had a good-sized walnut in its mouth.

Paul pulled into the daycare parking lot and turned off the engine. He was glad things had worked out for Sophia at the daycare. She loved going there, and it made life easier knowing his little girl was content during the day while he taught his second-graders. It hadn't always been that way. Just a year ago, Sophia had cried whenever Paul dropped her off. Since then, she'd become more settled and content being with some of the other children. That eased Paul's guilt for having to leave her each day while he earned a living. If Lorinda were still alive, Sophia would have been home with her mother all day.

Switching his thoughts once more, Paul reflected again on his phone call from Carmen. Maybe he'd take her to meet Emma Saturday morning.

Shipshewana

"I hope you won't be disappointed, but it looks like we won't be making a trip to Florida this fall after all," Emma said to Lamar as he sat in the living room, reading the latest issue of *The Budget.*

He looked up and blinked a couple of times. "Why's that?"

Emma pointed to the sheet of paper she held. "I already have two people signed up for my quilting class, and I have a feeling there will soon be others." She took a seat beside him on the sofa. "I hope you'll be able to help me with the classes again. I'm sure the students would be interested in seeing some of the quilts you've designed, not to mention gaining from your knowledge of quilts."

"I have to admit I'm a little disappointed that we won't be making any trips in the near future. On the other hand, I look forward to seeing who God will send our way." Lamar reached for Emma's hand and gave her fingers a gentle squeeze. "Of course you can count on me to help with the classes."

"*Danki*, Lamar. I always appreciate your help and input in the classes."

"Well now," he said, rising to his feet, "if there's gonna be another class starting next week, then I'd better look through some of my quilts and decide which ones to display in your quilting room."

As Lamar left the room, Emma leaned her head against the sofa cushion and closed her eyes. *Heavenly Father,* she silently prayed, *I don't know the two women who'll be coming to my class on Saturday, nor do I know who else may sign up. But as with all the other students who've come here before, I pray that I can teach them more than just how to quilt.*

Chapter 4

Do we have everything we need for class?" Emma asked Lamar as she paced back and forth in the spacious room she used for quilting. Lamar didn't know why, but she seemed a bit nervous today. It was silly, really, since she'd taught several classes since that first one a year and a half ago.

In his usual calm manner, Lamar gave Emma's shoulder a gentle squeeze. "Now try to relax. I'm sure everything will go as well with this class as it has with the others."

Emma sighed. "I hope so."

Lamar motioned to the cup of chamomile tea Emma had placed on the table. "Why don't you finish that before your students arrive? It might help settle your nerves."

Emma took a seat and picked up the cup. "All right, I'll try to relax."

"How many people did you say are signed up for this class?" Lamar questioned.

"As of yesterday, only three—two women and one man."

Lamar rubbed the bridge of his nose. "Seems like the classes are getting smaller. We had only five people for our last class. Maybe folks aren't as interested in quilting as they used to be. Maybe it's time for us to retire."

Emma set her cup down so hard that some of the tea splashed out. "*Ach*, Lamar, I'm not ready to do that. I enjoy teaching others to quilt, and it doesn't matter how many people are in the class. Besides, the smaller classes allow me to give more one-on-one attention to each person."

Lamar sat quietly, then patted Emma's shoulder and said, "You teach them quite well, I might add."

Emma smiled. "I think my students get even more from the class when you help me, Lamar."

Sure hope I won't let you down, Lamar thought, staring at his stiff fingers. With the colder weather, his arthritis was acting up. It was one of the reasons he wanted to vacation in Florida—along with thinking it would be a nice break for both him and Emma. He'd purposely not told Emma about his pain and stiffness because he didn't want her to worry or feel guilty about teaching another quilting class. He just hoped he could get through these next six weeks without letting on.

"Are you certain your Amish friend won't mind us dropping by unannounced?" Carmen asked as she climbed out of Paul's minivan and spotted a large, white house at the end of the driveway.

"I'm sure it'll be fine," Paul said, stepping onto the porch. "Emma's very hospitable, and Sophia and I have come by here many times when Emma didn't expect us. We were always welcomed with open arms."

Carmen didn't know why, but she felt a bit apprehensive. She'd conducted many interviews and never had a nervous stomach before—not even in her early days as a reporter. Today, however, she felt jittery.

She glanced around the yard, and her gaze came to rest on a black, box-shaped buggy parked near the barn. *I wonder how it would feel to ride in one of them,* she mused. Carmen knew from the things she'd read that the horse and buggy were the Amish people's primary mode of transportation.

The *ba-a-a* of a goat drew Carmen's attention to the other side of the yard, where a few goats frolicked in a pen. Nearby were several chickens pecking in the dirt, and just as Carmen and Paul stepped onto the porch, a fluffy white cat streaked across the yard, chasing a smaller orange-and-white cat.

I can't imagine what it would be like to live in this rustic-looking place. It's a far cry from the fast pace of Los Angeles. It might be interesting to be here for a while, but I wonder how long it would take for me to become bored or restless with the solitude.

Carmen stepped to one side as Paul knocked on the door. A short time later, an elderly Amish man with a long gray beard greeted them. His green eyes sparkled as he shook Paul's hand. "It's good to see you. It's been awhile."

Paul grinned widely. "It's good to see you, too, Lamar." He motioned to Carmen. "This is my sister-in-law, Carmen Lopez. She's visiting from California. Carmen, this is Emma's husband, Lamar Miller."

Carmen offered the man her best smile, while shaking his hand. "It's nice to meet you, Mr. Miller."

"Good to meet you, too, and please, call me Lamar." He opened the door wider. "Come in and say hello to Emma. I'm sure she'll be happy to see you," he said.

"If you're busy, we won't stay long," Paul was quick to say. "I just wanted you both to meet Carmen."

"We have a quilting class in an hour, but we can visit till then." Lamar motioned them inside and led the way down the hall. They followed him into a spacious room filled with several sewing machines, an empty quilting frame, and a large table with four chairs on both sides. Several colorful quilts draped over wooden stands were scattered around the room, which was lit by a few overhead gas lanterns. A slightly plump woman wearing a long navy-blue dress and a white cap perched on her head was seated in front of one of the machines. She was so intent on her sewing project that she didn't seem to notice when they came into the room.

"Look who's here," Lamar said, placing his hands on the woman's shoulders.

She turned her head and smiled at Paul. "It's so good to see you," she said, rising from her seat. "Where's that sweet little girl of yours?"

Paul gave the woman a hug. "It's always good to see you, Emma. Sophia is with my sister Maria, this morning." He turned to Carmen and said, "This is Emma Miller. She's the talented woman who taught me how to quilt. Emma, I'd like you to meet my sister-in-law, Carmen Lopez. She lives in Los Angeles, where she works at a newspaper."

Emma smiled as she greeted Carmen with a gentle handshake. "It's nice to meet you."

"I'm happy to meet you, too," Carmen said sincerely. "I was interested when Paul told me you'd taught him how to quilt."

"And she's an excellent teacher," Paul interjected.

Emma's cheeks colored as she dipped her head slightly. "Thank you, Paul. I enjoy sewing, and it's a pleasure for me to teach others how to quilt." She looked up at her husband and smiled. "Now that Lamar's helping me with the classes, people are learning even more."

"Lamar designed all these quilts," Paul said, motioning to the ones on display.

"They're quite impressive." Carmen moved to stand beside a quilt with muted shades of brown and green.

"That one I call Pheasant Trail." Lamar beamed. "It's one of my favorites."

"I can see why." Carmen leaned down to get a closer look. "The details in this quilt are amazing. I wish I could make something like that."

"Have you ever done any quilting?" Emma asked.

Carmen shook her head. "No, but I know how to do some basic sewing. My mother made sure both of her daughters learned how to sew." She glanced at Paul, but he was staring at the floor. Was he thinking about Lorinda and how much he still missed her? Well, Carmen missed her, too. She and Lorinda had been five years apart, but the age difference never mattered; they'd always been close.

As if sensing Carmen's discomfort, Emma touched her arm lightly and said, "Would you care to stay and be part of the class?"

"Oh yes!" Carmen couldn't believe her luck. If she was allowed to sit in on the class, she'd have the perfect opportunity to ask questions about the Amish—maybe even find out some details concerning the young people's time of running-around.

Paul quirked an eyebrow as he looked at Carmen strangely. "You won't learn much in just one class. It took me a full six weeks to be able to make a quilted wall hanging."

"How long will you be in the area, Carmen?" Emma asked.

She shrugged. "I don't know. I guess that will depend on how long my boss allows me to be gone."

"Emma's class goes for six weeks, and that's a long time to be away from work. Staying at a hotel, even an extended stay, like the one you're at now, can be expensive," Paul said before Emma could respond.

"Could you stay in the area for six weeks, Carmen?" Emma questioned.

"Yes, I think so. I'll step outside and give my boss a call." Carmen pulled her cell phone from her purse and scooted out the door.

"Hey, Carmen. How's it going there?" Carmen's boss asked after answering her call.

"Okay, Mr. Lawrence. I'm in Shipshewana, and. . ." Carmen paused and moistened her lips. "I was wondering. . . Would it be all right if I stayed here for six weeks?"

"Six weeks! Why so long?"

Carmen leaned against the porch railing. "I want to take a quilting class."

"Are you kidding me? I sent you there to get a story, not spend your time with a needle and thread." Mr. Lawrence's voice raised a few notches. "This is not a vacation, you know."

"I—I realize that, sir, but the quilting class is held in an Amish woman's home, and I think if I can get acquainted with her, I might be able to find out what I want to know about rumschpringe."

"Is that so?"

"Yes, and if I'm able to take the quilt class, which starts today and ends in six weeks, I'm sure I'll have a good story."

"Well, it better be, because the paper can't afford to send reporters on wild goose chases—especially for that length of time."

"I don't think it'll be a wild goose chase, Mr. Lawrence."

There was a long pause. Then, "Okay, if you think you're going to need six weeks, that's fine. Just make sure you come back with a top-notch story."

"Thanks, I'll do my best. Good-bye, Mr. Lawrence." Carmen hung up, drew in a deep breath, and stepped back into Emma's house.

"It's all set," she said, smiling at Emma. "Just tell me how much I'll owe for the classes, and I can get started today."

Once Emma discussed the price, Carmen turned to Paul and said, "I know you have other things you need to do today, so you can just leave me here and pick me up when the class is over."

Paul stared at her with a look of disbelief, but finally he nodded.

"I can't believe I'm doing this," Blaine mumbled as he parked his SUV on a graveled driveway where a white minivan was about to pull out. If he just hadn't lost that bet with Stuart when they'd gone fishing last Saturday. Blaine had been so sure he would catch the biggest fish that he'd stupidly agreed to take a six-week quilting class if he lost the bet. He'd never expected Stuart to pull a twenty-eight-inch largemouth bass from Lake Shipshewana. If he hadn't actually seen Stuart land the fish, he wouldn't have believed it, but even before his friend pulled the fish out of the water, Blaine knew it was going to be big. It had practically bent Stuart's fishing rod in half, and surprisingly, it didn't break.

Inwardly, Blaine had hoped the fish would roll and detach itself from the hook, but that didn't happen. Why would it? The week had been rotten. Earlier, he'd almost caved in when he'd been forced to give the fly-fishing demonstration to a large group of people. Somehow, dry mouth and all, Blaine had managed to get through it without letting on how uncomfortable he'd felt. And now he was stuck going to a quilting class of all things!

The fish Blaine caught had only been twenty-two inches long. What a disappointment that had been, especially when Stuart looked at Blaine's smaller fish and grinned at him in a teasing way.

Sure wish I could get out of taking this class, Blaine thought. *Maybe I could go inside, sit through the first few minutes, and then develop a sudden headache.*

Blaine was about to get out of his vehicle when his cell phone rang. He glanced at the screen and saw that it was Stuart. *Oh great. What's he doing. . .calling to check up on me?*

Blaine was tempted to let his voice mail answer the call, but changed his mind. If he didn't answer, Stuart would probably think he'd chickened out and wasn't going to take the class after all.

He snapped open his cell phone. "What's up, Stuart? Are you calling to check up on me?" Blaine's tone was harsher than he meant it to be.

"Hey, man, don't get so defensive," Stuart said. "I just wanted to make sure you were able to find Emma's house okay."

"Yeah, I found it. I'm sitting in her driveway right now."

"That's good. I'll be anxious to hear how your first class goes. I'm sure it'll be a walk in the park."

"I'll bet."

"What was that?"

"Nothing." Blaine glanced at his watch. "I'd better go. It's almost ten o'clock, and I sure don't want to be late for class."

"Okay, see you Monday morning."

"'Bye, Stuart." Blaine clicked off his phone and climbed out of his vehicle. He'd just started for the house when an older model Chevy rumbled into the yard. A few minutes later, an elderly woman stepped out. She wore baggy gray slacks, a green turtleneck sweater, and a floppy beige canvas hat. She glanced at him briefly, stuck her nose in the air, and tromped up the porch steps.

"Terrific," Blaine muttered under his breath, running his fingers through his thick, wavy hair. "I'll bet she's here for the quilt class. This is going to be anything but a walk in the park!"

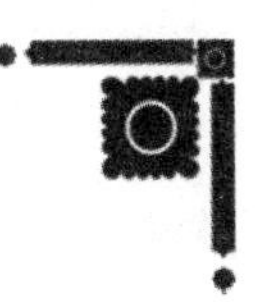

CHAPTER 5

Selma was surprised when a gray-haired Amish man with a long, full beard answered her knock. She'd expected a woman. "Is this the home of Emma Miller?" she asked, eyeing him suspiciously.

He offered her a cheery smile. "That's right. Emma's my wife, and I'm Lamar. Are you one of her quilting students?"

Selma gave a quick nod, thinking he seemed nice enough. "My name is Selma Nash, and I came prepared." She lifted the canvas satchel she'd brought along and gave it a confident pat. "I have everything right here that I'll need to make a quilt."

"Oh, there was no need for you to bring anything," Lamar said. "Emma has all the required supplies. If you'll follow me, I'll lead the way to her quilting room."

Selma clutched her satchel as she walked with Lamar into the next room. Despite what he'd said, she was sure she'd be able to use most of what she had brought along. *Maybe they'll be impressed with all the research I've done beforehand about quilting,* she thought.

As Selma entered the room, she noticed that the inside of the house was as tidy as the outside. She detected a scent of lemon in the air. An older Amish woman sat at the table with a young Hispanic woman, whom Selma assumed was also here to learn how to quilt. But it seemed strange that there were no other students in the room.

"This is Selma Nash," Lamar said to the Amish woman. "She's one of your quilting students."

The woman stood and shook Selma's hand. "I'm Emma Miller, and I'm pleased that you've joined our class." She gestured to the other woman. "This is Carmen Lopez. She's here to learn how to quilt as well."

"Are we the only two people in the class?" Selma asked, feeling rather perplexed as Emma motioned for her to sit in one of the extra chairs.

Before Emma had a chance to respond, the young man Selma had seen outside shuffled into the room. He looked uncomfortable, like he might want to turn and run.

"You must be Blaine Vickers," Emma said, extending her hand.

He gave a brief nod.

"Welcome to our quilting class." Emma motioned to Carmen and then to Selma. "This is Selma Nash and Carmen Lopez, and we're waiting for Anna Lambright to arrive. As soon as she gets here, we'll begin."

Blaine's eyes widened. "So I'm the only guy in the class?"

"You're the only male student," Emma said, "but Lamar will be with us. In fact, he'll be helping me teach the class."

Lamar motioned to one of the quilts in the room. "I've designed many quilts, and I also know quite a bit about the history of quilts."

"I've studied up on them, too," Selma interjected, rather proudly. "As soon as my neighbor, Jan, said he'd paid for me to come to this class, I went straight to the library and checked out a book on Amish quilts."

Selma reached into her satchel and pulled out the book. "See, this one is a Dahlia pattern," she said, flipping through the pages and pointing to one of the pictures. "I love flowers, so that's the kind of quilt I would like to make."

"Perhaps you will someday," Emma said, moving to stand at the head of the table. "But during the next six weeks, I'll be teaching each of you how to make a quilted wall hanging with a simple star pattern combined with Log Cabin quilt blocks with an Eight Point Star layout. The finished square hanging will measure thirty-five inches."

Selma frowned, feeling her forehead wrinkles deepen. "I don't care for that idea. Can't we make the Dahlia or some other floral pattern?"

"Those would be too difficult," Lamar spoke up.

"Well, I'm confident that I could handle any pattern at all, because I'm a proficient seamstress."

"I'm sure Emma has a reason for choosing the simple star pattern," Carmen spoke up. "Since she's the teacher, she obviously knows what's best for us."

Selma glanced at Blaine to see if he was going to comment, but he just stared at the table. He obviously didn't want to be there. *His wife probably forced him to come,* Selma thought. *But then, I wonder why she didn't sign up to take the quilting classes herself.*

"Actually, I chose the pattern for two reasons," Emma said calmly. "First, because it's a bit different from other star patterns. And second, because it will be easy to make. But we'll get into all the details about making the quilt after my other student has arrived."

Selma grunted and folded her arms. "Seems to me if people are going to sign up for a class, the least they can do is be here on time."

"It was the young woman's mother who signed her up," Emma explained. "And I'm thinking perhaps—"

"Maybe she didn't want to come," Selma cut in. "Some daughters can be stubborn like that. They just don't appreciate their mothers."

Everyone looked at Selma with curious expressions, and the room got uncomfortably quiet. Had she said something wrong? Should she explain about her relationship with Cora? No, it was best to leave that alone. After all, it wasn't in her nature to talk about her personal life to a bunch of strangers.

Emma cleared her throat a couple of times, and then she looked over at Lamar and said, "Since Anna's not here yet, why don't you go ahead and share some things about Amish quilts?"

"I'd be pleased to do that." Lamar joined Emma at the head of the table and proceeded to talk about the history of Amish quilts. "Quilt patterns are a reflection of our daily living and can sometimes resemble things found in nature or on the farm." He pointed to one of the quilts on display. "This one I designed myself, and I call it simply, 'Horseshoes.' As you can see, the shape of a horseshoe is patterned throughout."

"How about that one?" Blaine asked, pointing to the quilt closest to him.

"I designed it, too, and it's called 'Pheasant Trail,'" Lamar replied.

"If you ask me, it looks more like 'chicken scratch,'" Selma said with a snort. "Can't you show us some pretty floral designs?"

The room went quiet again, and everyone stared at Selma as if she had pointed ears. What was wrong with these people, anyway? Didn't they want to see something beautiful, or were they content to look at quilts with bland and blah colors?

"You don't have to be so rude," Carmen spoke up with her hands on her slender hips. "I think Lamar's designs are quite unique."

"Yeah, that's right," Blaine agreed. "You shouldn't be putting them down."

Selma's face heated. She had a notion to gather up her things and head out the door. But if she did that, she'd miss out on learning how to make a quilt. "Sorry," she mumbled. "I didn't mean that the quilts weren't nice. I'd just prefer to see something more to my liking."

"The thing about Amish quilts," Emma explained, "is that there's a variety of patterns, which means there is something to fit everyone's taste."

"That's right," Lamar agreed. "Some people prefer the more traditional patterns, like the Lone Star, and some enjoy making something unusual like my Pheasant Trail or Horseshoe pattern."

"When did quilting first begin?" Carmen asked.

"In a traditional sense, not until the 1870s," Lamar replied.

"At first the fabrics were solid and dark, much like our plain choice of clothing." Emma smiled, as she pointed to another quilt made with maroon, brown, and off-white colors. "But later, pastels and whites were added to many of our quilts."

"Do all Amish women quilt?" Selma asked, realizing she'd better stay low-key.

Emma shook her head. "Many do, but some women keep busy with other things and don't have time to quilt."

Selma was about to comment, when the door to the quilting room swung open, and a young, auburn-haired Amish woman rushed in. Her long green dress had several splotches of dirt on it, and there was a large tear near the hem. The stiff white cap on her head was askew, and her cheeks were red as a ripe cherry. "S–sorry I'm late," she panted. "I had a little accident on my bike."

Emma was relieved that Anna had made it to class, but she felt concern seeing the state of disarray the poor girl was in. "Are you all right?" she asked. "Were you hurt?"

Anna shook her head as she reached up to push her head covering back in place. "I think my knees are scraped up a bit, but I'm okay."

"How'd it happen?" Lamar questioned. "Did you spin out in some gravel, or what?"

Anna frowned. "When a stupid black dog started chasing me and tried to get a hold of my skirt, I got scared and pedaled faster to get away. That's when I lost control of the bike and ran into a ditch beside the road."

"What happened when you fell?" Emma asked. "Did the *hund* bite you?"

"No, but I was afraid he might. Some English man pulled up in his car to see if I was all right, and when he hollered at the dog, it took off like a shot."

"Why don't you go down the hall to our bathroom and make sure you're not bleeding," Emma suggested, noticing the look of embarrassment in Anna's light brown eyes. "Washcloths are in the cabinet, and the bandages are in the medicine chest by the sink."

"I'll do that right now." Anna scurried out of the room, muttering something under her breath.

Poor girl. She's probably self-conscious. Emma turned her attention back to the class, although she wondered how much information she would get through to her students today. They'd gotten a late start, and with Selma's know-it-all attitude, this might be a difficult class to teach. *I've never had one like her before,* Emma thought, cringing inwardly. *Of course it can't be any harder to teach this class than it was my very first one, when I had such a mix of unusual characters.* Emma remembered how surprised she'd been that first day when a young English woman with a sour attitude; a preacher's wife with church problems; a man and his wife struggling with marital discord; a Hispanic teacher, recently widowed; and a tattooed biker on probation had showed up at her door. If she could teach them how to quilt and deal with some of their personal problems, maybe it wouldn't be so hard to work with this group of people. At least she hoped that would be the case. After all, there were just four students. Surely they couldn't all have issues.

I'll need to remind myself to take one week at a time and just do my best, she told herself. *With God's help, nothing is impossible.*

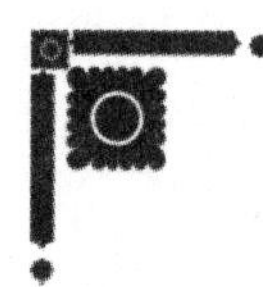

Chapter 6

Sure wish we didn't have to work today," Terry complained as Jan pulled his truck and utility trailer into Emma's yard. "I'd rather be out riding my Harley."

"Same here, but we can't leave those shingles we tore off the Millers' roof yesterday lying in the yard." Jan popped all five fingers on his right hand—a habit he'd started lately. "When we show up here on Monday morning, I want to be able to start on the new roof right away. Of course if we had a gofer things would move along faster."

Terry scratched his head. "A gopher? What are you talking about?"

"You know. Having another guy to take care of the odd stuff, like picking up the old shingles, instead of us having to do it," Jan explained. "Someone who'd bring us stuff when we're working on the roof. Tools and such. Like I said, a gofer." He grinned. "They'd go fer this and go fer that."

Terry chuckled. "Oh yeah. . .that kind of gopher."

Jan thumped Terry's arm. "Well, since we don't have one, I think we oughta get these old shingles picked up."

"Guess you're right. I'll just have to make plans to go riding next Saturday. Do you and Star want to go along?"

Jan shrugged. "I don't know. I'll have to wait and see what she's up to. She may have to work, or she could be in Fort Wayne, visiting her mom and stepdad."

"Do you ever wish you and Bunny could've gotten back together?"

"Sometimes." Jan sighed. "But I guess it's better this way. There was a certain kind of chemistry between me and Bunny when we were teenagers, but after Star was born, her mom changed. She couldn't have really loved me back then if she could just run away and take our baby without looking back or letting me know where she was going. Even if Bunny had tried to start something up with me after Star came back into my life, I don't think I could have ever trusted her again." He groaned. "I'm not sure marriage is even right for me. Think me and my dog, Brutus, are better off without a wife telling us what to do."

"I know what you mean." Terry slapped his knee. "Don't think I'll ever tie the knot." He slowly shook his head. "Not with the way things turned out for my folks."

"It's a shame they split up after being married so many years," Jan said, running his finger over the film of dirt clinging to the dashboard of his truck. "Figured after they'd gone to see a counselor that things might get better."

"Yeah, me, too. They were doing better for a while, but then Dad started drinking pretty heavy, so Mom kicked him out."

Jan gave the fingers on his left hand a good pop. "Life is full of disappointments, ain't it?"

"That's for sure. Sometimes it stinks."

"But some things we just can't change, and right now we'd better quit yammering and get to work." Jan opened the truck door and stepped out.

Terry hopped out, too, and went around and opened the back of the utility trailer. The sooner they got the shingles picked up, the sooner he could return to the single-wide trailer he rented from his uncle Ted. Not that there was anything great waiting for him there. It would just be nice to flake out for the rest of the day. Sometimes he wished he had a home of his own—maybe a log cabin surrounded by trees.

Maybe I oughta look into buying a small piece of land, Terry thought. *Then I could start building a cabin during my free time.* He grabbed some shingles and pitched them into the trailer. *Well, I can't think about that right now. I've got work to do.*

Terry and Jan had only been working a short time, when a sporty-looking, silver-gray car pulled into the yard. A slender young woman with short blond hair worn in a bob stepped out of the car. She was dressed in beige slacks and a rose-colored pullover sweater that showed off her womanly curves. She glanced up at the house, then opened her trunk and removed a cardboard box. Glancing briefly at Terry and Jan, she headed for Emma's house, walking with an air of confidence.

"Now there's a real looker," Terry said, as the woman stepped onto the porch.

Jan rolled his blue eyes. "She's probably here for Emma's quilt class, and don't get any dumb ideas, 'cause she's most likely married. Even if she's not, she looks too sophisticated for a guy like you."

"What are you sayin', man? You think I'm not good enough for someone like her?"

"I ain't saying that at all. Just don't think you'd have anything in common with the woman." Jan motioned to her car. "For crying out loud, she drives a Corvette. How's that compare to your beat-up truck?"

"Well, there's only one way to find out if she's married or not,"

Terry said, ignoring Jan's remark.

"Oh yeah, what's that?"

Terry rubbed his hands briskly together. "I'll go in the house and check things out."

Jan grunted. "Check out what, Terry? Are you just gonna barge into Emma's home and ask the blond-haired chick if she's married? And if she's not, are ya gonna ask her out?"

Terry shrugged. "I might."

"Don't be such a sap. Emma would be shocked if you did something like that, and the cute little blond would probably laugh right in your face."

"Maybe not. Maybe she likes the strong, silent type."

Jan leaned his head back and roared. "You, the silent type? Now that's a good one!"

"Well, maybe I'm not silent all of the time, but I am strong." Terry gave his ponytail a flip and chuckled. "Could be, too, that the pretty little thing likes men with flaming red hair."

Jan pointed to the shingles nearby. "Just get busy picking these up and quit fantasizing."

Terry's eyebrows lifted. "*Fantasizing?* Where'd you pick up a word like that?"

"I ain't stupid, ya know." Jan shook his head. "For your information, being around Star so much and listening to some of the song lyrics she's written has broadened my vocabulary."

Terry bent down and grabbed an armful of shingles. "If you say so."

After heaving the shingles into the bed of the trailer, Terry turned to Jan and said, "Just as soon as we're done here, I think I'll go inside and see what I can find out about the blond. Is that okay with you?"

Jan turned his hands palms up. "Suit yourself. Just don't say I didn't give you fair warning if someone throws you out on your ear. I'd hate to have to say, 'I told you so.' "

When Emma heard a knock on the front door, she turned to Lamar and said, "Would you mind getting that? It's probably Jan. I saw him and Terry pull into the yard a bit ago."

"Sure, no problem. You go on teaching the class, and I'll be back in a minute." Lamar shuffled out of the room, moving at a slower pace than usual. Emma hoped his back wasn't hurting again. He'd had trouble with it since he'd bent the wrong way to pick something up two weeks ago. A few visits to the chiropractor and Lamar said his back felt better, but maybe he just didn't want her to worry.

Turning back to her students, Emma was disappointed that Anna seemed bored. Rather than looking at the samples of material Emma had shown them a few minutes ago, the young woman sat staring out the window as though in a daze.

She doesn't want to be here, Emma thought. *I don't know why Anna's mother thinks I'll be able to teach her to quilt. She won't learn a thing unless she wants to, so the money Ira and Linda spent on the classes for their daughter might be a complete waste. Well, all I can do is try to get through to her and hope for the best.*

When Lamar returned to the quilting room, a slender, attractive woman was with him. Her pretty blond hair reminded Emma of one of her earlier students, Pam Johnston, only this woman's hair was shorter and worn in a bob.

"Emma, this is Cheryl Halverson," Lamar said. "She brought you a quilt."

"It's my grandmother's quilt," Cheryl was quick to explain. "It's in pretty bad condition, and I was wondering if you could repair it for me."

Cheryl set the box she held on one end of the table and opened the lid. When she lifted out a tattered old quilt, Emma slowly shook her head. "Oh my, that does need to be mended."

Lamar's forehead creased. "Can you do it, or is it beyond repair?"

"The ends are quite frayed, and there are several tears, but I think it's salvageable."

Cheryl smiled at Emma with a look of relief.

When Emma opened the quilt more fully, she saw the pattern in it. "Why, this looks like a traditional Amish wedding-ring quilt. Is your grandmother Amish?"

"Oh no," Cheryl said with a shake of her head. "It's a quilt someone gave her when she got married."

"They most likely bought it in an Amish quilt shop," Anna interjected.

Emma was pleased to see the girl taking an interest in the quilt. Well, maybe not an interest, but at least she was offering her opinion.

"Yes, that's probably how it happened alright." Cheryl glanced at Emma's students, sitting around the table with curious expressions. "I apologize if I've interrupted something. I really should have called first and made an appointment to bring the quilt by."

"That's all right. We're having a quilt class," Emma explained. "This is the first one, and we'll meet every Saturday for the next six weeks."

"That sounds interesting."

Emma smiled. "Would you like to join us?"

"Oh, I don't know about that." Cheryl hesitated, tapping her fingernails on the table. "I'm all thumbs when it comes to sewing."

"Join the club," Blaine put in. "None of us here knows anything about making a quilt."

"Except for me," Selma spoke up. "I—I mean, I've never made one, but I do know how to sew. Quite well, I might add."

Emma turned her attention back to Cheryl. "If you'd really like to join the class, we'd be happy to have you."

Cheryl smiled, revealing a small dimple in each of her cheeks. "Yes, I would," she said, taking a seat. "And I'll be happy to pay whatever the cost."

Carmen couldn't believe how kind Emma was to a complete stranger. But then, she'd been kind to her, too. In fact, when Paul had introduced Carmen to Emma, she'd been welcomed as though she was a good friend.

Carmen's conscience pricked her a bit. *If Emma knew the real reason I decided to take this class, she probably wouldn't have been so welcoming. I need to make sure to keep that a secret—from Emma as well as Paul.*

"Now I want to show all of you what your quilted wall hangings will look like when they're done," Emma said, holding up a small colorful quilt with various shades of blue. "We'll begin today by choosing the colors we want and then cutting out the log cabin squares and the points for the star."

Carmen snuck a peek at Selma, just waiting for her to complain about something. What was with that woman, anyway? Did she always walk around wearing a scowl? *She probably doesn't realize how much older it makes her look. She does have beautiful white hair, though.*

Carmen couldn't help wondering what Selma must have looked like years ago and what made her seem so unhappy. Her wrinkles seemed to be a part of the frown embedded on her face. She certainly had the remnants of a nice tan, and if you took away those deeply etched lines, Selma probably hadn't been a bad-looking lady in her younger years.

Regrettably, Carmen could relate in some ways with whatever was making Selma so touchy. She, herself, had things to overcome. And soon, if she wasn't careful, she'd end up looking older than her twenty-four years.

Carmen glanced at Anna as they started picking out colors. She was definitely the age for rumschpringe and seemed to have a chip on her shoulder. Could she be like one of those rebellious teenagers portrayed on the TV show Carmen had seen last week?

Maybe I'll get the chance to question the girl. If not today, then perhaps next Saturday. I'm confident that by the end of six weeks, I'll have my story.

"Okay, man, I'm going inside now," Terry said once he and Jan had finished loading the shingles.

"You're really going into Emma's house?"

"Yeah, that's right."

"What excuse are you gonna use for going in there?" Jan asked.

"I'll ask for a glass of water, or say that I need to use the bathroom. I'm determined to find out if that blond is available."

Jan's eyes narrowed. "Are you serious?"

"Yep."

"Give me a break, man. I mean, you can't just waltz in there and start plying the woman with a bunch of personal questions."

"I'm not gonna ask a bunch of questions. Just need to find out whether she's single or not."

"How do you aim to do that? Are you just gonna introduce yourself and then blurt out, 'Oh, and by the way, are you married?'"

"No way! I'm not dumb enough to do that. I'm gonna get to know the woman first."

"How's that gonna happen in the few minutes you'll be in the house? It don't take that long to drink a glass of water, you know."

Terry rubbed the side of his face. "Hmm. . . You're right. That could be a problem, unless I take a slow drink." He tapped his foot and contemplated things a bit more. Suddenly an idea popped into his head. "I've got it! If I can't get the answers I want right away, then I'll see if Emma has room for one more in her quilting class."

"*Ha! Ha! Ha!* Now that's a good one!" Jan rocked back and forth on his heels, laughing so hard, tears ran down his cheeks.

"It's not funny," Terry mumbled. "If you can learn to quilt, then so can I. And if I find out the little gal's not married, I'm gonna ask her out."

"Well, if you're determined to do this, then I'm going in with you, 'cause this I've just gotta see!"

CHAPTER 7

"Shouldn't we have knocked first?" Terry asked when Jan opened Emma's back door and stepped into her kitchen.

"Nope," Jan said, going to the cupboard and getting two glasses down. "When I told Lamar we'd be coming by today to pick up the old shingles, he said if we needed anything, the back door would be unlocked and to just walk right in." He handed Terry one of the glasses. "Here you go."

"Any ideas how I can find out whether the little blond's married or not?"

Jan filled his glass with water and took a drink. "Beats me. This was your dumb idea, so you figure it out."

"Maybe we could go in there and tell Lamar and Emma that we've finished picking up the shingles and will be back Monday morning to start putting on the new roof. Then, maybe one of 'em will introduce us to their quilting students." Terry filled his glass with water, took a drink, and set it on the counter. "But then, even if we are introduced, I'll only know the blond's name, not whether she's married or single."

Jan snickered. "If you wanna know bad enough, I'm sure you'll figure out some way to find out."

Terry rubbed the side of his face. This could be a challenge. He'd have to think fast on his feet. He released his hair from the ponytail, letting it hang loosely around his shoulders. "Do I look okay?"

Jan eyeballed him a few seconds, then shook his head. "I'd put the hair back in the ponytail if I was you."

"How come?"

"Some gals might not like guys with long red hair."

"Well, I can't do nothing about the color, since I was born with it, but if you think it'll improve my chances, I'll put it back the way it was." Terry pulled his hair back and secured it with a rubber band. "Is that better?"

Jan gave a nod. "Looks good to me. Let's go."

Terry picked up his glass and followed Jan into Emma's quilting room, hoping this wasn't a mistake and that the blond wasn't married. If she was, he'd bow out real quick.

When Terry and Jan entered the room, Emma looked up with a startled expression. "Oh, I didn't realize you two had come in. Is there something we can do for you?"

"Just came in for a drink of water," Terry said. He glanced at the cute little blond looking curiously at him, then turned to Lamar, who stood near one of the quilts on display. "Also wanted to tell you that we've got all the old shingles picked up and will be back Monday morning to start on the new roof."

Lamar smiled. "That's great. Thanks for letting us know."

Terry cleared his throat a couple of times, unsure how to proceed. Should he just come right out and ask to be introduced to Emma's quilting students? Hoping for assistance, he poked Jan's back.

Jan glared at him. "Hey, what's up with that?"

"Is something wrong, Jan?" Emma asked, looking at him over the top of her metal-framed glasses.

"Uh, no. I'm good." Terry smiled at Emma and said, "Looks like you're teaching another quilting class."

Emma nodded. An awkward silence filled the room, so facing her students, who sat around the table, she motioned to Jan and said, "This is Jan Sweet. He was one of the students in my very first quilting class."

"That's right, and I can tell you that Emma's one fine teacher," Jan responded. "If you do everything she says, you oughta have a nice wall hanging to take home at the end of six weeks." Jan grinned and winked at Selma Nash. "I'm glad to see ya here today."

She offered him a half smile. "Yes, thanks to your generosity."

Terry nudged Jan again. "Ain't ya gonna introduce me?" he asked, trying to keep his voice low.

With a disgruntled-looking frown, Jan finally said, "This is my friend and coworker, Terry Cooley."

"It's nice to meet you," Terry said, glancing briefly at each of the students, then settling his gaze on the blond.

All heads nodded, but no one offered their names. This wasn't going quite the way Terry had hoped. He'd made it inside, now he sure couldn't leave here without finding out if the blond woman was available or not.

"So, ladies," Terry said smoothly, "what do your husbands think of you taking this class?"

"Actually," Emma spoke up before any of the women could respond, "none of my students are married this time."

"I *was* married," Selma said. "I've been widowed for several years."

Terry knew that already, since Jan had given him the lowdown on his irritating neighbor. But instead of responding, he gave the blond his best smile and hoped she might say something. He was disappointed when she didn't.

"Jan's told me a lot about the quilting class he took," Terry said, pulling his gaze from the blond and glancing back at Emma. "Sounds like he not only learned how to quilt, but had a lot of fun in the process."

"That's true, I did," Jan agreed.

"Well, Emma, if you've got room for one more, think I'd like to sign up," Terry announced.

"We actually have room, don't we, Emma?" Lamar spoke up, moving closer to the table.

"Yes—yes, we do," Emma said, looking a bit flustered as her cheeks turned pink.

Lamar grinned. "It'd be nice for Blaine and me if there was another man in the class."

Terry glanced at the dark-haired guy sitting at the table with his shoulders slumped. He didn't look too thrilled to be here. Maybe it was because he was the only male student.

"You know," Terry said, grinning widely. "Since you do have the room, I'd like to take the class. Can I start today?"

"Of course," Lamar said, pulling out a chair for Terry. "Take a seat and join the others."

Terry looked over at Jan. "Would you mind coming back for me when the class is done?"

Jan gave a nod, looking at Terry as if he'd lost his mind. "Sure, why not?"

Terry rubbed his hands briskly together. "Great! I can't wait to get started!"

"Okay, I'll see ya later then." Jan gave Terry's back a solid thump, said good-bye to Emma and Lamar, and left the room, chuckling as he went out the door.

Sure hope I didn't make a mistake saying I'd do this, Terry thought as he took a seat at the table and checked out all the quilts in the room. It looked like a lot of detailed work went into them, and he wasn't sure he was up to the task of making one. Well, now that he knew the cute little blond was single, he couldn't see any way to ask her out except by taking the quilting class. He might not be interested in getting married, but he was more than eager to go out with someone as good-looking as this little gal. He couldn't help noticing her creamy complexion, slightly turned-up nose, and the thick, long lashes framing her light brown eyes.

He forced himself to concentrate on what Emma was saying, which wasn't easy, since he'd taken a seat right beside the blond-haired beauty.

"Now, class," Emma said, pushing Terry's thoughts aside, "with the templates I just handed out, I'd like you to begin marking the patterned pieces on the back of your fabric with either the dressmaker's chalk or a pencil."

"What do we do after that?" Terry asked, scratching his head. Putting on a new roof seemed like a piece of cake compared to this.

"When you're done marking, you'll cut out the pieces of material you'll be working with." Emma smiled. "Beginning next week, you'll start sewing together the pieces you've cut."

"That sounds like a lot of work," the other guy, sitting across from Terry, said.

He looks as out of place here as I feel, Terry thought. *At least I'm not the only guy here, though. Sure hope this gets better.* He was beginning to question his sanity. The blond might be dating someone already or have no interest in him. Of course Terry's intention was to win her over, and since he'd never had any trouble getting a date before, he was up to the challenge. He wasn't sure about the quilt-making, though.

"It is time-consuming to quilt," Emma said, "but it's well worth the effort. Nowadays, the patterned pieces are usually pieced by machine instead of by hand."

"That's a relief," the Hispanic woman at the end of the table said, heaving a sigh. "I can't imagine having to do everything by hand."

"I'm sure I could do it," Selma spoke up. "I've had a lot of experience mending things by hand."

Selma was the only one Terry knew by name, although he'd never spoken to her before. Most times when he'd gone over to Jan's, the nosy old woman was busy outside, pulling weeds, watering the flowers, or picking up things she didn't think should be in her yard. Terry had noticed that as soon as he pulled into Jan's yard, Selma would suddenly appear in her yard. She always acted as if she was busy with something but kept glancing their way, like a neighborhood snoop. After hearing some of the stories Jan had shared about Selma, Terry had decided it was best to give her a wide birth.

"Mending's not the same as quilting, though," Emma's husband, Lamar, interjected. "I'm sure everyone will find it much easier to use one of Emma's sewing machines."

"I don't know about that," the cute little blond said with a shake of her head. "I've tried using my mother's sewing machine several times and have never gotten the hang of it."

"You look like the type of woman who can do anything she sets her mind to," Terry said, leaning close to her.

She wrinkled her nose, leaned away, and reached for a piece of chalk Emma had placed in the center of the table.

Terry grimaced, while tactfully straightening in his seat. *Do I have bad breath or something? Stupid me, I shoulda put a breath mint in my mouth before I came in here.*

Turning his head and trying to remain inconspicuous, he cupped his hand over his mouth and cleared his throat. For the life of him, Terry couldn't remember what he last ate. Taking a quick glance around at everyone, he was glad Emma still had their full attention. So far so good. No one seemed to be looking at him. Hoping to remain unobserved, Terry expelled a little air into the palm of his hand. Cupping his hand over his nose, he inhaled deeply, and quickly lowered his hand before anyone noticed what he'd done. *Naw, don't think so. My breath smells okay to me. Maybe it's my body that stinks. I could be pretty ripe from cleaning up those shingles. I'll never get to first base with this gal if she won't even talk to me.*

"What will we do after our pieces have been sewn onto the quilt top?" the Hispanic woman asked, giving Terry a sideways glance and raising her eyebrows.

"Then the backing, the batting, and the quilt top will be layered, put into a hoop, and quilted by hand," Emma replied.

Perspiration beaded on Terry's forehead and upper lip. He really had bitten off more than he could chew. If he tried sewing anything, he was sure he'd look like a fool.

"When that step is done, the binding will be put on and your wall hangings will be done," Lamar interjected.

Emma nodded. "You should be able to complete the project in six weeks."

Six whole weeks? Terry groaned inwardly. Short of a miracle, it would probably take him a year to make a quilted wall hanging—if he could make one at all.

Cheryl tried to concentrate on what Emma was telling the class, but it was hard to focus when the red-haired fellow sitting beside her kept saying things to her, while checking her out. At least she thought that was why he kept staring at her and taking every opportunity to lean in closer. Between the two men sitting at the table, the scruffy-looking fellow beside her was the least appealing. Not that Cheryl was looking for another man. But if she was, the nice-looking guy across the table seemed to be more her type. Of course he hadn't said or done anything to make Cheryl think he was interested in her. It was just as well. She didn't need the complications, and she was here for only one reason—to learn from Emma and see that Grandma's quilt got repaired.

They all worked silently for a while, cutting out their squares and points for the stars. Then, reaching into his shirt pocket, Terry pulled out a pack of cigarettes.

Emma's mouth dropped open, and Lamar's bushy gray eyebrows shot straight up.

"Hey, now don't go lighting up in here. You ought to have more respect for Emma than that." The clean-cut guy across the table leveled the redheaded man with a look that could have halted a runaway freight train.

Cheryl felt relief. Earlier, when Terry first sat down, she'd noticed a stale cigarette odor on his clothing, and again, on his breath when he'd move in closer to speak to her. With the allergy she had to smoke, the last thing Cheryl needed was someone blowing smoke in her face.

"Sorry. Guess I wasn't thinking." Terry rose from his chair. "I'll go outside for a smoke."

"Why smoke at all?" Selma asked, wrinkling her nose. "It's a nasty habit, not to mention bad for your health."

"Yeah, well, I enjoy smoking. Besides, it's my health I've gotta worry about, not yours," Terry retorted.

"You don't have to be so rude," Selma huffed, crossing her arms. "A guy like you doesn't even belong in this class."

Neither does a busybody like you, Cheryl thought, watching as Terry hurried from the room.

Emma knew she'd have to do something soon with this class, or things would get out of control. She remembered back to her first quilting class, when Jan and Stuart had nearly gotten into a fight because of their hostilities. She couldn't let that happen again.

After Terry returned, Emma remembered that proper introductions hadn't yet been made. "Why don't we start at this end of the table and each of you can share something about yourselves—where you live and anything that might help us get to know you better. After all, we will be spending the next six Saturdays together." She motioned to Carmen. "Would you like to go first?"

Carmen moistened her lips with the tip of her tongue. "My name is Carmen Lopez, and I live in Los Angeles." She hesitated a minute, looking a bit anxious. "I'm visiting my brother-in-law, Paul Ramirez, and his little girl, Sophia. I'm taking the quilt class because it seems—uh—interesting."

Emma nodded. "Paul was part of my first quilting class, and we've become good friends. It's always a joy when he stops by with his little girl." She touched Carmen's shoulder. "Is there anything else you would like to share?"

"I think that's all," Carmen replied, staring down at the table. She appeared to be a bit uncomfortable all of a sudden.

Emma motioned to Anna. "It's your turn."

"There's not much to tell," the young woman mumbled. "My name's Anna Lambright, and I live in Middlebury. I came to the quilt class because my mom signed me up, but I really don't want to be here."

Emma was stunned. She hadn't expected Anna to be so blunt.

"Blaine, why don't you go next?" Lamar suggested, as though sensing Emma's discomfort.

"My name's Blaine Vickers. I work at a sporting goods store in Mishawaka." A patch of pink erupted on Blaine's cheeks. "I'm here because I made a bet with my friend, Stuart, about who could catch the biggest fish. I lost, so now I have to learn how to quilt."

There were a few murmurs from the ladies, and a snicker from Terry, but before anyone could say anything, Emma moved on. "Selma, you're next."

"My name is Selma Nash, and I live here in Shipshewana. I'm here because my neighbor, Jan Sweet, paid for me to take the class. I thought I'd better take advantage of it, because I doubt something like that will ever happen again."

Emma glanced at Lamar, to get his reaction, and he gave her a quick wink. They'd both gotten to know Jan rather well since he'd taken the quilt classes, and they knew that despite his rough exterior, he was a kind, generous man.

Emma then asked Cheryl to introduce herself.

"My name is Cheryl Halverson, and I live in Goshen." She motioned to the tattered quilt she'd brought along. "At the suggestion of my pastor's wife, I brought my grandma's old quilt to Emma for repair. After I got here, I decided to take the quilting class."

"Guess it's my turn." Terry spoke up before Emma had a chance to say he was next. "I'm Terry Cooley, and I also live here in Shipshe." He grinned at Cheryl. "In case you didn't know it, Shipshe's what many of the locals call Shipshewana. Oh, and I'm a roofer by trade."

"What made you decide to join our quilting class?" Lamar asked.

Terry scooted around in his chair, giving his ponytail a quick twist. Then he blew out his breath in a noisy, almost snort. "Well, uh. . . I just thought to myself, if Jan could take the class and like it, then maybe I would, too." He glanced over at Cheryl and grinned. "Thought it might be a chance to make a few new friends as well."

No words were needed as the rhythm of Cheryl's nails clicking on the table spelled out her annoyance with Terry.

Oh dear, Emma thought, seizing the moment to glance out the window, then turning to look at Lamar. His gentle-looking eyes reassured her, even though she couldn't tell what he was thinking. Emma didn't want to feel discouraged, but she couldn't help wondering if this was going to be another challenging class. *If so, Lord, please give me the right words to help these students.*

CHAPTER 8

How'd things go with the quilt class?" Jan asked Terry as they headed to Emma and Lamar's Monday morning to begin putting on the new roof.

"I would have told you on Saturday if you'd come back to get me," Terry muttered, reaching into his pocket for his cigarettes.

"I couldn't help it. When Star called and said one of her tires went flat, I had to rescue her. I tried calling, but you didn't answer your cell phone, so I left a message."

"I didn't realize my phone was turned off. Then when I did turn it on, the battery was dead. Selma saw me walking home, so she stopped and offered me a ride." Terry groaned. "It was nice of her to drive me home, and it sure beat walking, but that woman nearly drove me nuts with all her snide remarks about nearly everyone in the class. She even had something mean to say about Cheryl."

"Who's Cheryl?" Jan asked.

"That hot-looking blond I plan to take out," Terry proclaimed, blowing rings of smoke.

Jan cranked his head as they drove past the parking lot of the local grocery store.

"Hey! You'd better watch where you're going!" Terry shouted.

"Oh, yeah, sorry. I was checking out that Harley in the parking lot back there."

Terry glanced back at the cycle. "It's a nice one, all right."

"About that date," Jan said, "did you get anywhere with it?"

Terry shook his head. "Not yet."

"Did she show any interest in you at all?"

"No, and I don't wanna rush it. Just give me a chance to work my charm on her."

Jan shook his head. "I still say she's not your type, and I think you're barking up the wrong tree."

"Well, you know what they say. . .opposites attract." Terry swallowed as he flicked what was left of his cigarette out the window. "She sure is pretty and seems really nice, and I'm definitely attracted to her."

"You know, I do have an ashtray," Jan muttered.

"I didn't think there was room in there. Not with all the gum wrappers and stuff you have jammed inside. When was the last time you cleaned out this truck anyways?" Terry asked.

"Been awhile, I guess."

"Been awhile?" Terry looked at Jan, raising his brows and pointing at the dashboard. "I'll bet I could tell you every burger joint you've stopped at within the last month by all the Styrofoam cups and wrappers you have stuffed up there. It looks like you've been living in this truck."

"S–weet, isn't it?" Jan snickered. "This rig is sorta like my man cave, you know." He poked Terry with his elbow. "Anyways, back to this Cheryl gal. What if the interest you have in her ain't mutual? Then what are you gonna do?"

"Let's change the subject, shall we?"

"Sure, whatever. Why don't you tell me about Selma? How'd she do at the quilt class?"

Terry grunted. "I don't even know why she came. She already knows everything about making a quilt."

Jan's eyebrows furrowed. "She does? Then why she'd agree to take the class?"

"Maybe she didn't want to hurt your feelings. Or maybe she really doesn't know much about quilting and was just trying to act like she does."

Jan gave his index finger a quick pop before grabbing the wheel again. "You know, I'll bet that's it. It don't surprise me, neither. Selma probably acted like a know-it-all to cover up for what she doesn't know. She's one complicated woman."

Selma set her plate of scrambled eggs on the kitchen table and heaved a sigh as she took a seat. Another day of having breakfast and wishing she had someone to share it with. She missed her husband and daughter so much. She couldn't bring John back from the dead, and she'd all but given up on ever seeing Cora again. Selma attended church on a regular basis, yet she had no real friends. Everyone had their own families, like she'd had once, and what would anyone want to do with a lonely old woman?

Selma took a bite of her scrambled eggs and tried not to let images from the past clog her brain like they'd done so many times before. The last thing she wanted to do was stir up old memories. All it did was make her yearn for the past. And she knew all too well that the past was the past, and there was no getting it back.

She glanced at the calendar on the wall near the sink. *Well, at least*

I have another quilting class to go to. I just wish I didn't have to wait until Saturday.

Selma had all of her squares cut out and couldn't wait to start sewing them together. If she weren't afraid of her teacher's reaction, she'd use her own sewing machine and sew them this week instead of waiting to do them during class.

A thump on the back porch drove Selma's thoughts aside, and she pushed away from the table. Since the thump wasn't followed by a knock on the door, she figured it wasn't someone coming to visit. *Don't tell me one of the neighbor kids threw something on my porch.*

Draping a sweater around her shoulders so she wouldn't get chilled, she opened the door and was surprised to see a mangy-looking gray cat staring up at her. *Meow!*

"Go away. Shoo!" Selma clapped her hands, but the cat didn't budge. "Go on now, get!" She stamped her feet and reached for the broom leaning against the wall near her door. "Go back to wherever you belong!"

The cat hissed and bounded off the porch. Selma stepped back inside and slammed the door. "Stupid neighborhood pests," she mumbled. "You'll never catch me owning a cat or a dog!" Shuffling her slipper-covered feet back to the table so she could finish her breakfast, Selma realized that the cat didn't have a collar. Maybe it was just a stray. Well, she hoped it didn't come around her place again!

Mishawaka

"How'd things go at the quilting class?" Stuart asked when Blaine arrived at work Monday morning.

Blaine frowned. "Let's just say that I've had more fun sitting in the dentist's chair than I did during those two grueling hours. And that's saying a lot, because I hate going to the dentist."

"That bad, huh?"

Blaine nodded. "No wonder you dreaded going to that class."

"I did at first," Stuart admitted, "but after I got to know everyone, they kind of became my friends. At least most of them did. I never got that close to the biker or his newfound daughter, though."

"Well, I doubt anyone attending Emma's class will ever be my friend. There were too many people eyeballing me, and it made me sweat."

Stuart's eyebrows lifted. "How many people are taking the class?"

"Six, counting me."

"That's the same number that were in my class. You shouldn't feel nervous around that small of a group. It's not like you're teaching the class or anything."

"I know, but it wasn't just the amount of people there."

"What was it then?"

"I felt some sort of undercurrent going on, and you know I don't like conflict—even when I'm not personally involved."

"What kind of conflict?" Stuart wanted to know.

Blaine leaned against the wall and folded his arms. "Let's see now. . . this white-haired lady, Selma, acted like she knew more than Emma. She was a bit snippy, too. Oh, and the young Amish woman who came in late obviously had a chip on her shoulder and even said she didn't want to be there. Then there was the Hispanic woman who seemed kind of nervous. Oh, and the redheaded roofer was obnoxious and kept trying to hit on the pretty blond woman, who clearly didn't like him or his ashtray aroma."

"So the guy's a smoker, huh?"

"Yeah. He actually tried to light up in Emma's house, but I put a stop to that. He ended up going outside for a smoke, and I was hoping he wouldn't come back."

Stuart laughed. "Sounds like another group of challenging characters for Emma and Lamar to deal with." He gave Blaine's arm a reassuring tap. "Just relax and enjoy the ride. By the end of the six weeks, you might feel differently about things. Believe me, I never thought so at first, but it does get better."

"I doubt that," Blaine muttered. "And I probably won't know any more about quilting than I do right now."

Goshen

Cheryl gripped the steering wheel tightly as she headed for work. She'd awakened with a headache and had thought about calling in sick. But she wasn't going to give in to it. She'd taken an aspirin with a strong cup of coffee and told herself that she could get through the day. Maybe by the time she got to the office, the aspirin would take effect.

As Cheryl drove along, she was thankful that on Friday she'd gotten all her work done and had left her desk clean. She hoped this morning would start out quiet, with only e-mails to answer and phone calls to return. Most likely it would be that way, as long as her boss, Hugh Edwards, hadn't worked on Saturday, like he did on occasion.

Cheryl slipped in one of her favorite Christian CDs and tried to relax. She'd been uptight since she'd attended her first quilt class. When she'd decided to take the class, she hadn't figured that some overbearing guy who smoked like a diesel truck would be sitting beside her, asking a bunch of nonsensical questions.

Cheryl glanced at her cell phone, lying on the leather seat beside her. She'd called her folks Saturday evening, and again on Sunday, wanting to find out how Grandma was doing, but all she'd gotten was her parents' voice mail. She'd left messages every time, but no response. Surely Mom and Dad couldn't both be too busy to call. Had they gone out of town for the weekend? If so, why hadn't they let her know? Cheryl had been tempted to call again this morning, but with the three-hour time difference between Indiana and Portland, Oregon, her folks would still be in bed, assuming they were home.

She drew in a deep breath and exhaled slowly. *I'll try again when I get home this evening. I really want to know how Grandma's doing, and I need to ask Mom not to tell her about the quilt. I want it to be a surprise.*

Just then her phone rang, so she pulled over to answer, hoping it was her mother. Instead, it was her pastor's wife, Ruby Lee.

"Hi, Cheryl," Ruby Lee said cheerfully. "I'm calling to see if Emma was able to fix your grandmother's quilt."

"Yes, she took the quilt in to repair it," Cheryl replied. "Oh, and I ended up signing up for Emma's six-week quilting class."

"I'm glad to hear that. I'm sure you'll enjoy it as much as I did."

"I hope so. I'm not that good with a needle and thread, so I don't know if I can make a wall hanging as beautiful as the one you made when you took Emma's class."

"Now, Cheryl, remember what the Bible says in Philippians 4:13," Ruby Lee reminded. " 'I can do all things through Christ which strengtheneth me.' "

Cheryl smiled. "I'll try to remember that. Thanks for the pep talk. I needed it."

"You're welcome. Oh, and one more thing."

"What's that, Ruby Lee?"

"I believe that meeting new people—especially people like Emma and Lamar, will be as good for you as it was for me."

Chapter 9

Shipshewana

I've been meaning to ask, how did things go at your quilting class last Saturday?" Emma's daughter Mary questioned as she helped Emma do the dishes. Mary and her family lived next door, but one of the children had been sick last week, so Mary hadn't been over to see Emma for several days. This evening they'd all gotten together at Emma and Lamar's for a haystack supper.

Glancing out the window as the sun settled in the western sky, Emma sighed and placed another clean plate in the dish drainer. "Let's just say the class could have gone better."

"What happened?" Mary asked, reaching for the plate to dry.

Emma lifted her hands from the soapy water and held up one finger. "The first problem was Anna Lambright. She came in late and announced that she didn't want to be there." A second finger came up. "Then there was a lady named Selma Nash, who kept interrupting and acting as if she knew more about quilting than anyone else in the room—including me." Emma extended a third finger. "Jan's friend Terry Cooley was also in the class, and I'm afraid he didn't make a very good impression."

"With you?"

Pushing up her glasses, and leaving a small trail of soap bubbles running toward the tip of her nose, Emma shook her head. "I've met Terry before, so I already knew about his smoking habit. But Cheryl Halverson, who brought her grandmother's quilt for me to fix, ended up sitting right next to Terry." Emma wrinkled her nose. "He smelled like cigarette smoke, which I suspect is why she kept leaning away from him."

"Oh dear." Mary handed Emma a tissue to blot the suds on her nose. "I hope he didn't smoke here in the house."

"He was about to but ended up going outside. Thank goodness Lamar or I didn't have to say anything to Terry about it, because Blaine Vickers, one of the other students, spoke up."

"Who are the others who came to your class?"

"Well, Blaine Vickers is one of Stuart Johnston's friends, and a young woman named Carmen Lopez was also here. She's Paul Ramirez's sister-in-law."

"Sounds like quite a varied group of people," Mary said, reaching for another plate to dry. "Apparently some of them are connected with the first group you had."

"They certainly are. I sure hope things go better during our class tomorrow. I want to be able to help each of my students learn how to quilt."

Mary placed her hand on Emma's arm. "If these classes go like all the others you've taught, I'm sure your students will learn a lot more than quilting from you and Lamar. By the end of six weeks, I can almost count on them being thankful they took your class."

Goshen

Cheryl had just taken a seat at the table to eat the Caesar salad she'd fixed for supper, when her cell phone rang. She was going to ignore it until she realized the call was from her mother.

"Mom, where have you been?" Cheryl asked, reaching for the bottle of ranch dressing to drizzle over her salad. "I've been trying to get a hold of you all week."

"There's no need to be upset, Cheryl," Mom said in a matter-of-fact tone. "Your dad and I needed a little time away, so we went to the beach for a few days."

"To the beach? What about Grandma?" Cheryl's voice rose with each word she spoke. "Who checked up on her while you were gone, and why didn't you let me know you were leaving town?"

"Your uncle Don stopped by the nursing home to make sure she was okay, and we didn't call because going to the beach was a spur-of-the-moment decision."

Cheryl clenched her teeth, forking a crouton and watching it crumble. "I would have appreciated a call. I was worried about you."

"I'm sorry," Mom apologized. "When your dad suggested we go to the beach, I got caught up in the idea and didn't think to call."

"How'd you manage to get time off from the bank?" Mom always used her work as an excuse not to do things with Cheryl, but apparently spending time with Dad was a different matter.

"I had some vacation time coming. Why are you asking so many questions? Don't your dad and I have the right to get away by ourselves once in a while?" Mom sounded upset, and Cheryl knew she'd better not push it any further.

"I'm sorry, Mom. I hope you and Dad had a good time."

"We did. The weather was a bit chilly, but the sun was out, and we had fun walking the beach, looking for shells and agates. You know very well that we don't do something like this often, and it was nice to just go off like we did with no real planning involved." There was a pause. Then Mom said, "How are things going with you?"

"Okay. I found an Amish woman to repair Grandma's quilt, and I signed up to take a six-week quilting class. Please don't tell Grandma I'm having the quilt repaired. I want it to be a special birthday surprise."

"Oh, that's nice, and I won't say a word. Uh, listen, Cheryl, your dad just came in, and I need to talk to him about a few things, so if there's nothing else, I'd better go."

"Sure, Mom. Tell Dad I said hello. Oh, and give Grandma a hug from me when you see her the next time."

"I will. 'Bye, Cheryl."

Cheryl clicked off her phone and stared at her salad. For some reason, she'd lost her appetite. It was just like Mom to be too busy to talk. She never seemed to have enough time for her one and only daughter.

Elkhart

As Carmen stepped onto Paul's porch, her palms grew sweaty. Paul had invited her to join him and Sophia for supper tonight, and even though she looked forward to spending time with her niece, she was nervous about visiting Paul. What if he didn't accept her apology for blaming him for Lorinda's death? What if he quizzed her about the quilt class, and she ended up blurting out the real reason she'd signed up for it? She was sure he'd be upset if he knew she was taking the classes in order to gather research for an article that could shed a bad light on the Amish. And she certainly couldn't mention that she planned to talk privately with Anna Lambright, hoping to get information about her running-around years.

Taking in a quick breath, Carmen rang the doorbell. One glance at the yard told Carmen how the flower beds had been neglected over the past summer. Remnants of weeds where flowers had once bloomed were now dried and bent over.

I'll bet Paul has his hands full, being both mom and dad to Sophia, not to mention his full-time teaching job, Carmen thought. She didn't recall his yard looking so neglected when she'd been here before.

Paul answered the door, wearing a dark blue shirt and a pair of blue jeans. Noting the apron tied around his waist, Carmen suppressed a giggle. She'd never thought of him as the domestic type, but then when he'd had to take on the role of caring for the house, she supposed he'd learned to wear many hats. It couldn't be easy for him raising Sophia on his own. If Carmen lived closer, she would offer to do some things with Sophia. But at least Paul's folks, as well as his sister and her family, lived nearby. From what Paul had said in his e-mails, they often took Sophia to give Paul a break.

"Come in," Paul said, offering Carmen a nervous-looking smile. "You're right on time."

Carmen stepped into the house and removed her coat. "It was nice of you to invite me over. I hope you haven't gone to any trouble preparing the meal."

"Not really," he said, leading the way to his kitchen. Carmen could see it still had Lorinda's touch with the cheery decorations. "I fixed a taco salad for us, and Sophia will have scrambled eggs." He chuckled. "It's one of her favorite things to have for breakfast, but truth is, she likes eggs and could eat them most any time."

"I'm with her on that. Sometimes I like to make breakfast for dinner.

Speaking of Sophia, where is she right now?"

Paul motioned to the door leading to the living room. "In there, watching her favorite TV show with the giant puppets."

Carmen smiled. "I've always enjoyed puppets, too."

"Why don't you go watch the show with her while I get everything on the table?" Paul suggested. "I'll call you when it's ready."

"Are you sure there isn't something I can do to help?"

He shook his head. "I've got it under control."

"Okay." Carmen started out of the room but turned back around. "Uh, Paul, there's something I'd like to say, and if I don't say it now, the evening might go by without another opportunity."

Paul leaned against the counter and folded his arms. "What is it, Carmen?"

She took a step toward him. "I'm sorry for blaming you for Lorinda's death and sorry for not offering more support when she died. I was angry that my sister had been taken from me and needed someone to blame. I realize now that it wasn't your fault, and I don't want there to be hard feelings between us."

Paul stared at the floor. When he lifted his gaze, tears filled his eyes. "Thank you for saying that, Carmen. It means a lot."

Carmen was tempted to give Paul a hug but thought better of it. She wanted to offer comfort, but didn't want him to take it the wrong way. So instead, she merely smiled and said, "I feel better having apologized, and now I'm going to see my sweet little niece."

As Carmen hurried from the room, struggling with tears of her own, she felt a sense of relief for having apologized to Paul. At least that heavy weight had been lifted from her shoulders. Now if she could just get rid of the guilt she felt for not telling him the truth about why she'd come to Indiana.

Middlebury

"How'd things go at work today?" Anna's mother asked as she began dishing up for supper.

"It was okay, I guess." Anna grabbed some silverware from the drawer near the sink and proceeded to finish setting the table.

"Your daed was here almost two hours before you got home," Mom said, reaching around Anna to put a bowl of salad on the table. "Where'd you go after he closed the shop?"

Anna squirmed under her mother's scrutiny. "I. . .uh. . .went to visit one of my friends."

"Which friend, Anna?"

"Mandy Zimmerman."

Mom's eyes narrowed. "You know we don't like you hanging around her. She's a bad influence with all her worldly notions."

Anna went to the cupboard to get down the glasses.

"Mandy's rebellious, too. I wish you would stop seeing her, Anna."

Anger boiled in Anna's chest. *Here we go again. Mom's being critical and telling me what to do.*

"Anna, did you hear what I said?"

"Jah, I heard, but I think I ought to have the right to choose my own friends."

Mom shook her head vigorously. "Not if they're trying to lead you astray."

"Mandy's not doing that. She doesn't push anything on me. She's a lot of fun to be with, and I enjoy our times together." Anna went to the sink, filled a pitcher with cold water, and placed it on the table. "Mom, some of the young people I know are planning a trip to the Fun Spot amusement park tomorrow, and I want to go along."

"You can't, Anna. Have you forgotten about the quilting class?"

"No, but I don't want to go. I'd rather spend the day having fun with my friends than sitting in a room full of weird people and being forced to learn how to quilt."

"I'm sure the other students aren't weird."

"Jah, they are. There's a redheaded guy who tried to light up his cigarette in the Millers' house and an old lady who thinks she knows more than the teacher does. Oh, and then there's—"

Mom held up her hand. "That's enough, Anna. You're going to the quilting class tomorrow, and that's all there is to it. Now go call your sisters and brothers to the supper table."

Anna clenched her fingers so tightly that her nails dug into her palms. Tomorrow morning she would wake up with the flu or a cold, because there was no way she was going back to the quilting class!

Chapter 10

The next morning, Anna entered the kitchen, still wearing her robe and slippers. "I can't go to the quilt class today, because I'm *grank*," she announced.

Mom turned from her job at the stove and frowned. "You're sick? What's wrong, Anna? Is it the flu?"

"Umm. . .jah, I think so." Anna hated lying to her mother, but she had to do something to get out of going.

With a worried expression, Mom stepped away from the stove and hurried over to Anna. "You don't have a *fiewer*," she said, placing her hand on Anna's forehead. "If you had the flu, I'm sure you'd feel warm. Your cheeks aren't even flushed."

"Well, maybe it's not the flu, but I don't feel well." Anna dropped her gaze to the floor. It was hard to lie to Mom when she was looking at her with such concern. *I shouldn't have let her feel my forehead.*

"Anna, are you pretending to be sick so you don't have to go to the class today?" Mom asked, lifting Anna's chin.

Tears pricked the backs of Anna's eyes, but she held her ground.

"I don't want to go, Mom. I don't like it there, and I don't care if I ever learn how to quilt. I'm not a child, you know—I'm eighteen. I should be able to make my own decisions about something like this."

"I'm sorry you don't like the class, but I think it'll be good for you to learn how to quilt. Your daed and I have already paid for the class, so you need to go." Mom stared at Anna and then added, "Now go get dressed. As soon as breakfast is over and the dishes are done, your daed will hitch his horse to the buggy and take you to Emma's."

"Since you've already paid for the class, why can't Arie go instead of me? She likes to sew."

Mom rolled her eyes. "For goodness' sakes, Anna, your sister doesn't need sewing or quilting lessons. You're the one I've never been able to teach."

"Well, if I have to go, why can't I ride my bike, like I did last week?" Anna asked, knowing she wasn't going to get out of this. She also suspected that Mom didn't trust her to go on her own. She probably thought Anna would skip the class and sneak off for the day with her friends, which was exactly what she would have done if she'd been able to ride her bike.

"Your daed has some errands to run in Shipshewana, so it only makes sense for him to take you—especially if you are feeling poorly."

Anna grimaced. Like she was some sort of a little child, now she was stuck being taken to Emma's and then sitting through another boring class. *Why do Mom and Dad treat me like a baby?* she wondered as she tromped up the stairs to her room. *Can't they see that the more they force me to do things their way, the more determined I am to gain my freedom? If they don't let up on me soon, I might leave home for good!*

Shipshewana

"Are you ready for today?" Lamar asked, washing his hands after coming in from tending the goats.

"Jah, I suppose," Emma responded.

When his hands were cleaned and dried, Lamar helped Emma set things out on the sewing table. "I have high hopes that the quilt class will go better today," he said, offering her what he hoped was an encouraging smile. "First classes are always a bit awkward, with everyone getting to know one another."

She gave a slow nod. "I prayed this morning before breakfast that things would go well with the class."

"I prayed the same thing." Lamar placed his hands on Emma's shoulders and looked into her eyes. "Even if things don't go as we might like, I'm sure God will give us the right words to share with our quilting students."

Emma smiled and kissed his cheek. "One thing I've always appreciated about you is your positive attitude. When I'm filled with doubts, you make me feel hopeful."

"Just remember, our hope is in the Lord. Psalm 71:14 reminds us: 'But I will hope continually, and will yet praise thee more and more.'"

"You're right," Emma said. "Danki for that reminder."

"That must be one of our students," Lamar said when a knock sounded on the door. "Would you like me to get it?"

Emma nodded. "Jah, please."

"One of your goats is out," Selma said when Lamar answered her knock. She turned and pointed to the left side of the yard, where a frisky goat nibbled on the grass. "Unless you're trying to replace your lawn mower, you ought to keep that critter in its pen."

Lamar frowned. "Oh great. I must have left the gate open when I fed Emma's goats this morning. Go ahead into the house. Emma's in her sewing room." He hurried past Selma and into the yard, hollering and waving his hands at the goat.

"Sure don't know why anyone would want a bunch of goats. All they do is strip your yard clean, grass and all," Selma muttered as she stepped into the house. "Dogs, cats, goats—they're nothing but a nuisance."

When Selma entered the quilting room, she found Emma sitting at the table with her head bowed. Was she praying or sleeping? Selma waited several seconds, then cleared her throat real loud.

Emma lifted her head and smiled. "Oh, good morning, Selma. I was just getting my thoughts together before teaching the class. How are you today?"

Selma shrugged. "Okay, I guess." She motioned toward the window. "Your husband's outside chasing after one of your goats."

Emma rose from her seat and hurried to the window. "Oh dear, I'll bet it's Maggie again. I hope that critter isn't causing any trouble. She can be an escape artist when she wants to be."

"Lamar said he thought he'd left the gate open when he fed the goats this morning," Selma said, taking a seat at the table.

Emma sighed. "I hope he doesn't have any trouble catching Maggie. She can be a frisky one at times. Do you have any pets, Selma?"

Selma shook her head. "And I don't plan on having any, either."

"Are you allergic to most animals?"

"No, not really. I just can't be bothered with the messes they make."

"Oh, but think of the company a cat or dog offers."

Selma brushed the idea aside. "*Puh!* A barking dog or a yowling cat isn't the kind of company I need. I'd rather be alone than have some animal leaving hair all over my house and making little messes. I just happened to shoo a scraggly-looking cat off my porch this week. You know, once you feed them, they never leave."

Emma opened her mouth, then closed it and looked back out the window.

Selma glanced at the clock on the far wall. It was almost ten o'clock. Were the others going to be late? If so, she would let them know what she thought about that. Like a thorn in her side, tardiness had always been an irritation for her.

Cheryl had just gotten out of her car when a truck pulled into Emma's yard. Terry stepped out, puffing on a cigarette.

"Oh great," she mumbled under her breath. She was hoping he might not show up today.

"Are you ready for another lesson?" Terry asked as he approached her.

She took a step back, hoping to avoid the smoke from his cigarette, but it was no use. The smoke wafted up to her nose. She sneezed and coughed at the same time.

"Have you got a cold?" Terry asked, with a look of concern.

She shook her head, while hurrying along. "I'm allergic to cigarette smoke."

"Oops. Sorry about that." Terry dropped the cigarette on the ground and stomped it out. "So how'd your week go?" he asked, following as Cheryl hurried toward the house.

Before Cheryl could respond, an energetic goat zipped right between them. *Ba-a-a!*

"Come back here, Maggie," Lamar panted, red-faced, as he ran after the critter. He looked exhausted, like he might fall over any minute.

"I'll get her!" Terry shouted, tearing across the yard after the goat.

Cheryl stepped onto the porch and watched in amusement as Terry skirted back and forth across the grass in hot pursuit of the lively animal. Lamar stood by watching and catching his breath.

Terry, on the heels of the goat, raced through the front yard, then the side of the house, and back again. It didn't take long for Terry to grow winded as well. *If he didn't smoke he might not be so out of breath,* Cheryl thought.

As she continued to watch, Cheryl knew she would have given up on catching the goat long ago. But Terry was persistent, even when a coughing fit sent him into spasms. Back and forth he and Maggie went, like they were playing some unending game of tag. Finally, as the ornery animal got closer, it seemed that Terry was about to outwit her.

Cheryl's mouth dropped open when Terry took a flying leap, as if he were about to make an impressive tackle, and missed grabbing Maggie's back legs by mere inches. Covering her eyes with her hands, Cheryl peeked through her fingers just in time to see Terry land facedown in a patch of mud.

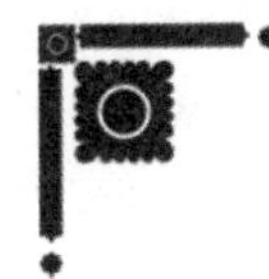

Chapter 11

As Blaine's SUV approached Lake Shipshewana, he fought the urge to stop. The lake was home to native bass and had been named after the chief of a small group of Potawatomi Indians who had used the location for their main camp. It was one of his favorite places to fish, and today the air was crisp yet calm—perfect for fly-fishing. Blaine had seen it many times—those still waters mirroring the azure sky.

Growing up in Canada, where lakes and streams were plentiful, Blaine had developed his love of fishing. He had many fond memories of his parents loading up the family car with picnic foods and fishing poles and taking him and his brothers for a day of fishing. From the first time Blaine could remember going fishing, he was hooked. Fly fishing was his favorite, but any type of fishing provided solitude. Like a true sportsman with heightened senses, nothing went unnoticed.

Blaine made his own lures and had pretty good success with them because they mimicked natural bait. There was nothing like having a pan of fresh-caught trout or bass frying up for dinner. But most times, Blaine just enjoyed catching and releasing, using barbless hooks, so as not to injure the fish. It was the thrill of feeling that tug on his line, reeling it in, and seeing his catch up close. Then, watching as the released fish gave a quick shimmer of its scales before the water swallowed it up in its depths.

Pushing the control to roll down his window, Blaine drew in a deep breath of air. Soon he'd be at the entrance to the turnoff for the lake, and the idea of forgetting about going to Emma's grew more appealing. Would missing one class hurt?

"I'll bet the fish are biting this morning," he said aloud as he hit the button again to close the window. It wasn't fair that he had to go to the stupid class. If he wasn't worried that Stuart would find out, he'd skip it and go fly-fishing instead. But with his luck, Stuart would probably talk to Lamar or Emma this week, and the truth would come out. *I should have known better than to make that stupid bet.*

Blaine thought about the fishing gear in the back of his SUV. He kept it there most of the time so he could fish whenever he got the chance or was in the mood. *Maybe it wouldn't hurt if I stopped and fished for half an hour or so,* he told himself. *I doubt that I'd miss out on much if I arrived at the Millers' a little late.*

Bearing off the main road, Blaine turned his rig into the parking area and shut off the ignition. A few minutes sitting on the dock with his line in the water and he'd feel like a new man.

Terry clambered to his feet, embarrassed that he'd made a fool of himself in front of Cheryl. So much for trying to make a good impression. The worst of it was that he hadn't even caught the stupid goat!

"Are you all right?" Lamar and Cheryl called in unison, as they made their way over to Terry.

"I'm fine. Not hurt. Just dirty and feeling a bit defeated." Terry brushed at the mud on his jeans, wishing he hadn't let his ego get the best of him. "Guess I must look like a real mess."

"Don't worry about that. I appreciate your help. Why don't you go in the house and get cleaned up?" Lamar suggested.

"What about the goat?" Terry asked, unwilling to give up the chase. If he could capture the goat, it might impress Cheryl.

"There's no need for that; looks like Maggie's found her way back into the pen on her own." Lamar pointed to the goat pen, where Maggie scampered about with the other goats. "I just need to go close the gate."

When Lamar headed in that direction, Terry started for the house.

"Are you sure you're okay?" Cheryl asked, catching up with him when he reached the porch.

"Yeah, I'm fine. It's just a good thing my buddy Jan wasn't here to see me make a fool of myself. He'd probably never let me live it down."

"It was just an accident, and you were trying to help." Cheryl offered Terry a sympathetic smile.

He grinned while opening the door for her. Even though Cheryl rolled her eyes, trying to squeeze past him, and then tripped over his big feet, at least she'd seemed concerned about him. Maybe he was making some headway with the pretty blond after all.

As Carmen neared Shipshewana, her thoughts went back to supper at Paul's the night before. The meal was good, and she'd enjoyed getting to know Paul and Sophia better. This visit had been the best so far, being able to spend more time with her niece and not feeling like she had to rush off so quickly. The little girl had taken to Carmen right away and had spent most of the evening sitting on Carmen's lap, while Carmen read from one of Sophia's storybooks. When Paul said it was time for his daughter to go to bed, she'd cried and held her arms out to

Carmen. Then Carmen had helped Sophia change into her pajamas, and afterward, she read the child a bedtime story.

Carmen smiled, reflecting on how she and Paul had tucked Sophia into bed and then spent the rest of the evening drinking coffee, while Carmen shared stories about when she and Lorinda were girls. It was bittersweet, talking about her sister to Paul, and seeing the sad look on his face, but she thought in some way it had brought healing to both of them. Lorinda had been a special woman, and Carmen knew she would always miss her. She was sure that Paul would, too.

Pushing her thoughts aside, Carmen followed a horse and buggy up the Millers' driveway. It stopped near the barn, and Anna stepped down. *Great. This is the perfect time for me to talk to her.*

Carmen parked her rental car and got out. Then she hurried over to Anna, who walked slowly toward the house, head down and shoulders slumped.

"How was your week?" Carmen asked cheerfully.

Anna shrugged and kept walking.

"I noticed you didn't ride your bike today."

Anna motioned to the horse and buggy, pulling out of the driveway. "My dad brought me instead."

Carmen couldn't miss the look of discomfort on Anna's face. She was almost sure the young woman was dealing with some sort of problem.

"I was wondering if you'd like to go to lunch with me after class today," Carmen said as they stepped onto Emma's porch.

Anna's eyebrows arched. "You want to have lunch with me?"

"That's right. I'd like to get to know you better, and it's hard to visit during the quilting class." *At least the kind of visiting I want to do.*

Anna studied Carmen before answering. "That sounds nice, but I can't go to lunch today because Dad will be picking me up as soon as class is over."

"Maybe we can go some other time. Would you be available any time next week?"

Anna looked hesitant, but she finally nodded. "I'd like that. Could you meet me for lunch on Wednesday at Das Dutchman in Middlebury?"

Carmen knew exactly where that restaurant was because she'd had supper there a few nights ago. "Sure, that'd be fine. I'm looking forward to it."

"Me, too." Anna sighed. "Guess we'd better get in there, or they'll be starting the class without us. Not that I'd mind," she quickly added.

That's the second time she's said it, Carmen thought as they entered the house. *Anna Lambright does not want to be here. I hope I can get her to open up to me when we have lunch next week.*

Chapter 12

While Terry was in the bathroom cleaning up, Cheryl went to the quilting room to speak with Emma.

"How's my grandma's quilt coming along?" she asked.

"I'm sorry," Emma said, "but I've been busy this week and haven't had much time to work on the quilt. I'm sure I'll be able to get more sewing done on it next week, though," she quickly added.

Cheryl smiled. "I'll be anxious to see the quilt when it's done. And I can't wait to see the expression on Grandma's face when I give it to her."

"Tell me about your grandmother," Emma said, as Cheryl took a seat at the table. "Does she live near you?"

Cheryl shook her head. "Grandma lives in a nursing home in Portland, Oregon. It's not too far from my folks' house, but with Mom and Dad both working all day, they don't go to visit Grandma that often." Cheryl's eyes filled with unwanted tears, and she blinked to keep them from falling onto her cheeks. "I—I don't think Mom really cares that much."

Emma's eyes widened. "About your grandmother?"

Before Cheryl could respond, Terry entered the room and took a seat beside her. His face and hair were wet, and so were the knees of his jeans. Unfortunately, the scrubbing he'd done hadn't removed the odor of smoke from his clothes, but at least the mud was cleaned off.

"So what'd I miss?" Terry asked, leaning close to Cheryl.

Cheryl leaned away. "Nothing. Emma and I were just talking about my grandmother's quilt." She hated to be rude, but the smell of smoke on Terry's clothes made her feel sick.

"Okay. Okay. I can take a hint." Terry leaped out of his chair and found a seat on the other side of the table just as Carmen and Anna entered the room.

Cheryl was relieved when Anna sat on one side of her, but she wished Carmen had taken the seat on the other side instead of sitting at the end, next to Anna. She hoped Terry remained where he was, but when Selma showed up and sat beside her, she wasn't so sure about that. Last week Selma had criticized the way Cheryl held her scissors. Who knew what she might find fault with today?

A few minutes later, Lamar entered the room. "Maggie's back in her pen, and the gate's closed. Hopefully she won't figure out how to get it open," he said to Emma.

She smiled. "You know my Maggie. She's one schmaert little goat."

"Schmaert? What does that mean?" Terry asked.

"It's Pennsylvania Dutch for the word *smart*," Lamar replied.

"Oh, I see. So what's the opposite of schmaert?" Terry questioned.

"*Dumm*," Emma responded.

"That's interesting and all," Selma spoke up, "but we didn't come here to learn a new language. We came to make a quilted wall hanging."

"That's right," Emma agreed, "and we'll get started with today's lesson as soon as Blaine arrives."

Selma wrinkled her nose and grumbled, "Last week Anna came in late, and now Blaine's not here. Can't people be on time? It's inconsiderate when they show up late and make the rest of us wait."

"Have you been out to the phone shack to check for messages this morning?" Emma asked Lamar, ignoring Selma's comment. "Maybe there's one from Blaine, letting us know he won't be here or is running late for some reason."

"I haven't checked yet," Lamar said, "but I'll run out there now. You can begin teaching the class while I'm gone. If Blaine is coming, he can catch up when he gets here."

Emma and her husband are sure patient, Cheryl thought. *If I were teaching this class, I'd call Selma up short for being so rude.*

"I think we should wait to get started until Lamar returns and we know if there's a message from Blaine," Emma said facing the class.

"What are we supposed to do until then?" Selma asked with a look of agitation. "Sit and twiddle our thumbs?"

"Of course not," Emma said, watching Selma take supplies out of her mint-green tote bag. "We can visit and get to know each other a little better."

"Puh!" Selma swiped the air with her hand as if she was after a pesky fly. "I didn't come here to get to know anyone. I came to quilt!"

Emma was taken aback by Selma's rudeness. The poor woman was certainly not the friendly type. "As I said before, we'll begin as soon as Lamar returns from the phone shack." Emma looked over at Terry and smiled. "How was your week?"

"It went fine till I fell in the mud chasing your goat." He leaned his head back and chuckled. "Guess I got what I deserved, thinking I could run faster than that frisky critter."

"If it makes you feel any better, you're not the only one of my students who's gotten bested by Maggie. During my first quilting class, Maggie got out, and Blaine's friend Stuart thought he could catch her. He ended up on his face in the grass. Then your brother-in-law went out to help him," Emma added, looking at Carmen.

"I'm not surprised Paul would do something like that. From the things my sister used to tell me about Paul, he's always been one who likes to help out."

"Yes," Emma agreed. "Paul has many fine qualities, and he was good with Maggie. I never saw that goat react to anyone like she did Paul. She went to him when he held out a handful of grass and didn't resist when he guided her back to her pen. Some people have a special way with animals."

"Jan's good with his dog," Terry spoke up, "but I guess goats ain't my thing."

"No animal is *my* thing," Selma said, wrinkling her nose. "They're nothing but pests."

Feeling the need for a change of subject and wanting her students to get better acquainted, Emma suggested that they go around the table and share something about what they had done during the week. Cheryl, Carmen, and Selma willingly shared a few things, but when Emma asked Anna how her week had gone, she merely shrugged and mumbled, "Same as always."

I wish there was something I could say or do to make Anna open up, Emma thought. *She seems so sullen and withdrawn. Even though Selma's a bit opinionated, at least she's willing to talk.*

Emma was relieved when Lamar returned. "No message from Blaine," he said, "but there was one from my daughter, Katie. She strained her back and asked if I'd give her a ride to the chiropractor's.

It's Dr. Clark's day off, of course, but he kindly said he'd meet us there. Emma, can you manage okay while I take Katie?"

"I'll be fine." Emma patted Lamar's arm. "You go along and help your *dochder*."

"Danki, Emma. I'll see you later." Lamar said good-bye to the class and hurried from the room.

"Since we don't know when or if Blaine will be here, I suppose we'd best get started," Emma said, reaching for a piece of material that had been cut and was ready to sew. "Today we'll begin sewing the pieces of fabric you've already cut. You can take turns using the battery-operated sewing machines, and if anyone wants to try out my treadle machine just let me know and I'll show you how."

"I already know how to use a treadle," Selma announced. "My grandmother had one when I was a girl, and she taught me how to sew on it."

"That's good. Maybe you'd like to use mine today." Emma smiled. "Some of my Amish friends and relatives prefer to use the battery-operated machines or one that's hooked up to a generator, but I've always enjoyed using the treadle."

"My *mamm* uses a treadle machine when she sews, too," Anna said. "But I'm not interested in that."

"You can use one of my battery-operated ones," Emma said, glad that Anna was conversing a bit. Maybe after she'd done some sewing and saw how her wall hanging was taking shape, she'd actually enjoy the class.

"I'd like to try the treadle machine for a few of my patterned pieces," Carmen said.

"Same here," Cheryl agreed.

"Not me," Terry said with a shake of his head. "I'm not even sure I can use the battery-operated machine." He frowned. "I'll probably end up sewing my fingers together instead of the material."

"You'll do fine," Emma said. "I'll make sure of that."

Terry had been fumbling with his pieces of material for ten minutes when Blaine showed up.

"Sorry I'm late," Blaine apologized to Emma. "I stopped at the lake and ended up dropping my line in the water. Guess I sort of lost track of time."

"What do you mean, 'sort of'?" Terry pointed to the clock on the far wall. "You're forty-five minutes late!"

Blaine glanced briefly at the clock; then he smiled at Emma and said, "I caught a largemouth bass, and it's in a bucket on the porch. If you like fish, I'd be happy to give it to you."

Emma nodded. "Lamar and I both like fish, but don't feel obligated to give it to us."

"No, I want to," Blaine insisted. "Should I go out and get it or wait until after class?"

"Just wait until Emma's finished teaching the class," Selma interjected. "In case you haven't noticed, the others have already started sewing, so you'd better take a seat."

Terry looked over at Blaine and said, "You knew you had class today, didn't you?"

Blaine gave a nod. "Of course."

"Then you oughta get your priorities straight, instead of going fishing and showing up late." He plugged his nose. "Phew! No wonder you smell so fishy."

"It's better than reeking of smoke," Blaine countered. "Besides, if you want to catch anything, you have to go when the fish are biting.

And they sure were hungry today," he added. "I caught a bigger fish than the one I'm giving Emma, but it rolled just as I was about to net it, and off went the hook."

Emma was surprised at Blaine's change of mood, and how his face lit up when he talked about fishing. It was nice to see this side of his character, but while she hated to burst his bubble, she'd better do something quick, or these two men who were acting like boys might end up in a fight. It was becoming more obvious to Emma that some sort of duel was going on between Terry and Blaine. She was sure it had nothing to do with Terry's smoking or Blaine's fishing, and everything to do with a certain blond woman in her class.

"Here are the pieces of material you cut out last week," she said, handing them to Blaine. "All you need to do is pin them in place, and you can begin sewing."

Blaine shook his head. "I don't know anything about using a sewing machine."

"I'll show you how," Emma said.

As the others took turns at the sewing machines, Emma instructed Blaine on how to pin his pieces of material together before sewing them. Once she was sure he could handle things on his own, she went to the kitchen to get some refreshments.

She'd just placed some banana bread on a platter, when her nine-year-old granddaughter, Lisa, who lived next door, rushed into the kitchen. "Mama wants to know if you have any *zucker* she can borrow," she told Emma. "We're gonna bake some chocolate-chip *kichlin*, but we don't got enough zucker."

"Of course you can borrow some sugar." Emma lovingly patted Lisa's head, then went to the cupboard and took down the plastic container she kept her sugar in.

"Did you do some baking this morning?" Lisa asked, pointing to the banana bread.

"I made it yesterday," Emma explained. "I'm getting ready to serve it to my quilting students."

Lisa grinned. "Are you gonna teach me how to quilt someday?"

"Of course. Unless your mamm decides she'd rather teach you."

Lisa shook her head. "I'd rather you teach me, *Grossmammi*. You're the bestest quilter in Shipshe."

Emma chuckled. It was nice to know her granddaughter felt that way, but she was sure others could quilt equally well. "I'd better get back to my students now, and you'd better go home. You'll never get any cookies baked if we keep gabbing." She handed the sugar to Lisa, then bent down and kissed her cheek. "I'll see you later this evening when Lamar and I come over for supper."

Lisa nodded and skipped out the door.

Emma was about to carry the tray of banana bread to the other room, when Carmen entered the kitchen. "I came to see if you needed any help," she said.

Emma handed the tray to Carmen. "You can take this into the quilting room, while I get some coffee and mugs."

"Okay." Carmen paused near the kitchen door. "I've been wondering about something, Emma."

"What's that?"

"Since I've been in the area I've heard some things, and one of them is that all Amish young people go through a time of running-around after they finish the eighth grade and are done with their formal schooling."

"That's right. It's called rumschpringe."

"That's what I thought; although I can't pronounce it correctly." Carmen shifted the tray in her hands. "What can you tell me about—"

"I came to tell you that Selma doesn't want any coffee," Lamar said, entering the room. "She said she'd prefer a cup of tea."

"Oh good, you're back. How'd Katie's chiropractic appointment go?"

"It went fine. She's home resting now with an ice pack."

"That's good. Now about Selma's request. . . Did she say what kind of tea she wanted?"

Lamar shook his head. "But to be on the safe side, maybe you should give her a cup of hot water and offer a choice of tea bags."

"That's a good idea." Emma looked at Carmen. "What was it you were about to ask before Lamar came in?"

"It was nothing important. I'll talk to you about it some other time." Carmen hurried from the room.

"Have things gone any better with the class today?" Lamar asked, reaching into the cupboard to get the tin filled with tea bags.

Emma sighed. "Not really. There seems to be some undercurrent going on between Terry and Blaine, and Selma's still a bit overbearing. Then there's Anna. I can't seem to get through to her, Lamar."

"Just give it more time. I'm sure things will improve. This is only the second class." He gave her arm a loving pat. "Remember how it went with your first class, Emma?"

"Jah. It was a bit rocky at first, but as time went on things got better."

"And so they shall again. Just remember to ask God for guidance."

"Yeow!" Blaine hollered. "I stuck my finger with a pin!"

Cheryl reached for her purse. "I have a bandage if you need one."

"Yeah, that'd be good." Blaine smiled at Cheryl in a way that nearly made Terry gag.

Terry rolled his eyes. *I'll bet he did that on purpose, just to get some attention.*

"You need to be careful with pins," Cheryl said as she put the bandage on Blaine's finger.

"I know that now." Blaine pointed to the pieces of material he'd already sewn. "I'm no better at sewing than pinning. Look how crooked my stitches are."

"They're not that bad," Cheryl said, leaning closer to Blaine. "It just takes a little practice to get the hang of it."

Hearing the conversation between the two of them was almost Terry's undoing. It was irritating watching how comfortable Cheryl seemed with this guy who smelled like fish. *I wonder if Cheryl's interested in him. If so, could the feeling be mutual? And Blaine—just look at him.* Terry had noticed before that Blaine didn't make eye contact with anyone much, but he sure wasn't having trouble looking into Cheryl's beautiful, doe-like eyes. The worst part of it was she was looking back.

She does seem to be better suited to him than me. Of course, opposites are supposed to attract, so there might still be some hope, Terry told himself. *If I could just get her to go out with me, maybe she'd see that I'm not half-bad. The biggest problem I see is that I smoke, and since Cheryl's allergic to smoke, that's a strike against me. There's only one thing to do,* he decided, reaching for a piece of banana bread. *I need to quit smoking. But can I do it?*

CHAPTER 13

Elkhart

Would you say that again?" Jan asked as he and Terry headed to a job on Monday morning. "I think I might've been hearing things."

"You heard me. I'm gonna quit smoking."

Jan quirked an eyebrow. "Oh yeah? What made you decide that?"

"Cheryl's allergic to smoke," Terry replied, trying to sound nonchalant. "Don't think she'll ever go out with me if I smell like smoke. Besides, as you've pointed out many times, it's bad for my health."

"Funny, but you've never worried about that before." Jan's deep laughter bounced off the roof of his truck. "Boy you must really have it bad!"

"What do you mean?"

"All the times I've tried to get you to quit, and you've just ignored me."

"That's 'cause I wasn't ready," Terry retorted.

"So you meet some gorgeous blond who you'll probably only date once or twice before you dump her, and suddenly you're ready to throw away your cigarettes? I'll have to see that to believe it."

"You can laugh all you want, but I will quit smoking, and if Cheryl agrees to go out with me, I'm sure I'll wanna date her more than a few times."

"You sound pretty confident. Have you even tried asking her out?"

"No, but I will. . . Next Saturday, in fact."

"And when are you planning to quit smoking?" Jan pointed to the pack of cigarettes in Terry's shirt pocket. "I see you're still toting them around."

"I'll quit as soon as I've smoked my last cigarette."

"When will that be?"

"When I've emptied this pack," Terry said, pulling out a cigarette and lighting up.

"Well, you'd better smoke it up quick then, 'cause there's only four weeks left before your quilt classes end, and that don't leave you much time to win Cheryl over."

"I can do it," Terry said with a vigorous nod. "Just wait and see. Besides, I'll bet I can quit smoking before you get this dirty truck cleaned out."

Jan grunted. "I'd be more worried about your smoking habit than my truck. And you know what?"

"What's that?"

"I think you oughta stop right now, so you have some time to get the smell outta your clothes. I mean, why wait around? If you expect Cheryl to take notice of you, then you oughta get right on it."

"I don't know." Terry scratched his head. "It's not gonna be easy."

"Maybe God wants you to quit. Did you ever think of that?" Jan elbowed Terry in the ribs. "I've invited you to attend church with me and Star many times, but you always come up with some sort of excuse.

Maybe if you sat in church once in a while and let God into your life, you'd have the strength and willpower it takes to quit smoking."

"I'll give it some thought," Terry said, blowing smoke out of his mouth and breathing it back up his nose.

Goshen

Cheryl had no more than taken a seat at her desk when the phone rang. "Edwards' Law Firm," she said after she'd picked up the receiver.

"Hey, Cheryl, it's me, Lance."

"Why are you calling me here at work?" Cheryl asked with irritation. She didn't know why her ex-boyfriend would call her at all, much less at her place of employment. She didn't want Mr. Edwards to think she was using the office phone for personal use. He probably wouldn't appreciate it.

"I tried your cell number but all I got was your voice mail," Lance said.

Cheryl reached into her purse and realized that she'd left her cell phone at home. "What do you want, Lance? I have a lot of work staring me in the face and don't have time to talk."

"I won't keep you long, but April's birthday is next week, and I need a suggestion as to what I should buy her."

Cheryl tapped her fingernails on the desk. "Why ask me?"

"You and April used to be good friends—college roommates, in fact. So if anyone should know her likes and dislikes it ought to be you."

"You're the one spending time with her now. April and I don't see each other anymore, so you should be able to figure it out on your own." Cheryl clenched her teeth, struggling to keep her emotions in check.

"I know that, but you used to be best friends, so I thought—"

"Well, you thought wrong. April's your girlfriend, so figure it out.

And please, stop calling me!" Cheryl hung up the phone before Lance could say anything more. It was bad enough that he'd dumped her for April. Did he have to rub it in her face?

She grabbed the morning's mail and thumbed through it, anxious to get her mind on something else. As a Christian, Cheryl knew she needed to forgive April and Lance, but with him calling her like this, it was hard to control her temper. Whenever Lance called, it felt like someone had poured salt into her wound. Just when Cheryl thought she was over Lance's rejection and April's betrayal, he'd call again, wanting to know something about April so he could make a good impression.

What was that verse Ruby Lee told me about? Oh yes, "I can do all things through Christ. . . ." I surely ought to be able to take control of my emotions and not get so angry like this. Maybe I should talk to Ruby Lee or Pastor Gene about it.

Middlebury

When Anna arrived at work Monday morning, the first thing she did was boot up the computer to check for e-mails from any of their English customers, who often placed their orders online.

After she'd taken care of that, since no one but her was in the office, she decided to surf the Internet and check out some sites that sold English women's clothes. She was fascinated with the bright colors, fancy scarves, pretty blouses, slacks, and jewelry. One of these days when she went shopping in Goshen, she planned to try on some English clothes. A few of Anna's friends like Mandy, who hadn't yet joined the church, dressed in English clothes whenever they were away from home and out having fun. Anna spent most of her time at work and didn't have much free time to spend away from home, so she hadn't been able to do all the fun things her friends did since they'd gotten out of school.

At least I can look at pretty things online, she mused, admiring a fancy pair of women's platform shoes. The shoes featured suede and tweed uppers, dotted suede details at the heel, and a vintage-looking bow. "Those are amazing," Anna murmured. *Of course I probably wouldn't be able to walk in them without falling over. It'd be fun to try, though.*

Anna had taught herself how to use the online search options, and the more she used the computer, the more fascinated she became. She was amazed at the information available by simply typing in a word or two in the search window. She could visit places she'd only dreamed about, see clothes she longed to wear, and take part in some chat rooms, where she could converse with others outside the scope of her Amish community. Since the computer was in a separate room, away from where the windows were made, Anna used it for her own enjoyment whenever no one else was around. If a customer came in, she could easily minimize whatever page she'd been looking at. And she could usually hear Dad's footsteps when he was approaching the office, so there was time to click out of whatever site she'd been exploring before he discovered what she was up to.

Anna wished she could have a computer at home, but of course that was against their church's rules. And it wasn't bad enough that the church had rules. Mom and Dad had their own set of regulations, which was why Anna felt like a little girl so much of the time. If only they'd give her the chance to explore the English world, she might not feel so frustrated.

"Anna, what are you doing?"

Anna jumped and tried to downsize the website she'd been on. In the process, the mouse flew right off the desk, as Dad's booming voice echoed in her ear.

"*Ach*, Dad, you scared me! I—I didn't hear you come in. I thought you were in the other room."

"I was, but I'm here now, and I don't like what I see!" His finger shook as he pointed at the computer. "I was afraid when I bought that thing that it'd be a temptation for you. Guess I was right because I see that you're looking at fancy English shoes." His forehead creased as he looked at her sternly. "What's it gonna take before you become trustworthy, Anna? You hang around with Mandy even though we don't approve, you've made excuses for not going to church, and now this? I can't believe you, Anna."

Anna dropped her gaze to the floor. "I'm sorry, Dad. I just wanted to see—"

"I know what you wanted to see. You have worldly ways on your mind, and this is not a good thing. I think it'd be best if you let me manage the orders and e-mails from customers from now on. You can work in the back on windows."

"But Dad..."

"No buts, Anna. I will not have you, or any of my other *kinner*, using the computer to look at fancy things!" Dad pointed to the other room. "Now go in there and ask your uncle Sam what you can do to help."

Tears welled in Anna's eyes. If she couldn't use the computer anymore, she'd be miserable. It was the only thing she had to look forward to at work every day. She needed to find another job. It was the only way she would be free from so many rules.

Anna squeezed her fingers tightly together. *If Mom and Dad would stop treating me like a child and let me make my own choices, I might not be so interested in fancy things.*

Chapter 14

Shipshewana

On Wednesday, shortly before noon, Selma decided to rake the leaves that had fallen from the trees in her front yard. She'd had a late breakfast and wasn't ready to eat lunch, so this seemed like a good time to tackle the job.

When John was still alive, he'd always kept the yard cleaned up, while Selma concentrated on her flower and vegetable gardens. Now the burden of everything fell on her shoulders. It was a lot of work, but she enjoyed being outside, which at least made the time go by quickly.

Selma went to the shed and got out the rake. Then, pushing her floppy-brimmed hat off her forehead a bit, she went right to work. She'd been raking for about thirty minutes when she spotted her neighbor, Frances Porter, who lived across the street, and noticed that she was also raking leaves. Frances was in her forties and worked from home, decorating cakes. Her husband, Earl, was a sales representative for a pharmaceutical company, so he was on the road a lot, leaving many of the chores to Frances and their twelve-year-old daughter, Gretchen. Frances didn't complain, though, at least not to Selma. Of course, most of the neighbors said very little to Selma, unless she spoke to them first.

After Selma had worked her way to the edge of the lawn with her rake, she hollered across the street, "I hope you've insulated your roses against the cold weather we'll soon be having. Some of those leaves in your yard would work well for that."

Frances waved but gave no response. Was she avoiding Selma, or just too busy to talk?

"Humph!" Selma grumbled. "Wouldn't you think she'd have the decency to say she appreciated my suggestion?"

Selma turned aside and continued raking the rest of the leaves. When she was done, she put the rake back in the shed and headed for the house to fix lunch. She'd worked up a hearty appetite, and the thought of that ham sandwich she planned to make sounded pretty good about now.

She'd just started up the porch steps when she spotted that same mangy-looking gray cat she'd chased away the other day, sitting on her porch near the door.

Selma stomped her feet and clapped her hands. "Go on now! Shoo! Shoo!"

The cat tipped its head to one side and let out a loud, *Meow!*

"Don't think you can soft-soap me into feeding you," Selma said, shaking her finger at the cat. "I give out free lunches to no one—least of all to a flea-bitten feline like you!"

Selma reached for the broom she kept near the door, but before she could pick it up, the cat took off like it had been shot out of a cannon.

"Good riddance," Selma muttered as she hurried into the house. "I hope I've scared you enough that you'll never come back here again!"

Mishawaka

Blaine was just getting ready to take his lunch break, when he caught sight of his ex-girlfriend Sue heading his way. *Oh great*, he thought. *I wonder what she wants.*

Sue stepped up to Blaine and touched his arm. "Hi. How are you?"

"Do you really care, or are you just being polite?" he muttered, hoping none of the employees had heard him. The last thing he needed was for word to get out that he'd been rude to a customer. Stuart might be his friend outside of work, but here in the store, all employees were treated equally—and that meant being courteous to every customer.

"Of course I care. We're still friends, right?" she asked, looking up at him with an innocent smile.

"Yeah, sure. Now what can I help you with?" Blaine asked, trying to ignore his rapid heartbeat. Looking at Sue's soft brown eyes and curly auburn hair made him miss what they'd once had together. And it hadn't helped when she'd touched him, either.

"I came to buy a present for my grandfather," Sue replied. "His birthday is next week."

Blaine made a sweeping gesture. "As I'm sure you can see, there are lots of things to choose from here in the store, so why don't you browse around for a while?"

"I was hoping you'd have some suggestions, since you and Grandpa both like to fish."

Blaine's stomach knotted. He'd been convinced that Sue was the right woman for him, and now. . . Well, he just needed to get over her and move on with his life, because there was no point in moping about their breakup and letting it consume him.

"What exactly did you want to get your grandfather?" Blaine questioned.

"I don't know. That's why I asked for your help."

"How about a hunting vest, a hat, or a new fishing pole?" he suggested.

"Maybe. Let's look at those things, and then I'll decide."

"I really don't have time to show you everything," Blaine said, struggling to remain patient. Didn't Sue realize how hard it was for him to be with her? Didn't she care how badly she'd broken his heart by not agreeing to marry him?

She sighed. "Well then, if you'll point me in the right direction, I'll go look for myself."

Blaine showed Sue the sections of the store where she could find the items and then said good-bye and hurried off in the direction of the break room.

When he stepped inside, he saw Stuart sitting at one of the tables with a cup of coffee and a doughnut. It didn't take Stuart long to spot Blaine and wave him over.

"How's it going?" Stuart asked when Blaine took a seat beside him. "You look a little harried right now."

"I'm a lot more than harried; I'm upset." Blaine took a handkerchief from his pocket and wiped his sweaty brow.

"How come?"

Blaine explained about Sue coming into the store and asking his help in choosing a gift for her grandfather. "Wouldn't you think after our breakup that she'd find somewhere else to shop?" he grumbled.

Stuart frowned. "You want to send our customers elsewhere?"

"Just Sue. I wish she'd find a job in some other part of the country so I'd never have to see her again. It's too painful, not to mention a reminder that I must have done something wrong because our relationship failed."

"You didn't do anything wrong."

"Yeah, well, something sure went haywire, or she wouldn't have broken up with me."

"Want to know what I think?" Stuart asked, placing his hand on Blaine's shoulder.

"What's that?"

"You ought to start dating again. It would help get your mind off Sue, and you'd probably smile more often, too."

"I might consider that if there was someone I wanted to ask out."

"What about the pretty little blond you mentioned who's taking Emma's quilt class with you?" Stuart asked. "Didn't you say she was single?"

Blaine nodded. "I'm not sure she'd be interested in going out with me. Besides, I don't know her that well, and we may not have anything in common."

Stuart thumped Blaine's shoulder a couple of times. "There's only one way to find out—ask her out."

"Where would we go?"

"Use your imagination. Take her out to dinner, to the movies, or go bowling. She's bound to like one of those things. And who knows—maybe she's the type who likes to go fishing, the way you and Sue used to do." Stuart took a drink of his coffee. "If you hit it off, she could end up becoming Mrs. Blaine Vickers, and then you can stop worrying about your brothers having families and not you."

Blaine reached for a cup of coffee, savoring the aroma as he lifted it to his lips. "I'll give it some thought."

Middlebury

Carmen had just entered Das Dutchman restaurant Wednesday afternoon when she spotted Anna near the door. She smiled and touched Anna's arm. "I'm glad you could meet me here today."

"Me, too."

After their hostess seated them at a table along one wall, Anna leaned close to Carmen and whispered, "I'm in big trouble with my dad right now, so I wasn't sure I could meet you at all."

Carmen's ears perked up. "How come you're in trouble?"

Anna proceeded to tell how she'd been caught surfing the Internet and was made to work on windows instead of greeting customers and taking care of orders in the office. "I'm gonna look for a new job," she added.

"What kind of work would you like to do?" Carmen asked.

Anna shrugged. "I'm not sure. I've worked in the window shop ever since I graduated from eighth grade, so I don't really know how to do much else."

Carmen's mouth dropped open. "You didn't go to high school?"

Anna shook her head. "Amish children only get an eighth-grade education."

Carmen wasn't sure how she missed this basic fact, so she decided to question Anna about rumschpringe, asking what it was like to run around with her friends and experience the English world.

"My folks don't approve of most of my friends—especially Mandy Zimmerman—but I still see her whenever I can." Anna sighed. "I can't help but wonder what it'd be like to wear an English dress or a pair of blue jeans, like some of my friends do when they're not at home."

"I saw a little dress shop near the hotel on this property," Carmen said. "Would you like to go there when we're done eating lunch?"

"I wish I could," Anna said wistfully, "but Dad will expect me to be back from lunch by one, so there's no time to look at clothes."

"Maybe we could go on Saturday when we're finished with the

quilting class. Would you be free to do some shopping then?" Carmen asked.

"I–I'm not sure. Maybe, if my dad doesn't take me to Emma's again. Sometimes I feel like running away and never coming back. My parents control my whole life."

Carmen could see by Anna's anxious expression that she wasn't happy. Could her parents be holding such a tight rein on her that she was on the verge of rebellion? Carmen looked forward to visiting with Anna again and getting additional information for the story she planned to write. Maybe there was more to this rumschpringe thing than most people knew about. If so, she planned to find out as much as she possibly could.

Goshen

As Jan directed his truck into town, Terry reached into his pocket and pulled out a cigarette.

"I see you're still smoking," Jan said, looking at Terry with disgust. "I figured you wouldn't be able to hack it."

Terry lit the cigarette and blew the smoke out the open window. "Hey, man, get off my case! I'm doing the best I can with this."

"I don't call blowing smoke out the window doing your best. If you ask me, the only way to quit is to go cold turkey."

"I tried that already. It didn't work. I got shaky, and I couldn't think straight. I just need to taper off."

"Why don't ya try taking only one drag of smoke each time you reach for a cigarette, and then put it out? Maybe that one drag would satisfy you till the next one."

"Guess I could try that, but I don't know. This is harder than I thought."

"It's gonna take you a lot longer to quit if you try to do it with that attitude." Jan reached into his pocket and pulled out a pack of gum. "Here, chew one of these. If you don't quit smoking, your teeth and fingertips will turn yellow."

Terry grunted. "Like gum's gonna take away my craving. It'll probably end up giving me cavities."

"It's sugarless, and it might help you quit smoking. That's what got me over the hump when I used to smoke."

Terry's eyes widened. "When was that? I've never known you to smoke."

"Started when I was sixteen, but I quit before Star was born. I didn't want my little girl breathing any secondhand smoke. That all happened way before I met you."

"But you said Star was less than a year old when her mom ran off with her. I'm surprised you didn't start smoking again after that."

"I was tempted to—many times. But I figured it was a nasty habit, and I hoped Bunny would come to her senses and return to me, so I never went back to smoking."

Terry knew that Bunny was the nickname Jan had given Nancy, his ex-girlfriend. "Guess you've got more willpower than I do," Terry said. "But I'm gonna lick this thing, just wait and see." He popped a piece of gum in his mouth and handed the package back to Jan.

"What are you gonna do if you're still smoking by Saturday?" Jan asked as he turned his truck into the parking lot of the Wal-Mart store in Goshen.

Terry shrugged. "I don't know. Guess I'll chew plenty of breath mints and wear some cologne so I don't smell like smoke." He glanced out the window. "Why are we stopping here?"

"Star's working today, and I want to stop and say hello. You wanna go in with me?"

"Naw. I'll wait for you here. Tell Star I said hi, though."

"Will do." Jan turned off the ignition and hopped out of the truck. "I'll be back soon."

Terry leaned his head back and sat with his eyes closed, thinking about Cheryl and fighting the urge to smoke. Feeling more edgy by the minute, he finally opened his eyes and lit up, making sure to keep his window rolled down so the smoke would blow out. Maybe he wouldn't be able to quit smoking. Maybe he was stupid thinking he could get Cheryl to go out with him. It might be best just to forget the whole thing; then he wouldn't have to take any more quilting lessons. But if he did that, he'd be admitting defeat, and he'd never been a quitter.

"Nope," he muttered, snuffing out the cigarette. "I'm gonna snag a date with Cheryl, and I'll do whatever I need to do in order to make it happen."

Chapter 15

"I appreciate your taking the time to see me on such short notice," Cheryl said when she entered Ruby Lee and Gene's house Friday evening.

Ruby Lee gave Cheryl a hug. "We had no other plans this evening, and we're always happy to have a visit from any of our parishioners."

"You have a lovely home," Cheryl said, glancing around the cozy but spacious living room. "These hardwood floors are beautiful, and it would be hard to draw me away from those cozy-looking window seats. I don't think I'd get much done, wanting to watch outside all the time."

"We've lived here almost two years, but it still feels new to us." Ruby Lee laughed. "Maybe that's because we lived in a church-owned parsonage for so many years and waited a long time to have a home of our own. About the only thing I've never really gotten used to is the dog next door. He seems to bark at anything that moves—especially the scampering squirrels."

Cheryl sighed. "Where I grew up, outside of Portland, Oregon, my parents had a big backyard, and we were always watching some sort of animal or bird that ventured onto our property. We had squirrels and birds at the feeders my dad built, and occasionally we'd see some deer come out of the woods adjoining our place. They liked to nibble on the shrubbery and grass in the yard."

"That sounds nice, Cheryl," Ruby Lee said as they both went to the window. "Time stands still when I stop to watch the birds at our feeders. The activity there is ongoing." She smiled at Cheryl. "Are there a lot of different birds in Oregon?"

"Oh yes. We have several species, much like you have here. Grandma used to make her own suet, and we'd hang it out during the winter months. The downy woodpeckers and northern flickers loved it." Cheryl pointed to Ruby Lee's backyard. "We have goldfinches, too, like those on your thistle feeders. Some of the birds that came into our yard stayed all year. Other birds came only at certain times of the year. Also, there's a place called the Oaks Bottom Wildlife Refuge, which is about ten minutes from our home. When I was a girl, Grandma and I used to walk the trails there, and we often saw great blue herons and egrets in the small lake and wetlands there. Sometimes we'd even catch a glimpse of a bald eagle flying overhead." Cheryl laughed. "I guess you can tell I could go on and on about the subject of birds and other wildlife."

"I think you and I have a lot in common," Ruby Lee said, lightly tapping Cheryl's arm. "But I guess we'd better get to the reason for your visit this evening." She motioned to the adjoining room. "Gene's in his study. Should we go in there to talk, or would you prefer that he come out here?"

"We can go in there," Cheryl said.

Ruby Lee led the way, and when they entered Gene's study, he turned off his computer and motioned for them to sit down.

"It's good to see you, Ms. Halverson. How are you doing?"

"Please, call me Cheryl." She cleared her throat a couple of times. "To tell you the truth, Pastor Gene, I'm not doing so well."

"What seems to be the problem?"

Cheryl explained her situation with Lance and April and ended by saying that she was still angry and hadn't forgiven them. "I know as a Christian I shouldn't feel this way, but with Lance calling me to ask questions about April, I'm having a hard time dealing with things. I feel like telling him to go jump in a lake. And if I never saw Lance or April again, it would be fine with me. I often find myself wishing I could do something to get even—make them pay for what they did to me."

Gene reached for his Bible, and after thumbing through several pages, he read, " 'Be ye angry and sin not: let not the sun go down upon your wrath.' That's Ephesians 4:26." He flipped back to the Old Testament. "Proverbs 15:1 says: 'A soft answer turneth away wrath: but grievous words stir up anger.' " He closed the Bible and looked directly at Cheryl. "It's our human nature to feel angry sometimes. People hurt us, injustices are done, and sin runs rampant in our world. But it's important to remember not to let our anger consume us or cause us to do something we'll later regret." He paused and laced his fingers together, leaning slightly forward with his elbows on his desk. "Would getting even bring you happiness or change what happened between you and Lance?"

Cheryl shook her head as she swiped at the tears rolling down her cheeks. "No, but I can't forgive their betrayal."

Ruby Lee, who had been sitting quietly beside Cheryl, patted Cheryl's arm. "It's important that we forgive those who have wronged us. Only then will your heart begin to heal."

"My wife's right," Pastor Gene put in. "In Matthew 6:14 we are told: 'If ye forgive men their trespasses, your heavenly Father will also forgive you.' "

Cheryl let Ruby Lee's and the pastor's words sink in. When she felt ready, she said, "You're right, I do need to forgive Lance and April. I also need to ask God to forgive me for the anger and bitterness I've been harboring toward them. If I don't, I know it will destroy my Christian testimony."

"Remember one thing," Ruby Lee said, clasping Cheryl's hand. "You don't have to condone what Lance and April did to you, and you certainly don't have to accept Lance's phone calls. But for complete healing, you may need to let them both know, perhaps through a letter or an e-mail, that you've forgiven them."

"That won't be easy," Cheryl admitted, "but with God's help, I think I can do it."

"There's one more thing I'd like to say before we pray with you," Ruby Lee said.

"What's that?"

"Don't be afraid to begin dating again. Not all men will treat you the way Lance did. When you find the right one, you'll know it. Just make sure he has the same moral values as you."

Cheryl smiled, glad that she'd come here tonight. "Thanks, Ruby Lee, I'll remember that. And thank you, Pastor Gene, for the scripture you shared."

Elkhart

"It's been a long time since I've had pizza," Carmen said, smiling across the table at Paul and Sophia. "Thanks for inviting me to join you tonight."

Paul's eyes twinkled as he tucked a napkin under his daughter's chin. "Once Sophia had her first taste of pizza, coming here to the pizza place became a weekly occurrence. Of course, the fact that her daddy would rather not cook every night played a small role in it, too," he added with a grin.

Carmen laughed and reached for her glass of iced tea, watching Sophia in her high chair, wearing a flowered bib, as she picked the pepperoni off the pizza and ate it first. Her face was a mess, but she was obviously enjoying herself. It was great getting to know Paul, and spending time with his daughter made it that much sweeter. Carmen liked it here in northern Indiana, too. It was different from Los Angeles, with its endless traffic and people rushing about.

"Are you still enjoying the quilt classes you're taking?" Paul asked.

Carmen nodded. "I'm anxious to see how my wall hanging turns out."

"I'm sure it'll be fine. With Emma and Lamar's guidance, I don't think anybody ever leaves one of their classes with a wall hanging they don't like. You'll never meet two nicer people than those good folks, not to mention having the opportunity of making new friends during the course of the six weeks."

"I hope that's the case for me."

"So besides the quilt class last Saturday, what else have you done this week?" Paul asked.

"Oh, I drove around the area, took some pictures, checked out some of the Amish-run stores, and had lunch with Anna Lambright on Wednesday." No way was Carmen going to admit her reason for doing those things.

"Isn't Anna the young Amish woman who's also in Emma's quilt class?" Paul questioned.

Carmen nodded.

"It's nice that you're getting to know some of the others in your class, but I'm surprised it would be the Amish woman and not Cheryl, because it seems like she would have more in common with you than Anna."

"Maybe so, but I'm fascinated with the Amish culture and have enjoyed spending time with Anna." Carmen cringed. Could Paul be on to her? Had he somehow guessed that she planned to write an article about the Amish?

Paul nodded. "You're right; the Amish way of life is fascinating. I think we could learn a lot from the Plain People, and I'm impressed by the way they put God first and care so much for their families."

Carmen reached over and gave Sophia's chubby little leg a gentle squeeze. "I think this little girl is pretty high on her daddy's list." She smiled at Paul. "You're doing a good job raising her. I know Lorinda would be pleased."

Paul sighed. "I hope so. I tend to worry about Sophia, and sometimes I'm a bit overprotective. I often wonder if Lorinda is looking down from heaven and shaking her head when she sees some of the blunders I've made." He chuckled. "Once when I was in a hurry, I tossed Sophia's disposable diaper in the bathroom sink, thinking I'd remember to throw it away after her bath, but I forgot and left it there. The first one to find it was my niece, Lila, who was seven at the time. She and her family had dropped by to visit, and Lila asked to use the bathroom." Paul wrinkled his nose. "Needless to say, my sister, Maria, razzed me about that one."

Carmen chuckled. "We all make silly mistakes."

"True enough, and I've made more than my share." Paul tweaked the end of his daughter's nose. "Isn't that right my little *niña*?"

Sophia giggled and grabbed Paul's thumb.

Carmen smiled. She'd never imagined spending time with Paul and Sophia could be so much fun. And to think, it wouldn't have happened if her boss hadn't sent her on an assignment.

A chill went up Carmen's spine. *I can't let Paul find out why I came.*

He'd never forgive me if he knew I planned to write a negative story about his Amish friends. Sometimes I wonder if I'm doing the right thing. How would I like it if someone were to write a not-so-nice article about my family and our way of life?

Chapter 16

Middlebury

On Saturday morning, Anna was almost out the door, when she remembered that she planned to go shopping with Carmen after the quilting class. "Uh, Mom," she said, poking her head through the kitchen doorway, "I wanted you to know that I'll be a little late getting home this afternoon."

"Why is that?" Mom asked, looking up from where she sat at the table, drinking a cup of tea.

"I want to do some shopping," Ann replied.

"How come?"

Anna grimaced. *Why can't Mom just say, "Oh, all right, have a good time," instead of making me explain everything all the time? Now I have to give some kind of explanation.*

"Mom, will you please fix my hair? A piece of it's sticking out the back of my head covering," Anna's sister Arie said, stepping into the room and rushing over to Mom.

Anna took advantage of the interruption and slipped quickly out the door, relieved that she didn't have to offer her mother an explanation. She was anxious to see Carmen again, but they couldn't go shopping in Shipshewana, where Anna could easily be seen by someone she knew.

Shipshewana

Terry's hands shook as he climbed into his truck and turned on the ignition. He hadn't had a cigarette since yesterday morning, and he struggled with the temptation. Besides being shaky and irritable, he'd had a hard time sleeping last night. What he wouldn't give for a smoke to take the edge off. He'd made sure to use mouthwash and splash on some cologne this morning, hoping to erase any telltale signs of cigarette smoke from the day before. He'd even dressed a little nicer today, choosing some khaki slacks and a beige button-down shirt, instead of his usual jeans and T-shirt. If all went well, he planned to ask Cheryl if she'd go bowling with him tonight.

"Maybe it wouldn't hurt if I just took one drag," Terry said aloud, as though trying to convince himself that it was okay. He opened the glove compartment and removed a pack of cigarettes, then fished around and found a book of matches under an assortment of maps and other things that had been jammed in there. At least his truck wasn't as filthy as Jan's. It just needed a little reorganizing. Terry's rig was old, but he kept it halfway tidy on the inside, and tried to keep the outside clean, too.

Striking the match, and then lighting the cigarette, he sat there awhile, letting the engine idle as he took a drag.

Ahhh. . .that sure feels good. Terry inhaled the air of the cab as it filled with more smoke. Feeling kind of drowsy, he leaned his head against the window and closed his eyes, hoping his urge for a cigarette would ease.

Suddenly, Terry's eyes snapped open. There was a different kind of smoke filling the inside of his truck now. "Oh no!" Terry hollered, turning off the engine and looking down at the seat. A thin pillar of smoke spiraled up from where the smooth vinyl once was. In its place was a hole the size of a quarter, darkened around the edges from the hot ashes still burning in the stuffing of the truck's seat.

Immediately, Terry unbuckled his seat belt, spotted a half-full water bottle that he'd left in the truck, and dumped the water onto the smoldering seat. It did the trick. "Guess that's what I get for taking a drag," he mumbled, rubbing his hand over the gaping hole. Looking at his cigarette pack, he was tempted to throw it out the window. But that would be littering, and with his luck, a cop would probably see him do it, and he'd end up with a fine. He'd toss the cigarettes as soon as he found a garbage can.

"Can't believe this happened," he muttered. Now he'd either have to get the seat re-covered or have the whole thing replaced. Not only that, but he probably smelled like the dickens, too. He really did need to quit smoking.

Terry got out of the truck and walked around for a bit, hoping the fresh air would get rid of the smoky aroma that might be lingering on his clothes.

Getting back into his truck, and sniffing the arm of his shirt, Terry knew if he didn't get going, he'd be late for class. The last thing he wanted was a tongue-lashing from Selma, like she'd given Blaine last week when he'd walked in late. "Well, here goes nothing," Terry said, pulling out into traffic as he popped a piece of peppermint gum in his mouth.

Selma peered into her canvas satchel, checking to make sure she had everything she'd need for the quilting class today. Scissors, seam ripper, tape measure, thread, pins, needles, and thimble. Yes, it was all there. Of course, Emma had each of those items available for her students to use, but Selma preferred her own things. She'd even thought about bringing her portable sewing machine along but knew that wasn't possible since Emma had no electricity in her home. Besides, last week Selma had used Emma's old treadle, and she'd enjoyed the sense of nostalgia from days when her grandmother was alive.

Emma had told them that this week they'd continue to sew the pieces they'd cut out the previous week. Selma looked forward to seeing the wall hanging take shape and couldn't wait for its completion. There was a sense of gratification that came from sewing, just as there was with floral arranging. Selma sometimes missed her position at the flower shop she used to manage, but continuing to work with flowers at home since her retirement three years ago had helped fill the void. Most of the bouquets she put together were for herself, but once a week when the flowers in her yard were blooming, Selma made lovely arrangements for the church she attended. It made her feel good to add some beauty to the table in the entrance; although she wasn't sure how much it was appreciated by others in the congregation. No one except for the pastor's wife had ever said anything to Selma about the flowers she brought.

Pulling her thoughts aside, Selma slipped into her sweater, picked up her satchel, and opened the back door.

Meow! The scraggly gray cat had returned once more, and he darted into the house before Selma could stop him. "Come back here, Scruffy!" she shouted, chasing after the cat as it raced into her kitchen.

The determined feline zipped around the table a couple of times, made a beeline for the hallway, and dashed into Selma's bedroom.

She moaned. If she didn't catch the critter soon, she'd be late. Aggravation tugging at her, Selma set her satchel on the table and headed down the hall. When she entered her bedroom, she gasped. The mangy animal was lying in the middle of her bed, curled up as if he thought he belonged there!

Selma's first instinct was to holler at the cat. But if she did that, he might run, and she'd be on another merry chase. Instead, she tiptoed quietly to the bed, slowly reached out, and scooped the furry cat into her arms. Selma wrinkled her nose, watching as clumps of cat hair floated through the air and onto her clean bedspread.

Prrr. . . Prrr. . . Prrr. . . The cat went limp the moment he was picked up, and nuzzled Selma's neck with his warm nose.

It softened Selma just a bit, but she wouldn't give in. This persistent critter had to go out!

"Why do you keep coming back here when you know you're not welcome?" Selma mumbled after she'd taken the cat outside and placed him on the grass. "Now go back to wherever you belong and stop coming to my house."

The cat looked up at Selma, as if to say, "You know I'll be back." Then it trotted down the driveway with its fluffy tail held high.

I can't figure out why Scruffy doesn't get the hint, Selma mused as she made her way back to the house to get her sewing satchel and use a lint roller on her clothes. She made a mental note to run the vacuum cleaner when she returned.

Does the cat think if he keeps coming around I'll eventually take him in? She shook her head determinedly. *That's never going to happen.*

"Everyone and their horse was at the bakery this morning, and look what I came home with," Lamar announced when he entered the quilting room, where Emma was busy getting things ready for her third class.

She looked up and smiled when she saw the box of doughnuts he held. "What'd they have on sale today?"

Lamar's green eyes twinkled as he grinned at her. "Maple bars and chocolate doughnuts, with vanilla-cream filling."

Emma smiled. "Two of your favorites."

"That's true," he admitted, "but they're not all for me. I plan on sharing."

"I'm glad to hear that. I might like at least one of those tasty-looking maple bars."

"You can have as many as you like, Emma. What I meant to say was, they're not all for us. Thought I'd share them with the quilting class when it's time to take a break today."

"That was thoughtful of you," Emma said. "Especially since all I have to serve are some of the sugar kichlin I made two days ago. I've been busy repairing the quilt for Cheryl's grandmother and haven't had time to do any more baking."

Lamar smacked his lips. "We can have some of those sugar cookies, too."

Emma motioned to the kitchen. "Why don't you put the doughnuts away until it's time to share them with our students?"

"That was my thought exactly, because if I leave them setting out, we'll be tempted to start eating right away, and no one will get much sewing done." Lamar started out of the room, but turned back around. "Isn't it amazing how we often think alike, Emma?"

She nodded. "I'm thankful for that." Emma knew that not all married couples were as compatible as she and Lamar. She felt grateful that God had brought such a kind, loving man into her life. Even though she hadn't planned to remarry after her first husband, Ivan, died, she'd never regretted her decision to marry Lamar.

When Cheryl pulled into the Millers' yard and saw no other cars in the driveway, she figured she must be the first one to arrive. That was unusual, but it was fine with her. She hoped this would give her some time to visit with Emma alone. From the first moment Cheryl had met Emma, she felt comfortable with her. Emma was so kind and easy to talk to. Cheryl felt relaxed around her—almost like she'd known Emma all her life. Maybe that was because, like Cheryl's grandma, Emma was easygoing and didn't just talk about herself. She seemed interested in others.

Not like Mom, Cheryl thought. *Everything always revolves around her job and social activities. Mom could learn a lot if she spent time among the Amish. Maybe she wouldn't be so focused on worldly things.*

Finished with her musings, Cheryl stepped out of the car and headed for the house. She was greeted at the door by Lamar, wearing his usual friendly grin. He, too, made Cheryl feel at ease and welcome in their home.

"Am I early, or is everyone else late today?" Cheryl asked, stepping into the house.

"You're a few minutes early, but I'm kind of surprised some of the others aren't here yet—especially Selma. She's usually the early one."

Cheryl couldn't argue with that. If there was one thing she'd learned about Selma Nash, it was that she liked to be punctual.

"Cheryl's here," Lamar announced as he and Cheryl entered the quilting room.

"Oh good." Emma smiled and motioned for Cheryl to come over to the table. "I did some work on your grandmother's quilt this week, and I want to show you how it's shaping up."

A sense of excitement welled in Cheryl's chest when she took a seat and watched as Emma spread the quilt on the table.

"See here," Emma said, pointing to one section of the quilt, and then another. "I've replaced some of the tattered pieces of material with new ones."

"They look new and yet old. How did you do that, Emma?"

"I used some old pieces of material I had that were still in good condition," Emma explained. "I want to make the quilt look like it did when it was originally purchased."

Cheryl smiled. "It definitely does, and the quilt's taking shape quite nicely. I'm sure Grandma will be pleased when she sees it."

"Will you be going to Oregon to give it to her?" Emma asked. "Or will you mail it and ask your mother to take it to your grandmother?"

"I have some time off from work coming the middle of November, so I'm hoping to take it there myself," Cheryl replied. "I want to give the quilt to Grandma on her birthday." She sighed deeply. "I can't count on Mom to do it. She's always so busy with her job and extracurricular activities. She doesn't even have time to talk to me for more than a few minutes whenever I call. And when I ask about Grandma, Mom either says she's doing okay or that she hasn't visited her in a while." Tears pricked the backs of Cheryl's eyes, and she swallowed around the lump stuck in her throat. "Wouldn't you think she'd want to visit her own mother as often as possible? And I don't understand why she can't take the time to really talk to me."

"I'm sorry, Cheryl." Emma put her hand on Cheryl's trembling shoulder. "It's hard to understand, but some people don't appreciate their family like they should. For me, though, I've always been close to my family. I'm grateful that my daughter Mary lives right next door. I can pop over there anytime I like, and it's always a joy whenever Mary or any of her children drop by here to see us."

"That must be nice," Cheryl acknowledged.

"If your family lives in Oregon, what brought you here?" Emma asked.

Cheryl clasped her fingers tightly together. "My ex-boyfriend is the reason I decided to move. I hoped we'd be married, until Lance admitted that he'd been secretly seeing my best friend, April, and wanted to marry her." She sniffed, struggling not to break down. "I needed a new start, so when the opportunity to work for a lawyer in Goshen came up, I took it."

"You're still hurt by your friends' betrayal, aren't you?" Emma asked. "I can see the pain in your eyes."

Cheryl nodded. "It does hurt, but thanks to my pastor and his wife, Ruby Lee, I've come to realize that I need to forgive Lance and April. In fact, I sent them both an e-mail, saying I'd forgiven them and moved on with my life."

"I'm glad to hear that. I know Ruby Lee, and she's a wise woman," Emma said. "God's Word says a lot about forgiveness. It's the only way we can truly find peace when someone hurts us."

"Ruby Lee thinks I should start dating again," Cheryl said. "But I'm not sure I'm ready for that."

Emma smiled. "You know, after my first husband died, I convinced myself that I'd never fall in love or get married again. Then Lamar came along, and it wasn't long before he won my heart."

"Do you think I should start dating again?"

"It might be a good thing," Emma said. "Of course, that's up to you." She gave Cheryl's arm a gentle squeeze. "Before the others get here, there's one more thing I'd like to say."

"What's that?"

"I have a good ear for listening, so if you ever need to talk about anything, I'm here."

Cheryl smiled. "Thanks, Emma. I appreciate that."

Chapter 17

Carmen was relieved when she pulled into Emma's yard and saw Anna parking her bike. Since Anna's father hadn't brought her this time, maybe she'd be free to go shopping after class. Carmen needed the extra time to visit with Anna, in order to find out more about her time of running-around—or perhaps the lack of it. She'd been surprised to learn that Anna's parents were so strict. The bitterness this young woman felt might make a good storyline, and maybe at the same time, Carmen could offer some suggestions to Anna. After all, she remembered her own teen years—those times when she thought she knew more than her parents, while her mom and dad struggled to keep the upper hand.

Now that Carmen was older and looking back, she realized how hard it must have been on her folks, remaining authoritative yet not wanting to let go. But at the same time, Carmen remembered her desire to start doing things on her own and make decisions without needing parental approval. It was a difficult adjustment for any parent and young adult.

For a few years, she and her parents had argued frequently. But once Carmen had proven that she could be trusted, they'd given her more freedom. Looking back on it, she realized that Mom and Dad had done a pretty good job of raising both their daughters. Since Carmen was the youngest, it had been harder for them to let her go, but after some time had passed, they slowly relented and came around to treating her like a responsible adult.

Carmen got out of the car and headed for the house. Anna met her on the porch. "It's good to see you, Anna. Will you be free to go shopping with me after class?" Carmen asked.

Anna bobbed her head. "I told my mom I'd be getting home late and that I had some shopping to do, but she doesn't know I'll be with you."

"Would she disapprove?" Carmen questioned.

"If she knew I planned to try on English clothes, she'd be very upset."

"If you'd rather not do that, I totally understand. I don't want to cause any difficulty for you. If you like, we could just grab a bite of lunch somewhere and visit awhile," Carmen suggested.

Anna shook her head vigorously. "No, I want to go shopping. We can have some lunch when we get to Goshen, if that's okay with you."

"That's fine." Carmen motioned to Anna's bike. "There isn't enough room in my rental car's trunk for that. Do you think Emma would mind if you leave the bike here while we're gone? I can drop you back off when we return from Goshen."

Anna rubbed her chin, looking thoughtful. "I suppose that would be all right. Maybe I could leave it on her porch until we get back. I'll tell Emma that you and I are going out to lunch. That's all she needs to know."

By ten o'clock, everyone but Selma had arrived at Emma's.

"I wonder if something came up for Selma and she couldn't make it today," Emma said to Lamar. "It's not like her to be late."

"Should I check our answering machine and see if she left a message?" Lamar asked.

Emma glanced at the clock. "If she's not here in the next ten minutes, you can go out to the phone shack. In the meantime, would you mind passing out everyone's projects, while I explain what we'll be doing today?"

"Sure, no problem."

While Lamar gave each of the students the patterned pieces they still needed to stitch, Emma explained that they would finish sewing today, and if there was time, they'd cut out the batting. "We may need the entire time to finish sewing the pieces of material you have cut out, though," she added. "And we'll want to take a break at some point, to enjoy the doughnuts and maple bars Lamar bought at the bakery this morning. I also have some cookies to set out."

Terry smacked his lips. "Sounds good. Sure won't turn any of that down. I've always had a thing for maple bars."

"Same here," Cheryl agreed. "Of course I never overindulge on sugary desserts."

"It's nice to know we have something in common." Terry winked at Cheryl.

Blaine cleared his throat real loud. "Can we just get on with our lesson?"

"For a guy who stuck himself with a pin last week, you're sure anxious to do it again," Terry said with an undignified snicker. "Oh, and I'm surprised you're not smelling like fish this morning."

Blaine glared at him. "It'd be better than reeking of cologne. What'd you do, take a bath in it to try and cover up that horrible smell? What is that smell, anyway? Are you smoking a different brand of cigarettes these days?"

Terry sneered back at Blaine. "No, I'm not! Fact is, I'm not smoking at all anymore."

"Oh yeah?"

There they go again, Emma thought. *I really need to put a stop to these snide comments before the situation gets out of control.*

"Terry, Anna, and Carmen, why don't you use the sewing machines first? While you're doing that, Cheryl and Blaine can take turns using my iron to press out the seams on the pieces of material they've already sewn."

"How are we going to do that when you don't have electricity in your home?" Blaine questioned. "Is your iron battery-operated like the sewing machines?"

Emma shook her head. "It's heated with a small propane bottle. I'll fire it up and show you how to use it." She glanced over at Lamar and said, "Maybe you should go out to the phone shack now and see if Selma's left a message for us."

"Jah, I'll do that."

When Lamar left the room, Emma set up her ironing board and lit the propane bottle on the iron, while Terry, Carmen, and Anna took seats in front of the sewing machines.

A few minutes after Emma showed Cheryl how to use the iron, Lamar returned. "There was no message from Selma," he said, "but as I was walking back to the house, her car turned up the driveway, so she should come inside any minute."

A short time later, Selma entered the room, red-faced and looking a bit disheveled.

"Sorry I'm late," she apologized, "but that stray cat I found on my porch last week came back." Selma's thin lips compressed. "Only this time Scruffy got into the house, and I had to chase after him."

Terry chuckled. "Scruffy, is it? Since you've already named the critter, maybe you oughta keep him. That way, you won't have to worry about chasing him off anymore."

"No way!" Selma shook her head. "I can't be bothered with a pet."

"A cat makes a nice companion, and they're really not that much work," Emma said.

"That's right," Cheryl agreed. "The nursing home where my grandma lives has a cat for the residents to enjoy. It's actually been proven that holding or petting an animal can bring down a person's blood pressure."

"My blood pressure's just fine," Selma said with a decisive nod. "Had it checked a few months ago when I had a physical."

"I'd have a cat if I didn't have to be gone from home so much for my job," Carmen interjected.

"We have cats, too," Anna said, "but they stay outside or in the barn because my younger sister, Becky, is allergic to cat dander. I do like to go out and talk to our kitties, though. They always seem to listen."

Emma was pleased that Anna had contributed so much to the conversation. It was a sign that she felt more comfortable with the class.

"Well, I'm not interested in having any pets," Selma said with a note of conviction. "I don't need cat hair all over everything."

Clearly Selma was not in a good mood, so Emma quickly gave her the material she still needed to sew. "Would you like to use my treadle machine again?" Emma asked. "You seemed to enjoy it last week."

Selma gave a quick nod. "That's fine with me."

While everyone worked on their projects, Emma went to the kitchen to put a pot of coffee on the stove. Once it had perked, she would lower the propane level to keep the coffee warm until it was time for refreshments.

Emma rubbed her temples and sighed. She felt like a failure with this class—not in showing her students how to make a quilted wall hanging, but in helping them work through their personal problems. Of course, other than Cheryl, most of them hadn't really opened up to her yet. But Emma suspected that each of them had something they were hiding. She hoped that within the next three weeks they would share their burdens with either her or Lamar. After all, Emma had felt from the very beginning that part of teaching these classes involved mentoring her students emotionally and spiritually. In the meantime, though, she needed to be patient and try to set a good example for all.

As Terry struggled to sew a straight line, his hands trembled and his head felt like it was stuffed with cotton, making it hard to think. Just one full day without a cigarette and he was a basket case. Lighting up in the truck earlier had probably made his symptoms worse, not to mention the bigger problem it had created for him. Now he'd have to spend money to get his truck seat fixed.

Terry would give just about anything to go outside for a smoke, but that was out of the question—especially since he'd announced that he'd quit smoking. Besides, after what had happened with the cigarette he'd dropped in his truck, he knew he really needed to quit, even if a date with Cheryl wasn't in the picture.

Every once in a while, Terry looked up from his sewing and watched Cheryl and Blaine as they took turns using the antiquated iron. They seemed to be talking quite a bit, but with the hum of three battery-operated sewing machines, plus the steady rhythm of the treadle, he couldn't make out what they were saying. Everyone seemed engrossed in what they were doing, and nobody seemed to notice Terry's agitation. *Who knew giving up cigarettes would be so hard? Why couldn't Emma have paired me with Cheryl, instead of putting her with Blaine?*

"Coffee and doughnuts are ready," Emma announced. "Why don't we all gather around the table?"

Terry was hoping to sit beside Cheryl, but Blaine beat him to it. *Rats! At this rate I'll never get to ask her out,* Terry fumed. *Sure can't holler it across the table. Guess I'll have to wait till class is over and catch her at the door.*

Lamar passed the box of doughnuts around, and Emma poured Selma a cup of tea and offered coffee to everyone else.

When Terry picked up his cup, his hand shook so badly that some of the coffee spilled. He jumped up, nearly knocking his doughnut off the table.

"Are you all right? Did you burn yourself?" Emma asked with concern as she handed Terry a napkin.

"Naw, I'm okay," he said, blotting up the mess and trying to make light of the situation. At this rate he'd never make a good impression on Cheryl—especially with the puzzled look she'd just given him. *So much for wearing nicer clothes today,* Terry thought, looking down at the splotches of coffee he'd managed to get on his pants.

"When you come here next week we'll add the batting to your wall hanging and begin the actual quilting process," Emma said. "Does anyone have any questions?"

"Is it all right if I begin the quilting at home?" Selma asked. "I have some batting, so I'm sure I could go ahead on my own."

"I'd rather you not do that," Emma said. "It would put you ahead of the others, and if you made a mistake, you'd have to spend extra time tearing it out."

"I don't think any of us should try working on our wall hangings without Emma's help," Carmen spoke up. "After all, we paid for the lessons, and she's the teacher."

"You know," Lamar added, "when Emma taught her very first class, she let the students take home their quilting projects to work on, but it didn't work out too well for some."

"Well, if that's the way you want it, then I suppose I'll just have to deal with it." Selma folded her arms and stared straight ahead.

No wonder Jan says his neighbor is a pain in the neck, Terry thought. *She's such a know-it-all. I can't understand why she bothered to take this class.*

When everyone finished their snacks, it was time to go, and they all moved toward the door. Terry jumped up from his seat to approach Cheryl, but Blaine got to her first.

"I was wondering, do you like to bowl?" Blaine asked Cheryl as they went out the door.

"I do enjoy bowling, but I'm not very good at it," she replied.

Blaine smiled. "That's okay; I'll coach you. Would you like to go bowling with me this evening?"

"That would be nice. There's a bowling alley in Goshen. Can we meet there around seven?" Cheryl asked, pulling her sweater around her as the October wind blew a chill across the yard.

"Sure, that'd be great." Blaine followed Cheryl out to her car.

Terry gritted his teeth. *That's terrific. Think I might show up at the bowling alley tonight. I wonder how he'd like that.*

CHAPTER 18

Goshen

"This is going to be so much fun," Anna said as she and Carmen entered a restaurant on the east side of town. "Thanks for taking the time to spend the afternoon with me."

Carmen smiled. "You're welcome."

After their hostess seated them, and a waitress came to the table to take their orders, Carmen placed her purse in her lap, opened it, and discreetly turned on her portable tape recorder. She wanted to be sure she got everything Anna said to her during their meal. This would be the best time to talk, because when they went shopping it would be harder to converse.

"So is there anything more you can share with me about rumschpringe?" Carmen asked.

"Well, as you know, it's the Amish young people's time before joining the church." Anna paused and took a sip of water. "'Course I'm not sure I'm going to join."

"Is it because you want to do worldly things, or are you unhappy being Amish?" Carmen glanced down at her lap to be sure the tape recorder was working.

"It's not that I have anything against the Amish way of life," Anna replied quietly, looking around, as if afraid someone might hear. "I'm just not sure it's meant for me. I mean, I don't feel accepted by my family."

"Why is that?"

"My folks treat me like a baby." Anna frowned. "Most of my friends do things other than getting together for games and singings. But my parents don't allow me to try anything new."

Carmen leaned forward. "What kind of things?"

Anna shrugged, glancing around again while twirling her napkin around her fingers. Carmen had a hunch this was something Anna didn't want to talk about. *But it's what I want to know. I need to keep pressing until she tells me more.*

"Anna, do your friends drink or do drugs?" Carmen questioned. That was the kind of thing she'd seen on TV, and she needed to know how much of it was true.

"A couple of my friends have done some of those things," Anna admitted. "But most just meet in town and do fun things together."

"What kind of things?" Carmen questioned.

"Some of the girls wear English clothes when they're away from home. Some wear jewelry and makeup, too."

"Have you ever done any of those things?"

The middle-aged waitress came with their orders. "Let me know if you need anything else," she said before turning away from the table.

Anna glanced around nervously, as though someone might be watching her. Then in a timid voice, she said, "I always say a silent prayer before meals. I hope that's all right with you."

"Of course. I'll do that, too." Carmen turned off the tape recorder and bowed her head. Even though she went to church occasionally, she'd never made a habit of praying in public. A silent prayer shouldn't draw as much attention, so she had no problem with bowing her head. However, instead of thinking of something to pray about, a sense of guilt overtook her. She was not only trying to get information for her story from Anna, but she'd invited her out for the afternoon, knowing Anna hadn't gotten permission from her parents.

But how else am I going to get the information I need? Carmen told herself. *I need to keep asking Anna questions for the rest of the afternoon, and sometime this week I'll stop by Emma's and ask her about rumschpringe.*

Shipshewana

Emma had just finished washing the lunch dishes when a knock sounded on the front door. Since Lamar had gone next door to visit Mary's husband, Emma dried her hands and went to see who it was.

When she opened the door, she was surprised to see Pam Johnston on the porch, holding a large paper sack.

"It's good to see you," Emma said, giving Pam a hug. "How have you been?"

"I am doing well, and it's nice to see you, too." Pam smiled, pushing a strand of long blond hair behind her ears. "If you're not too busy right now, I have a favor to ask."

"I was just finishing up with the dishes, but that can wait." Emma opened the door wider and motioned for Pam to come in. "What can I help you with?"

Pam lifted the paper sack. "I'm making a quilted table runner for one of my friends, and I'm having trouble with the binding."

"It's basically the same as you did for the wall hanging you made during the classes you took from me," Emma explained.

"But that was over a year ago," Pam said. "Since I haven't done any quilting since then, I can't remember how I did the binding. I think I'm supposed to sew the strips together at right angles somehow."

"Come into the other room, and I'll show you what to do," Emma said, leading the way.

Pam took the table runner out of the sack and placed it on the table. She'd used material with varied colors of purple and pink and placed them in a simple star pattern.

"This is lovely," Emma said. "You've done a good job so far."

Pam smiled widely, revealing perfectly straight teeth. "Thanks, Emma. That means a lot coming from you. I would have never learned how to quilt if it hadn't been for your patience and expertise."

Emma's face heated with embarrassment. "I enjoy what I do, which is why I've continued teaching quilting classes."

"Speaking of which, how are things going with your new group of students?" Pam asked.

Emma pursed her lips. "Not as well as I'd like, but then it's not the worst class I've ever taught, either."

Pam rolled her eyes. "I'm guessing the class Stuart and I were in was your worst, right?"

Emma gave Pam's arm a tender squeeze. "I wouldn't say worst. I was just new at teaching and wasn't quite prepared for the challenge of instructing such a unique group of people."

"It's true. We were people with problems," Pam said. "And you helped all of us learn a lot more than just how to quilt."

"I hope I can do that with this group of students, too. I'm just a bit worried because, with the exception of Cheryl, no one has really opened up to me yet."

"Do you think they all have a problem?"

Emma nodded. "I believe so."

"I can tell you what Blaine's problem is, if you want to know."

Emma hesitated a minute. As much as she did want to know, she didn't think it would be right to hear it from Pam. It might be like listening to gossip, and she'd always tried to avoid that.

Turning to face Pam directly, Emma smiled and said, "I appreciate the offer, but I think it might be best to see if Blaine chooses to share his burdens with either Lamar or me."

"Oh, I see." Pam's downcast eyes told Emma she was disappointed. "So who are your other students?" Pam asked, quickly revising their topic.

"In addition to Blaine, I have a young Amish woman named Anna. Then there's Cheryl, Carmen, Selma, and Jan's friend, Terry."

Pam snickered. "I've never met Terry, but if he's anything like Jan, I'm sure your class must be quite interesting."

"Oh, it is," Emma admitted. "But then I guess that's why I like the challenge of teaching." She motioned to the quilted table runner Pam had brought. "Now shall we get started with that?"

Goshen

When Cheryl entered the bowling alley that evening, she glanced around but didn't see any sign of Blaine. Well, it wasn't quite seven o'clock, so she'd just take a seat and watch the other bowlers until he showed up. Rubbing her hands, which had gotten quite cold, she realized a pair of gloves would have felt good driving over. It was almost the middle of October, but it felt more like November.

Cheryl watched the activity buzzing around her. The first couple of lanes were reserved for bowling leagues. It looked like the men were against the women. In another lane, an elderly couple seemed to be enjoying themselves.

Looking in the other direction, she noticed a young mother rocking her baby while cheering for her husband after he'd rolled a strike. Cheryl wondered how the baby could sleep with all the noise from people whooping and cheering, balls rolling down the lanes, and pins getting hit and scattering into the pit.

As food smells wafted from the snack bar in the eating area, Cheryl's stomach growled. Several people stood in line, waiting for their orders, while others sat at tables, enjoying the food. She remembered long ago when she'd first bowled with some friends, how good the food at the snack bar had tasted. Maybe she would treat Blaine to a hot dog and a shake after they did a little bowling.

Cheryl took a seat where she could watch the people bowl, but she'd only been there a few minutes when someone tapped her shoulder. She turned her head and was surprised to see Terry.

"How's it going?" he asked, grinning from ear to ear.

"Umm. . .okay. I didn't expect to see you here tonight."

"I come here a lot. Bowling's one of my favorite things to do on a Saturday night." He flopped down in the seat beside her. "Wanna join me in a game?"

She shook her head. "I can't. I'm meeting someone."

Terry quirked an eyebrow. "Blaine?"

Cheryl nodded. "How'd you know?"

"I saw the two of you talking today during class. Figured he might be trying to set up a date. When we went outside afterwards, I heard him ask you to go bowling."

"Oh, so you followed us here?"

"Uh, not really. I actually have bowled here many times."

Cheryl kept her focus on the bowlers in the lane in front of her.

"You thirsty? I could get us a couple of sodas," Terry offered.

"No thanks, I'm fine."

"You like to ride motorcycles?" he asked.

"I don't know. I've never ridden one, although it does sound exciting."

"Wanna try it sometime? I've got a nice bike, and—"

"Oh, there you are," Blaine said, stepping up to Cheryl and touching her arm. "Have you been here long?"

She smiled up at him. "Only a few minutes."

Blaine's forehead wrinkled as he looked at Terry. "What are you doing here?"

Terry lifted his shoulders in a brief shrug. "Came to bowl, same as you. Fact is, I'm meeting my friend Jan and his daughter soon. Any objections?"

Blaine shook his head. "It's a free country." He held his hand out to Cheryl. "Ready to bowl and have some fun?"

She quickly rose to her feet. "Ready as I'll ever be."

Chapter 19

Shipshewana

"Would you like a cup of mint tea and one of those chocolate *faasnachtkuche* left over from today?" Emma asked when she entered the living room and found Lamar seated in his recliner near the fireplace.

"That sounds good," he replied, "but I'm surprised there are any doughnuts left."

"Most everyone went for the maple bars," Emma explained.

"Guess I wasn't paying close attention to who ate what. I was more interested in the look on Terry's face when he was watching Blaine talk to Cheryl."

"What kind of a look?" Emma asked.

"Irritation. . .jealousy. . .desperation." Lamar gave his right earlobe a tug. "If I was a betting man, I'd say Terry's interested in Cheryl."

"What about Blaine? Do you think he likes her, too?"

Lamar shrugged. "He acts interested, but not in the same way as Terry. Blaine seems to be. . . Well, he wears kind of a placid expression when he looks at Cheryl. It makes me wonder if he's only showing interest in her to irritate Terry."

"Why would he do that?" Emma questioned.

"I don't know, but I'd like to find out."

"Pam Johnston came by this afternoon, and Blaine's name came up." Emma's glasses slipped down her nose, and she pushed them back into place. "Pam wanted to tell me something about Blaine, but I didn't think it would be right, so I moved our conversation in another direction."

"Maybe I should pay more attention to Blaine," Lamar said. "He might need a friend."

Emma nodded. "You could invite him to go fishing with you sometime. That's something you both have in common."

"That's a good idea, Emma. Maybe we could go some Saturday after class." Lamar rose to his feet. "But enough about your students right now. Let's head out to the kitchen and get our evening snack."

Goshen

"What are you doing over there?" Blaine asked when Terry plopped down in the scorekeeper's chair next to him.

"I'm gettin' ready to bowl, same as you. Besides, this is the lane I was assigned," Terry replied with a smirk. At least that was how Blaine interpreted the smug-looking smile on Terry's face. What was the guy really doing here, anyway? Could he have known they were coming and showed up at the bowling alley on purpose, just to make trouble? Did he request the lane next to them, or had it really been assigned?

"Where are your friends?" Blaine asked. "Didn't you say you were meeting them here?"

"I am. They just haven't shown up yet." Terry left his chair and took a seat on the bench beside Cheryl as she put on her bowling shoes. "Do you come here often?" he asked.

She shook her head as she finished tying the shoelaces. "This is my first time since I moved to Goshen. But even when I lived in Oregon, I didn't bowl that often. Back home at our local alley, I remember enjoying the hot dogs and milk shakes and just hanging out with my friends. It's fun to bowl, but I'm really not that good at it, and I've never had lessons."

"I'd be happy to teach you," Terry said, a little too eagerly.

"I'm Cheryl's date, so if there's any teaching to be done, I'm the one who'll be doing it," Blaine called over his shoulder. He'd be glad when Terry's friends arrived. Maybe then he'd mind his own business and quit bothering Cheryl.

Terry didn't seem to notice Blaine's irritation; he was too busy grinning at Cheryl. The guy was clearly interested in her, but Blaine was sure the feeling wasn't mutual. After all, she was too refined for a rough-around-the-edges kind of guy like Terry.

"Would you like me to help you pick out a ball?" Blaine asked, leaving his seat and standing next to Cheryl.

"No thanks, I brought my own," Terry quipped.

Blaine narrowed his eyes. "I was talking to Cheryl."

Cheryl, looking a little flustered, giggled and stood. "Thanks for the offer, Blaine, but I think I can pick out my own ball. I need one that's not too heavy and fits my small fingers." She hurried off toward the rack of balls, leaving Blaine alone with Terry.

"How many years have you been bowling?" Terry asked as he took his bowling ball out of the bag and wiped it down with a small towel.

"I bowled my first game when I was eight years old."

"Guess you must be pretty good at it then."

Blaine gave a nod, watching as Terry put his multicolored bowling ball on the ball return. "I used to play on a league, and my average is 190, but my highest score was 260."

Terry snickered, stuffing the corner of the towel in his back pocket. "That's nothing. My highest score was 275."

"I'll bet," Blaine muttered under his breath.

"What was that?"

"Nothing." Blaine put his own ball on the ball return and seated himself in the scorekeeper's chair again. He was beginning to wish he'd taken Cheryl out to dinner or to see a movie. He'd sure never expected to run into Terry here—not when the guy lived in Shipshewana.

Blaine inserted his and Cheryl's names into the computer scoring system and felt relief when Cheryl returned with her ball, saying she was ready to start bowling.

Terry watched as Blaine showed Cheryl how to stand, hold the ball, and make her delivery. Everything was so precise—almost stiff-looking. Not the way Terry would do it, free and easy. *Sure wish it was me teaching her, and not Blaine.*

Terry studied Cheryl as she rolled her ball down the alley. It knocked down three pins and left seven standing.

"It's okay, Cheryl," Blaine said. "I bet you'll pick them up on the next try."

When her bright green ball returned, Cheryl tried again. This time she knocked down three more pins. "Guess it's better than a gutter ball," she said, smiling at Blaine. Then she glanced over at Terry and smiled at him, too. "Is it best for me to aim at the pins or the marks on the floor?"

"Aim at the pins," Blaine said.

Terry shook his head. "I use the marks on the floor mostly."

Cheryl lifted her hands. "That wasn't much help. Guess I'll figure it out for myself. Either way, or doing both, might make it easier."

Boy, she sure is pretty—especially when she smiles, Terry thought. *Sure wish she was my date tonight.*

It was Blaine's turn to bowl, and Cheryl sat beside Terry. As Blaine stepped up to the line, Terry looked over at Cheryl and said, "Look at me over here by myself. I feel like the Lone Ranger."

"Not anymore." Cheryl gestured toward the entrance of the bowling alley. "It looks like your friend Jan just arrived."

Terry swiveled in his seat. Sure enough, Jan was heading his way, and Star was right behind him. When they joined him a short time later, he introduced Star to Cheryl. "And you've already met my boss and good friend, Jan Sweet," Terry added.

Cheryl smiled at Star. "It's nice to meet you." The young woman's hair was straight and black, and she sported a small nose ring. Cheryl also noticed a little star tattooed on the young woman's neck, but she wore a radiant smile and seemed quite bubbly.

"Same here," Star said, shaking Cheryl's hand. "Terry's told us all about you."

"It was all good, honest," Terry said, his face turning slightly pink.

It was unexpected to see him blush like that. Cheryl was also surprised to hear that he'd been talking about her. Well, maybe it wasn't just her he'd mentioned to Jan and Star. Terry might have talked about everyone in the class.

"Are we going to bowl, or stand around talking all night?" Blaine asked impatiently. He motioned to Cheryl's ball. "It's your turn now."

"No, it's not," Terry spoke up. "You were about to bowl when Jan and Star showed up."

Blaine's face flamed as he glanced down at the ball in his hands. "Guess you're right."

Cheryl could see how embarrassed Blaine was, so she made light of it. "It's no big deal. I do things like that all the time. The other day at work I went to the copy machine, and after I copied the document I'd taken there, I got distracted when someone asked me a question. Then when I went back to my desk I realized I didn't have the copy I thought I'd made. So back to the copy machine I went, where I discovered that the original, as well as the copy, were still in the machine."

Terry chuckled. "Once, when I was climbing a ladder to get on a roof, I stopped halfway up and couldn't remember what I was going up there for. So I told myself, 'I'm gonna stand right here on this rung till I remember.'" Terry tapped his forehead a couple of times. "I never did figure it out, but after some thought, I couldn't remember if I was going up or down that ladder."

Cheryl laughed. "You made that up, didn't you?"

He winked.

"I think we'd better get back to bowling." Blaine stepped up to the line, made his approach, and let the ball go. He knocked down eight pins, and the two left standing were side by side. "I should be able to get those easily," he said, glancing back at Cheryl.

"I bet you can." She cheered Blaine on.

In the meantime, Terry picked up his ball and stepped up to the line just as Blaine did. They both started their approach and released their balls at the same time.

"That's not good," Star said, glancing at Cheryl and shaking her head. "One of them should have waited for the other to go first. I don't think either of 'em knows anything about bowling courtesy."

Cheryl held her breath as she watched both men's balls roll down the alley toward the pins. Terry's ball, which had been released with a stronger hand, made it there first, knocking down nine pins. Blaine's ball hit his last two pins, and he turned to face Cheryl with a grin.

"Good job," she said, picking up her ball and waiting until Terry finished his turn. He missed the one pin that had been left standing, but instead of getting upset about it, he winked at Cheryl and said, "That was just my practice shot. 'Course practice makes perfect, and nobody's perfect, so really, why practice?"

Cheryl couldn't help but smile. Terry had such a humorous way about him. He was actually kind of a likable guy. Too bad he and Blaine seemed to be at odds with each other. They'd both been acting really testy tonight. "Guess it's my turn to bowl," she said.

The first ball she rolled, knocked down four pins, but on her second try she got three more. After Star took her turn and got a spare, Jan bowled, knocking down all of the pins. Everyone cheered.

Terry and Blaine both jumped up next, grabbed their balls, and lined up, neither of them waiting for the other to go first. Terry glanced briefly at Blaine, then let go of his ball. As it started rolling down the aisle, he shouted, "Come on, baby. . . . Come on. . . . Knock down those pins for me right now!"

Meanwhile, the ball Blaine released glided down the alley, with him coaxing it along. "That's it! That's it! Just a little more to the left."

Terry's ball hit eight pins this time, and Blaine knocked down seven.

"It's time for a spare," Blaine said, looking back at Cheryl.

Terry grabbed his ball and dashed up to the line. Blaine did the same. Once more, they released their balls at the same time.

Thunk! Both men's balls rolled into the gutter without hitting a single pin.

"Rats!" Terry slapped the side of his jeans, and Blaine slunk his way back to his chair.

Cheryl looked at Star and rolled her eyes.

"Men," Star whispered, leaning close to Cheryl. "They always have to show off, and if they don't win, they think it's the end of the world."

Cheryl nodded. To her, bowling, or any other sport, was about having fun. It was obvious that Terry and Blaine took the game more seriously, though.

Star and Cheryl took their turns next, and then Jan. Cheryl watched in fascination as the big burly man bowled one strike, followed by another. Star cheered and so did Terry. But Blaine just sat with his arms folded.

When Star took her next turn, she bowled a strike. Cheryl cheered for her, thinking, *Maybe I should have had her show me a few things about bowling.*

Cheryl went to her purse and dug out a few dollars. "Blaine, would you mind getting me a chocolate milk shake? If they taste anything like the ones back in my hometown, then I can hardly wait to have one. Get yourself something, too," she added, handing him the money. "It's my treat."

"I should be treating you, not the other way around," Blaine said.

"Don't worry about it. You paid for our bowling, so it's the least I can do."

"Okay. I'll be back soon with a couple of chocolate shakes." Casting Terry a quick glance, Blaine hurried away.

For the next two hours they continued to bowl, until Cheryl told Blaine she needed to go. "I plan to attend the early service at church tomorrow morning, so I need to go home and get to bed," she explained.

"Where's your church and what time does it start?" Blaine asked.

Thinking he might want to come, too, she smiled and said, "It starts at 8:45, and the church is here in Goshen. Gene Williams is the pastor, and his wife, Ruby Lee, took one of Emma's quilting classes."

"Oh, I see. Well, if you need to get home, I'll walk you to the car," Blaine said, making no comment about the church or asking for directions.

Disappointed, Cheryl smiled at Star. "It was nice meeting you."

"Same here." Star grinned. "Maybe the two of us can get together and bowl sometime," she whispered. "Without the men."

Cheryl gave a nod. "Sounds like that could be fun." She said good-bye to Jan and told Terry she would see him next Saturday at Emma's. "Oh, and I'm glad you've quit smoking. Keep up the good work," she quickly added.

"I will," he said with a twinkle in his eyes. "Think it'll be worth it."

As Cheryl and Blaine walked toward the door, she glanced over her shoulder and noticed Terry watching her. She couldn't explain it, but something about him was appealing, which was strange, since she hadn't felt that way when they'd first met. While Blaine was nice looking, polite, and seemed to be steady, Terry was funny and had a zest for life. He was different from any man she'd ever known.

When Cheryl stepped into the chilly evening air, a shiver ran through her. *Do I actually wish I'd gone bowling with Terry tonight instead of Blaine? No, that's ridiculous; Terry and I are worlds apart.*

CHAPTER 20

Shipshewana

Selma pulled the covers aside and shivered as she crawled out of bed. It seemed so cold in her bedroom this morning. Could the temperature have dipped lower than usual during the night? Maybe her furnace had quit working.

Wherever Selma could, she stepped on the throw rugs scattered across her bedroom floor, knowing the hardwood would probably be cold. It was the only room in her house, besides the kitchen and bathroom, that didn't have carpeting.

Selma padded across the room in her bare feet and bent down to put her hand in front of the floor vent. *Now that's odd.* Even though the slats were open, no heat was rising through the vent. She slipped into her robe and slippers, then stepped into the hall. It seemed warm enough there, and in the living room as well. She checked both living-room vents and discovered warm air drifting up. It made no sense that the vent in the bedroom wasn't directing heat into the room.

Selma checked a couple more vents—one in the spare bedroom, and one in the dining room. Warm air wafted up from both of them. She felt relief knowing her furnace hadn't given out.

"Guess I'll have to ask someone to crawl under the house and check the heat duct going up to my bedroom," she said aloud. "Maybe it got clogged somehow."

Selma headed for the kitchen to put the teakettle on the stove, and when she stepped into the room, she halted, shocked at the sight before her. That mangy gray cat was sitting in her sink, licking at the slow drip coming from the faucet.

"How in the world did you get in my house, and what are you doing in the sink?" Could she have left the door open last night during the short time she'd gone out to be sure her car was locked? But if the cat had gotten in then, why hadn't she seen it before she'd gone to bed? Maybe the sneaky feline had hidden out somewhere in the house. Whatever the case, Scruffy had to go out!

Meow! The cat looked at Selma as if to say, "Please let me stay in the house."

"I'll give you a bowl of water, but you have to go outside." Selma picked up the cat, unconsciously petting his head.

Prrr. . . Prrr. . . The cat burrowed his nose in Selma's robe and began to knead with his paws.

"Now, none of that, Scruffy," Selma said with a click of her tongue. "You're not going to soft-soap me this morning." She held the cat away from her, while scrutinizing him. *If you could talk, you'd probably tell me plenty,* Selma thought, wondering where this cat must have come from.

She opened the back door, set the cat on the porch, and quickly shut the door. When she returned to the kitchen, she took out a plastic bowl and filled it with lukewarm water. Then she took the bowl outside and placed it on the porch. Seeing that Scruffy was still there, Selma smiled, despite her agitation. If all the mats were combed out of the critter's fur, he wouldn't look half bad. In fact, he was kind of cute, even if he was nearly full grown.

Now don't go getting soft, Selma scolded herself. *I am not keeping this cat.* She opened the door and stepped quickly inside. She needed to eat breakfast and get ready for church, or she'd end up being late. She would deal with the faulty heat vent sometime this week, and she hoped giving the cat some water had not been a mistake. But she had a feeling it already was.

Middlebury

Anna yawned and forced herself to sit up straight, hoping to relieve her aching muscles. They were nearly halfway through Sunday worship, and she really needed a break. She'd wait until the reading of the Scriptures, though. Anna knew that would be when a few other people would slip out to use the restroom or walk around for a bit to get the kinks out of their stiff backs.

Anna barely heard the song being sung, as her mind took her back to yesterday and the time she'd spent with Carmen. She'd enjoyed the afternoon so much, and the interest Carmen had taken in Anna made her feel like she was important. Carmen seemed to care what Anna thought about things and didn't criticize, the way Mom often did. She'd enjoyed sharing information and answering questions Carmen had asked about their Amish traditions. Too bad Carmen didn't live in the area. If she did, she and Anna would probably be friends.

Of course, Anna mused, *Carmen's more educated than I am. She's much prettier, too. I'll bet she thinks I'm really plain.* Nevertheless, no one had ever taken an interest in Anna like Carmen had. It made her feel kind of special.

Anna looked down at her hands, clasped firmly over the skirt of her dark blue dress. *Even though I am plain, I'd still like to be pretty.* Was there such a thing as being pretty and plain at the same time? Anna's grandmother had told Anna on more than one occasion that her auburn hair was pretty. But the freckles dotting Anna's nose made her wish she had a clear, creamy complexion like she'd noticed Cheryl Halverson had.

Anna glanced to her right, where her friend Mandy Zimmerman sat staring out the window of Deacon Lehman's buggy shed, where church was being held today. Mandy looked bored and was probably ready for a break, too. She was a pretty young woman, with shiny blond hair, bright blue eyes, and a bubbly personality. She was also a bit rebellious, although her parents had given her the freedom to experience some worldly things. Mandy's boyfriend, David, had a car, and sometimes took Mandy for rides. Anna, on the other hand, had no boyfriend. She didn't care, though. None of the young men she knew had caught her interest. Besides, she was still young, and there was plenty of time for courting and flirting. Not that Anna wanted to flirt. She'd seen Mandy do it several times, though, with David and a couple of other young men.

Anna's thoughts turned to the piece of jewelry Carmen had bought for her yesterday while they'd been shopping. If Mom and Dad found out she had a fancy bracelet, she'd be in for a lecture, and maybe worse. They might say she couldn't see Carmen anymore outside of the quilt class. Anna was glad she'd hidden the bracelet beneath her underclothes in one of her dresser drawers. Since she cleaned her own room and always gathered up the laundry, she was sure the bracelet wouldn't be discovered.

As the congregation stood for the reading of Scriptures, Anna slipped quietly out and headed for the house. Mandy did the same.

Once in the house, Anna quickly realized there was a lineup in the hallway for the restroom, so she visited with Mandy as they stood in the living room, awaiting their turn.

"I have something to tell you," Anna whispered.

"What is it?" Mandy asked, leaning closer to Anna.

"I went to lunch in Goshen with Carmen Lopez yesterday, and afterward, we did some shopping."

"Carmen's that young Hispanic woman you told me about, right?"

Anna nodded. "Carmen's really nice, and she actually listens when I talk. Not like Mom and Dad. They don't listen or try to understand me at all."

"So what'd you buy when you went shopping?" Mandy asked.

"I didn't buy anything myself, but Carmen bought me a pretty bracelet."

"Why would she do that? She doesn't even know you that well."

Anna sucked in her bottom lip as she mulled things over. "I guess after I shared some things with her about how Mom and Dad have been holding me back, she felt sorry about my situation and decided to give me something nice."

"What'd you do with the bracelet? I'm sure you didn't go home and show your folks."

Anna shook her head. "I hid it in one of my dresser drawers."

"I hope your mamm doesn't find it there."

"I'm sure she won't because she never goes into my room."

Mandy smiled. "I'm anxious to see it. When can you show it to me?"

"How about tomorrow? Maybe we can meet somewhere after I get off work in the afternoon."

"Sounds good," Mandy said. "Let's meet at the Dairy Queen. I've been craving one of those chocolate-and-vanilla-swirl ice-cream cones. Think you can be there by four o'clock?"

Anna nodded, already looking forward to it.

Goshen

When Cheryl stepped into the church foyer, she spotted Ruby Lee, talking with an elderly woman. Cheryl didn't want to interrupt, so she waited until they were done before she joined Ruby Lee. "Guess what?" she asked, giving Ruby Lee a hug. "I took your advice and went on a date last night."

"I'm glad to hear that. Who'd you go out with?"

"Blaine Vickers. He's one of the men taking the quilt class with me." She paused, wondering how much to share with Ruby Lee.

"I sense there's more," Ruby Lee said, touching Cheryl's arm.

Cheryl nodded. "Blaine and I went bowling, and Terry Cooley, who also attends the quilt classes, showed up. He ended up bowling on the lane next to ours."

"Was he invited?"

"No, but he was meeting his friend Jan Sweet and Jan's daughter, Star. They came in after Terry had been there awhile." What Cheryl didn't tell Ruby Lee was that Terry had vied for her attention all evening and that she'd actually enjoyed it. She could hardly admit that to herself, because it didn't seem right that she'd be attracted to someone like Terry.

Ruby Lee smiled. "Sure wish I'd been there. I haven't seen Jan or Star for some time. They kept things quite interesting during our quilting classes, but by the end of our six weeks, we all came to care for each other."

"Terry keeps our classes interesting, too."

"Did I hear my name mentioned?"

Cheryl whirled around, surprised to see Terry, wearing black slacks, a white shirt, and a black leather jacket, standing behind her with a big grin.

"Wh–what are you doing here, Terry?" she stammered. She couldn't get over how different Terry looked today, dressed in nice clothes.

"I overhead you telling Blaine last night that you were going to church this morning."

"I did tell him that, but I didn't say the name of the church, or where it was located—just that it was in Goshen."

"But you did say it was the church Ruby Lee's husband pastored, and since Ruby Lee and Jan took the same quilting class, I figured Jan would know where the church was, so I got the directions from him."

Before Cheryl could respond, Ruby Lee extended her hand to Terry and said, "We always welcome visitors when they come to our church. I'm Ruby Lee. It's nice to meet you, Terry."

"Same here," Terry said, as he shook hands with Ruby Lee. Then he turned back to Cheryl and said, "If you don't mind, I'd like to sit with you during church."

Stunned, Cheryl couldn't seem to find her voice. All she could manage was a quick nod. Had Terry come here to be with her? If so, how did she feel about that?

Chapter 21

As Cheryl sat near the back of the church, she wondered what the people around her thought about the redheaded man with a ponytail, seated beside her on the pew. Even though Terry was dressed in nicer clothes today, he still looked a bit rugged. Of course, as she'd heard Pastor Gene say on more than one occasion, "A church is a hospital for sinners, not a home for the saints."

Cheryl thought about how Jesus had spent time with people like Zaccheus, whom many people hated because he was a tax collector. In God's eyes, people were all the same. Stereotyping and bigotry was man's choosing, not God's, and if the people attending this church chose to judge someone because of the way they wore their hair, then shame on them!

That goes for me, too, Cheryl thought. *When I first met Terry, I judged him based on how he looked and because he smoked. I really didn't give myself a chance to get to know him.*

One of the men in the church had just started to give the announcements when Terry leaned over to Cheryl and said, "Can I ask you something?"

Cheryl put her finger to her lips. Apparently Terry hadn't been to church that often. Either that or he didn't know enough to be quiet.

Terry reached for one of the visitor's cards, wrote something on it, and handed it Cheryl.

It read: *Would you go out to lunch with me after the service?*

Cheryl hesitated, then wrote back: *That would be nice.*

Terry couldn't believe his good fortune. He'd not only been able to sit beside Cheryl in church, but now they were eating lunch together at one of his favorite restaurants in Goshen. As far as he was concerned, this was definitely a date!

"This is really good chicken," Cheryl said, taking a bite of the drumstick she held. Terry was glad she wasn't one of those prissy women, afraid to pick up a piece of meat and eat it with her fingers.

He smacked his lips. "You're right about that. But then most of the food they serve here is good."

"Since you're a roofer and get around the area a lot, I imagine you've tried many of the restaurants."

Terry nodded as he reached for his glass of root beer. "When I'm out riding my Harley, I'm able to check out lots of restaurants."

"Do you go riding often?" she queried.

"Yeah, whenever I can." Terry paused to take a drink of his soda. He felt relaxed sitting here with Cheryl and felt no need for a cigarette. Being with her might be the motivation he needed to quit once and for all. "I usually go riding on the weekends, and I probably would have gone today if I hadn't come to church," Terry said, placing his glass on the table.

"So you don't go to church on a regular basis?"

"No, but Jan's always after me to go with him and Star."

"Do they attend church every week?"

Terry shook his head. "Sometimes they hit the road with their cycles. But they go as often as they can," he quickly added. "Jan mentioned one time that if they're near a church during one of their road trips, he and Star will go. Even dressed in their biker clothes, Jan said they've always been welcomed." Terry paused and took a bite of the fried shrimp he'd ordered. "Ruby Lee made me feel comfortable today, so I think I'll start going more regularly, too." He grinned at Cheryl and dipped another piece of shrimp into his cup of cocktail sauce. "I can always go riding on Saturdays, or even Sunday after church."

"I've never ridden a motorcycle before. What it's like?" Cheryl asked.

"Ever gone for a ride in a convertible?"

Cheryl nodded. "My ex-boyfriend had one."

"Well, it's sort of like riding in a convertible, but with no doors. You're open to nothing but the air around you." Terry was glad to know Cheryl had an ex-boyfriend. That meant he had a better chance with her. *Of course, Cheryl might not be interested in a guy like me. She might think Blaine's more her type.*

Cheryl shuddered. "I think I'd be scared to death on a motorcycle."

"Naw, you'd get used to it. It's hard to put into words, except that when I'm on my bike I feel free, like I'm in total charge of what I'm doing. It's great to be able to see everything around me, even the ripples and potholes in the pavement." Terry leaned back in the chair and crossed his arms. "I'm relaxed when I'm riding my Harley, and I enjoy the noise of the wind and even the smells from farms and cars. When I'm out on the open road, just me and my Harley, nothing seems wrong with the world. It's like some people enjoy reading a good book to relax. Well, riding my bike is like that for me. 'Course there are a few things that ain't—I mean, aren't so much fun about riding."

"Like what?" she asked with a curious expression.

"When it rains, it feels like hundreds of needles are hitting my face. Oh, and once a bumblebee crashed into my helmet when I was going at a high speed, and it felt like I'd been hit in the head by a rock. Then, too, after a long ride, my ears sometimes ring for an hour or so. I also learned a good lesson early on."

"What was that?" Cheryl asked, leaning forward.

"When I first got my bike, I thought it'd be neat to let my hair fly free in the wind." Terry scrunched up his face. "Boy was that ever a mistake."

"What happened?"

"When I got home, it took me over an hour to comb out all the tangles. Afterward when I looked at the floor, I thought I'd lost half my hair. 'Course I didn't, but now I never go riding without pulling my hair back into a ponytail."

Cheryl drew in her bottom lip. "I don't think I'd like any of that—especially getting whacked by a bug."

"When you think about it, it's really not so bad. I never ride my Harley without a helmet, and I also have a face shield attached to the helmet to protect my eyes. Over the years, I've found the good that comes from riding my cycle outweighs the bad." Terry snapped his fingers. "Say, I've got an idea."

"What's that?"

"How would you like to follow me back to Shipshe? Then I can give you a ride on the back of my Harley."

"Oh, I don't know. . . ."

"Aw, come on. It's not as bad as you might think, and you might even enjoy it."

"It does sound intriguing. Do you promise not to go real fast?"

"I won't break the speed limit, if that's what you mean, but we gotta pick up a little speed or we won't get the full enjoyment from the ride."

Cheryl looked down at the outfit she was wearing—a dark green skirt and a creamy off-white blouse. "I'm not dressed for riding."

"If you don't live too far from here, you can go home and change," Terry suggested. "I'll follow you there and wait in my truck till you're ready. Then you can follow me home in your car so you'll have a ride back to Goshen." Terry had thought about offering to give Cheryl a ride in his truck, but the seat still had that hole in it and didn't smell too good. "So what do you say? Should we go for a little joyride today?"

Cheryl sat staring at her plate, but she finally nodded. "Sure, why not? I need a little excitement in my life."

Shipshewana

"Okay, now," Terry said. "You need to keep your feet on the passenger pegs."

"Passenger pegs?"

"The footrests," Terry said, pointing at them.

Cheryl stared at the bike, wondering what in the world had possessed her to agree to go for a ride with Terry. This wasn't the type of thing she would normally do. Up close, his Harley looked bigger than she thought it would. It appeared to be a huge powerhouse on two wheels. And to think she was going to be sitting on that compelling piece of machinery, riding down the open road, with a man she'd felt a great dislike for when they'd first met. *What on earth has gotten into me, agreeing to do something like this?*

Terry handed Cheryl a helmet. "You'll need to wear this."

Cheryl's hair was short enough, so she didn't have to worry about tying it back as she reached for the plain blue helmet. Terry's helmet was a lot fancier. It was almost as colorful as his bowling ball and matched his Harley, which was a fiery red speckled with metallic paint. "What should I hold on to?" Cheryl asked, heart pounding, as she put the helmet on her head and took a seat on the back of the motorcycle.

"Me. You hold on tight to me." Terry grinned down at Cheryl as he stood next to the bike. "And if your back muscles get sore, just lean against the sissy bar behind you. It'll give you some added support."

Cheryl's face warmed as she thought once again, *Oh my, why did I ever agree to this? I must have been out of my mind.*

"Oh, and whenever we're at a stop sign, don't put your feet down; just keep 'em on the pegs. It's my job to make sure the bike stays upright when we're stopped."

Cheryl nodded. "I understand." She was glad she'd made the quick decision to put on her heavier leather shoes instead of the sneakers she'd almost decided to wear.

"One more thing," Terry said, throwing his leg over the bike, "don't wiggle around or shift your weight. Just lean with me, and since you'll be hanging on to me, that should be easy."

"Don't worry," Cheryl said, her voice trembling a bit, "I'll be too scared to do anything but hang on tight."

"You'll be fine; just try to relax and enjoy the ride."

Yeah, right, Cheryl thought. *Sounds like something I heard in a movie once.*

Terry fired up the bike, looking back as Cheryl wrapped her arms snugly around his waist. "By the way," he shouted over the roar of the engine, "you look real good in that helmet."

Cheryl couldn't help smiling. Watching Terry pull his face shield down, she did the same.

As they rode out of Terry's yard, Cheryl couldn't see much of anything except Terry's back. She was also aware of the smell of leather from his jacket, and when they turned onto the road, a drafty wind whipped up the back of her neck. She felt vulnerable, but it was also quite exhilarating. It was nothing like being enclosed in a vehicle, with four sides around her and a roof overhead. And it in no way compared to riding in a convertible.

As they ventured farther onto the open road, Terry picked up speed. Cheryl was glad her helmet had a shield. If not, Terry's ponytail would be slapping her in the face like a horse's tail swatting at flies.

"Whoo-hoo! Isn't this great?" Terry hollered into the wind.

Cheryl was afraid to open her mouth, and she thought for a minute to just lean her forehead against Terry's back and not look at anything at all. At the same time, she didn't want to act like a baby and miss the whole experience, so all she could do was hang on for dear life and try to enjoy this crazy ride.

CHAPTER 22

Selma's eyelids fluttered, but she couldn't quite open them. She'd been having a pleasant dream and didn't want to wake up. But something—she wasn't sure what—seemed to be pulling her awake.

She rolled her head from side to side, snuggling deeper under the blankets. She couldn't remember when she'd slept so well.

Prrr. . . Prrr. . . Something soft and warm pushed at Selma's face.

Selma's eyes snapped open. The furry gray cat was lying on her chest!

"Yikes!' Selma screamed and sat straight up. The cat hissed and leaped off the bed, looking like one of those frightened arched-back Halloween cats.

"How did you get in here?" Selma shouted as the cat raced out of the room. She pulled the covers aside and grimaced when her feet touched the cold floor. Her floor vent still wasn't sending up any heat, and now she had to deal with a cat in the house. This was not a good way to begin her Monday.

Without bothering to put on her slippers and wearing only her nightgown, Selma ran down the hallway, chasing the cat. She caught up with him in the kitchen, where he was crouched near the back door, looking up at her with big, innocent eyes. He looked scared, and Selma almost felt sorry for him. She wondered if someone might have abused the cat, or if he'd learned to defend himself after years of living on his own. She had to admit she had slept quite well last night and wondered if it was due to the warmth and comfort of the cat sleeping on her chest.

No, that can't be, she told herself. *It was the dream I had—that's why I slept so well.* "And you, Mr. Scruffy," she said, picking up the cat, "are going outside, where you belong!"

As Carmen's car approached Emma's house, she thought about how she'd gone to church with Paul and Sophia on Sunday. They'd eaten lunch afterward at a family-style restaurant, then gone to a nearby park. If anyone didn't know better, they might have thought the three of them were a family spending a Sunday afternoon together.

Carmen had enjoyed watching Sophia run and play. She could still hear the little girl's laughter as she sat on the swing, being pushed by Paul and Carmen. Sophia looked so much like her mother, and seeing her on the swing reminded Carmen of the times she and Lorinda were children and enjoyed swinging in their parents' backyard. Carmen looked forward to seeing Paul and Sophia this Saturday evening, when they would have supper at the home of Paul's sister, Maria. Carmen would miss the happy times she'd spent with Paul and Sophia when she went back to California, and she planned to keep in better touch through phone calls and e-mails. Maybe during Paul's summer break, he and Sophia could come to California for a visit. It would be fun to go to the beach and teach Sophia how to build sand castles and search for seashells.

Carmen pulled her thoughts aside as she turned up Emma's driveway and parked the car. When she got out, and started walking toward the house, she spotted Emma's goat Maggie lying on the porch swing, snoozing. The goat looked so cute, Carmen couldn't help but smile. She was sure Maggie had escaped from her pen again, and figured Emma and Lamar didn't realize it.

Carmen walked past the swing and knocked on the front door. Apparently unaware of her presence, Maggie slept on, snoozing like a dog on a lazy summer afternoon. A few seconds later, Lamar came to the door. After Carmen greeted him and said she'd come to visit Emma, she pointed to the porch swing. "Looks like Emma's goat is enjoying herself."

Lamar groaned. "That silly critter can sure be persistent." He opened the door wider. "Emma's in her quilting room, so just go on in. I'd better put Maggie back in her pen."

"Thanks, I will. Oh, and good luck with the goat," Carmen called over her shoulder as she entered the house.

When she stepped into the room, she found Emma working on the tattered old quilt Cheryl had brought for repair.

"I don't mean to interrupt," Carmen said, approaching the sewing machine where Emma sat, "but Lamar said I should come in."

Emma smiled and motioned to the chairs at the sewing table. "What a nice surprise. It's good to see you. Please, make yourself comfortable."

"When I got here, I discovered your goat lying on the porch swing, so Lamar's outside putting her away," Carmen explained. "That animal must keep you and Lamar on your toes."

Emma clicked her tongue while peering over the top of her glasses. "That's my Maggie. I'm beginning to think there's nothing that will keep her in the pen."

Carmen smiled, glancing out the window just in time to see Lamar walking Maggie back to her pen. "She does seem to be quite the escape artist, but I see your husband has everything under control."

"He's good with animals," Emma said. "Maggie can be a handful, but it's hard to stay mad at her. So what brings you by here this morning?" she asked.

"I was hoping we could talk awhile—if you have the time, that is."

"That sounds nice. Would you like a cup of tea?" Emma asked, rising from her chair and setting her sewing aside.

"Don't go to any trouble on my account," Carmen said.

"It's no trouble at all. It's nice that we can visit like this, other than just during the time we spend in the quilt class." Emma smiled and ambled out of the room.

Carmen left her seat and went over to look at the quilt Emma had been working on. Being careful not to touch it, she studied the detailed stitching. Each stitch was evenly spaced, and the pattern, with interlocking patches of color, was quite interesting. A quilting machine couldn't have done it any better than the quality she saw in Emma's work. Carmen remembered Emma saying that the design of this quilt was called Wedding Ring, and that many Amish couples received a quilt like this when they got married.

I wonder if I'll ever get married, Carmen mused. In high school, she'd had a few boyfriends but never gotten serious about any of them. Since her job kept her so busy, she really didn't have time for dating these days. Sometimes, Carmen wished she were married and raising a family or had at least found someone with whom she might want to pursue a meaningful relationship.

"Here we go," Emma said as she entered the room and placed a tray on the table.

Carmen motioned to the quilt. "I know this is old, but I think it's beautiful."

Emma nodded. "I agree. But then, I have a fondness for quilts, so most of them appeal to me."

"I'm glad I decided to take your class," Carmen said. "I'm anxious to see how my wall hanging turns out."

"Do you have a special place you'll want to hang it?" Emma asked.

"I'm thinking of giving it to my niece, Sophia, for her bedroom. The colors I chose are bright, and they nearly match her bedspread and curtains."

"I'm sure she'll appreciate the wall hanging as she gets older, and also the quilt that Paul finished for her after his wife died," Emma said.

Carmen flinched at the mention of her sister. If Lorinda hadn't been killed, she would have finished Sophia's quilt.

"Yes, my sister, Lorinda, had many talents. She could walk circles around me with all she knew how to do." Carmen looked down, wondering if she'd ever get over the loss. "Sophia was cheated, losing her mother before she had a chance to know her." Taking in a quick breath, she continued. "I feel cheated, too, after losing my sister, but I'll certainly make sure I share with my niece all the wonderful memories I've locked away in my heart, growing up with a big sister like Lorinda."

"I'm sure you will, Carmen, and I'm sorry if I've opened up a painful memory for you." Emma put her hand on Carmen's arm, patting it gently. "Your niece is fortunate to have a father like Paul. Even a stranger could see how much he adores his little girl. And from what I've observed, she's pretty lucky to have an aunt like you as well."

"Thank you, Emma. And don't worry, you didn't open any wounds. It's getting easier for me as time goes on to be able to talk about my sister and not get all choked up." Needing to change the subject, Carmen said, "Would you mind if I asked you some questions about the Amish way of life?"

"Of course not. You can ask me anything while we drink our tea."

Emma poured tea into their cups, handed one to Carmen, and took the other for herself.

Carmen took a sip of tea, savoring the delicate aroma and taste of peppermint. "This is really good," she said, letting it roll around on her tongue.

"I'm glad you like it. I grow the mint in my garden, and there was a lot of it this summer."

"I can't have a garden where I live." Carmen sighed. "That's what you get with apartment living."

"Maybe someday you'll have a home of your own." Emma set her cup on the table. "If you have a patio, perhaps you could plant a few herbs in a planter box. They don't need a lot of space. I've planted things in the window box outside the kitchen. It's nice to be able to pick whatever I need without having to walk out to the garden all the time."

"That sounds doable." Carmen's interest was heightened. "I may consider that when I get back home. In Los Angeles, the nights are sometimes cool in the winter months, but the days are pretty mild. In fact, wintertime is our rainiest season. The rest of the year it's quite dry."

"I can't imagine being able to have a year-round garden." Emma paused and took a sip of tea. "Now, on to another subject. What is it you want to know about the Amish life?"

"I've been wondering about rumschpringe. What can you tell me about it?"

Emma tapped her fingers on the edge of the table. "Well, it normally begins around the age of fifteen or sixteen and ends when an Amish young person decides to be baptized and join the church."

"Do most of the youth go wild during that time and do things their parents wouldn't approve of?" Carmen queried, thinking of her boss's insistence that her article focus on wild Amish teens.

"No, not all. In fact, most, at least those in our district, enjoy a time with others their age, where they attend Sunday night singings and get together for volleyball and baseball games. Some take trips together, and some never leave the area during their running-around years."

"So it's not just a bunch of wild parties or Amish young people leaving home to experience things in the world that their parents would disapprove of?"

Emma shook her head. "I'm sure there are a few who do that, but as I said, most of the young people I know have stuck close to home."

"What about their parents?" Carmen asked. "Do they approve of rumschpringe?"

"Some look the other way," Emma admitted, "but other parents hold a tight rein on their children."

"From what Anna's told me, her parents won't give her the freedom to explore the outside world," Carmen said. "Is that healthy?"

Deep wrinkles formed across Emma's forehead as her lips compressed. "It's not really my place to say, but I think they may be making a mistake by holding her back. Anna, like most others her age, is curious about the English world. In my opinion, if she's allowed to experience a few things outside of her community, she might find out, just as my children did, that there's much to appreciate about the Amish way of life."

Carmen mulled things over as she finished her tea. Emma was a wise woman, and this conversation had given Carmen a lot to think about. After learning what she had so far, it would be difficult to write a negative article about the Amish. But if she didn't write it, she could lose her job.

Chapter 23

Elkhart

"How come you've been so quiet today?" Jan asked as he and Terry removed shingles from the roof of an elderly couple who didn't have much money. Jan had given them a discount, which he often did when someone couldn't pay full price. It was a wonder he made any money at all, but he said that over the years he'd become aware of what a limited income many senior citizens struggled to live on and that it felt good to be able to help out whenever he could.

"Hey, man, did you hear what I said?" Jan repeated. "I asked how come you've been so quiet today."

"Yeah, I heard. I've just been thinking, is all."

"About what?"

"The weekend and how it went."

"If you're talking about Saturday night at the bowling alley, then I can tell you exactly how it went."

Terry tipped his head to one side. "Oh yeah? How's that?"

"You bent over backwards to get Cheryl to pay attention to you instead of her date." Jan grunted. "And you made a complete fool of yourself in the process."

Terry's face heated. "Oh really? What'd I do that made me look like a fool?"

Jan stopped what he was doing and held up one finger. "You tried to out-bowl Blaine, and you both acted like two roosters in a henhouse." Another finger shot up. "You talked more to Cheryl then you did me and Star, and we were the ones you were supposed to be bowling with." Jan held up a third finger, but before he could say anything Terry cut him off.

"Okay, I get it. You're mad because I paid Cheryl some attention." Terry planted his hands against his hips. "Did you forget that I've been trying to get her to go out with me?"

Jan shook his head. "'Course not, but you shouldn't be making a play for her when she's out with another man. That just ain't cool. Anyone watching could see you were pushing too hard, and I wouldn't be surprised if she noticed that, too. If anything, that might have turned her away."

Terry shrugged. "Think what you want to, but I had to get Cheryl to notice me somehow, and you know what? It worked!"

"How so?"

"Cheryl and I had our first date Sunday afternoon."

Jan quirked an eyebrow. "Is that the truth?"

"'Course it is. I showed up at Cheryl's church, and—"

Jan stared at Terry in disbelief. "I'm not hearing this. Did you just say you went to church?"

"That's right, and afterward Cheryl and I went out to lunch." Terry grinned widely. "When we were done eating, we drove back to Shipshe and got my Harley, so Cheryl could take her first ride on a motorcycle."

Jan whistled. "I've gotta hand it to you, buddy. All those crazy stunts you pulled Saturday night must have impressed that little gal. I woulda thought the opposite, though. And going to church. . . Well, if it took trying to land a date with the pretty little blond to get you in church, then I have to say, 'Amen' to that, 'cause I've tried everything but stand on my head to coax you into going to church, and you always come up with some lame excuse."

"You don't have to rub it in." Terry bent down, grabbed an armful of shingles, and tossed them into Jan's utility trailer. "You know what?"

"What?"

"I kinda enjoyed the church service. The preacher read some verses from the Bible that sorta opened my eyes to the truth about some things."

"Such as?"

"He talked about temptation. Even said Jesus was tempted, and that He's able to help those who are tempted." Terry scratched the side of his head. "I think he said the verse was found in Hebrows something or other."

Jan laughed and poked Terry's arm. "It's Hebrews, and it's a great verse for you—especially since you're struggling with the temptation to smoke."

"Yeah. I've been doing a little better with it today, though," Terry said. He patted his pocket. "Been chewing a lot of gum."

"That's good to hear." Jan loaded more shingles into the trailer and paused to wipe his damp forehead. Despite the autumn chill, they'd both worked up quite a sweat. "So where'd you go to church?"

"That church in Goshen, where your friend, Ruby Lee's husband, pastors. That's why I asked you where it was, remember?"

Jan smiled. "Star and I have been there a few times, but we mostly go to a church near my place in Shipshe. Pastor Gene's a good man, and Ruby Lee. . . Well, she's a sweetheart."

Terry bobbed his head. "She was real friendly and made me feel welcome. When church was over, she introduced me to her husband, and they both said they hoped I'd come back. I even saw a motorcycle in the church parking lot, so I know I'd have something in common with someone in the congregation."

"Think you'll go back?" Jan asked.

"Yeah, I'm pretty sure of it."

"That's good to hear, but you shouldn't be going to church because of Cheryl. There's a lot more to it than that." Jan thumped Terry's shoulder. "Can I offer you a piece of advice?"

"Sure. You usually do," Terry added with a snicker.

"I can see by the starry look in your eyes that you're pretty hyped up about Cheryl. Just be careful you don't get your heart broken. She might have gone out to lunch with you and taken a ride on your Harley, but she went bowling with someone else, so don't get your hopes up."

Terry shrugged. "Don't worry, I'm not. Even if I do go out with Cheryl again, it'll just be for fun 'cause I have no plans of getting serious about anyone."

Jan chuckled and thumped Terry's back. "That's what they all say before they're reeled in."

"Hey, wait up a minute, would you?" Stuart called as Blaine was about to leave the sporting goods store at the end of his workday.

Blaine halted near the door as he put on his hunter-green zip-up jacket. "What's up?"

"I haven't had a chance to talk to you all day and wanted to hear how things went with Cheryl on your bowling date."

"It was okay, I guess," Blaine replied in a nonchalant tone, anxious to get home after a grueling day. He'd been on his feet the entire shift, and between helping customers and stocking shelves, his recliner and a good DVD were all he could think about. Extra shipments of goods were starting to arrive for the upcoming holidays. A busy time of the year for the store was fast approaching, but for now, all Blaine wanted to do was get home and prop up his feet.

"Didn't you enjoy your date at all?" Stuart asked, nudging Blaine's arm.

"Cheryl's nice, but she's not Sue."

Stuart opened the door to let a late shopper out. "Do you think it's fair to compare the two women?"

"Maybe not, but—"

"You need to forget about Sue and get on with your life."

"I guess you're right," Blaine admitted. "And I did enjoy being with Cheryl—at least until Terry showed up and started showing off for her."

"Did she leave with him?" Stuart questioned.

"Well, no, but she didn't leave with me, either. She drove her own car to the bowling alley, and I met her there."

"Was Cheryl impressed with Terry? Did she pay him any attention?"

Blaine shrugged. "I don't know if she was impressed, but she did laugh at his corny jokes."

"Maybe you ought to ask her out again," Stuart suggested. "Take her someplace where Terry's not likely to show up."

"Such as?"

"How about one of the nice restaurants on Winona Lake? Pam really likes it when I take her there. With all the little stores in the village, she could spend hours shopping."

"I don't know. Winona Lake's in Kosciusko County, over an hour away."

Stuart thumped Blaine's back. "Exactly! I mean what are the odds that Terry would show up there?"

"Slim to none, I guess."

"Right. A guy like him probably wouldn't even go to a fancy restaurant, let alone drive that far to get there."

"Hmm. . ." Blaine pondered Stuart's suggestion. "Maybe when I see Cheryl at the next quilting class I'll ask her out to lunch. Better yet, maybe she'd like to go fishing with me sometime." Blaine had never been to Lake Winona, which was south of Mishawaka, but he was game to find new places where he might want to venture for some good fishing. He remembered one of his customers saying he went to Lake Winona every year and rented a cottage there, but Blaine couldn't recall what the man had said about the fishing.

"I don't know about Cheryl, but I know all too well how Pam resented me going fishing so much," Stuart said. "Maybe you'd better stick to taking Cheryl out to lunch for now. Since you'll be at the lake, the subject of fishing might come up, and you can ask her then. And I think it might be better if you asked her out over the phone. That way, Terry won't know about your plans."

Blaine nodded. "You're right. That would be better than asking her during class. I'll give Cheryl a call tonight."

"You're late. What took you so long?" Mandy asked when Anna entered the Dairy Queen and found her friend sitting at a table.

"Sorry, but it couldn't be helped. Dad made me stay longer than usual this afternoon because he had a couple of orders that needed to go out." Anna sank into the seat beside Mandy. "Have you already had your ice-cream cone?"

Mandy shook her head. "I was waiting for you."

Anna smiled. "Good, because I'm hungry and more than ready for a treat. Let's go order our cones now, and then we can visit."

Anna and Mandy returned to their table a few minutes later with chocolate-vanilla swirl cones. "This hits the spot," Anna said, swiping her tongue over the sweet frozen treat. "I love soft ice cream."

"Me, too," Mandy agreed. "Guess this will probably spoil my appetite for supper, but I probably won't eat much of it anyway, because Mom's fixing baked cabbage tonight, and I don't like it."

Anna wrinkled her nose. "Me neither. Besides tasting yucky, cooked cabbage stinks up the house."

"Have you had any luck finding another job yet?" Mandy asked, switching the subject and glancing at the English boys a few tables away.

"No, Dad keeps me so busy at the window shop that there's no time to go looking."

"I'm going down to Sarasota this winter," Mandy announced with a grin. "I'll be working at one of the restaurants outside of Pinecraft." She clasped Anna's arm. "Why don't you come with me? I'll see if I can get you a job there, too."

Anna's eyes widened. "Really? You'd do that for me?"

"Of course. What else are friends for? It would be more fun being there if we were together."

Anna smiled. This might be the opportunity she was hoping for—a chance for a new job—in a place where Mom and Dad couldn't watch every move she made. She'd be able to make her own decisions and not worry about anyone telling her what to do. She had a good head on her shoulders and could never understand why Mom and Dad didn't see that about her.

"So what do you think?" Mandy asked, bumping Anna's arm. "Will you go to Sarasota with me in December? Think about it—it's right by the Gulf, and we could go to the beach during our free time. Imagine getting a tan in December."

"That does sound appealing. Where will you stay while you're there?" Anna asked.

"I'll be renting a small house in Pinecraft." Mandy smiled widely. "Just think how much fun it'll be for us to spend the winter where it's warm."

"I would like to go." Anna paused to finish her cone. "You know what, Mandy?"

"What?"

"If I like it there, I may just stay and never move back."

Chapter 24

Shipshewana

Selma turned out the lights in her living room and padded down the hall toward her bedroom, dreading the coolness of the room. She'd called the furnace company, but they said they were swamped and couldn't send a man over until early the next week. Out of desperation, Selma had gone next door to see if Jan might be able to help her out, but he wasn't home; just that big mutt of his, barking and jumping at the fence in his dog run. She knew she shouldn't complain. At least Jan had remedied the problem, and Brutus hadn't found a way to break out of the pen Jan had built for him.

Selma stopped at the linen closet in the hall and grabbed a heavy blanket. The nights had been getting colder lately, and with no heat in her room, she would need the extra blanket. She'd switched to flannel sheets when she'd remade the bed last week, and since then, each morning it was harder to get out of her warm, cozy cocoon.

When Selma entered the bedroom, she placed the blanket on the bed, changed into her nightgown, and turned down the covers. She was about to climb into bed, when she heard an unfamiliar noise. Unexpectedly, the floor vent popped up, and the scruffy cat poked his head through.

Selma jumped. Then, trying hard not to laugh, she shook her finger at the cat and sternly said, "So that's how you've been getting in, is it? You're just full of surprises, aren't you, Scruffy?"

The cat gave a quick *meow!* Then he leaped onto her bed and curled into a tight ball. A few seconds later, seeming quite content, he began to purr, looking as if it would take more than a harsh scolding to change his mind about moving.

Selma couldn't believe how persistent this animal was. It didn't seem to matter how stern she was. Scruffy just wouldn't give up. For some unknown reason, he'd decided to make this his new home, and he didn't seem to care whether Selma liked it or not.

Should I weaken and let Scruffy stay? she wondered. Selma figured if she put the cat out he'd just find his way back in. *Guess I could set a box or one of my bedside tables over the vent, but then he'd probably sit under the house and meow all night.*

Leaning down, so she was eye level with the cat, Selma said quietly, "Okay, Scruffy, you win—you've got yourself a new home."

Middlebury

As Anna got ready for bed, she realized that in her excitement over the possibility of going to Florida in December, she'd forgotten to show Mandy the bracelet Carmen had gotten her. Anna had only been to Florida once, when as a nine-year-old, she'd gone with her grandparents for a few weeks in December. The one thing she remembered most was running barefoot on the white sandy beaches. It had been fun to look for shells, chase the seagulls, and wade in the warm water. Grandpa had even taken a kite along, and on windy days he'd shown Anna how to fly it.

The eighty-degree temperatures in Sarasota felt so good. Not having to bundle up like she would have been doing back home had been a plus, too. Summer had always been Anna's favorite time of the year, and she recalled how different it was to sip milk shakes during the warmth of a winter evening instead of watching snowflakes. On one of those nights, she'd sat with her grandparents on their front porch, watching as lightning illuminated the sky and thunder rumbled.

The idea of going to Sarasota with Mandy was exciting, but one thing bothered Anna. How was she going to tell her folks? They'd never give their blessing, because they thought her place was at home where they could tell her what to do and keep a close watch on her. Anna could already imagine the clash, trying to convince her folks that she should go to Sarasota, while listening to them give all the reasons she shouldn't.

Maybe I should just go and not tell them, Anna thought as she stared at the blank wall across her room. *I could head out during the night, and leave them a note on the kitchen table.* Anna knew that would be a cowardly thing to do, but wouldn't it be better than listening to Mom and Dad list all the reasons it would be wrong for her to go? She could already sense this would become one more wedge pushing her and her parents apart. *I don't need to decide anything right now,* she reminded herself. *December is still two months away.*

Anna went to get her purse, which she'd placed on her dresser when she'd arrived home that afternoon. Reaching inside to get the bracelet Carmen had given her, she was surprised when she couldn't find it. She dug around for a bit, but there was no sign of the bracelet.

Going over to the bed, Anna dumped the contents of her purse onto the quilt, but after sorting through everything, she realized the piece of jewelry wasn't there.

Anna's heart started to pound. What had happened to it? Could one of her siblings have sneaked into her room while she was helping Mom do the dishes and gone through her purse?

She sank to the bed with a moan. *What should I do? I can't accuse anyone when I don't know who did it. And what if I say something and no one admits to taking the bracelet? If Mom and Dad get wind of this, I'll be in trouble for sure.*

Anna pondered the situation. Maybe the best thing to do was snoop around in her siblings' rooms when they weren't there and see if she could locate the missing jewelry. If she didn't find it by the end of the week, she'd have to come right out and ask.

Shipshewana

As Emma followed Lamar down the hall toward their bedroom, she noticed that he was limping and walking slower than usual. Today he'd worked on one of the hickory rockers he made to sell at a local gift store. Perhaps he'd overdone it.

"Are you feeling okay this evening?" Emma asked after they'd entered their room. "I noticed you were limping and wondered if you might be in pain."

Deep wrinkles formed across Lamar's forehead as he turned to face her. "I'm stiff and my joints ache," he admitted, leaning against the dresser for support.

"Did you work too long on the rocker today?"

"Maybe, but I think it's my arthritis flaring up. These cold days we've been having don't help with the stiffness." Lamar rubbed his fingers. "My hands don't work well when my arthritis acts up."

Emma lowered herself to the bed as reality set in. "You wanted to go to Florida because you knew you'd feel better where it's warm, right?"

He nodded slowly as he released the suspenders from his trousers.

"Then why didn't you explain that to me? If I'd only known—"

"You would have agreed to go, even though you wanted to teach another six-week quilting class," he interrupted.

"Jah, that's right. I would have changed my mind had I known the reason."

"Which is why I didn't tell you." He sat beside Emma on the bed. "I knew you were looking forward to teaching another class, and I wouldn't have felt right asking you to give it up on my account."

"Oh Lamar," Emma said, tears welling in her eyes, "you're my husband, and I love you so much."

"I love you, too, Emma." Lamar placed a comforting arm around her shoulders.

"I appreciate you allowing me to teach another class, and I really do feel that the students who've come to my class have been sent for a reason. But your health and your needs come first, so. . ."

Lamar put his finger to her lips. "It's all right, Emma. We have just three more weeks of teaching your students, and maybe after that, if you're willing, we can head to Florida."

She smiled and leaned her head on his shoulder. "I'm more than willing, and if you like, we can spend the entire winter there, where it's nice and warm."

He reached for her hand and gave it a gentle squeeze. "I'm surely blessed to have a *fraa* like you."

Goshen

Cheryl took a seat at her kitchen table and booted up her laptop. While she ate a snack of apples and cheese, she planned to answer any e-mails that had come in over the weekend.

She was about to go online when her cell phone rang. She saw in the caller ID that it was Blaine.

"Hello, Blaine," she said, holding the phone up to her ear.

"Hi, Cheryl. How are you this evening?"

"I'm fine. How are you?"

"Doing okay." After a pause, Blaine cleared his throat a few times. "The reason I'm calling is I was wondering if you have any plans for Saturday."

"Just Emma's quilt class," Cheryl replied.

"I meant Saturday afternoon, when the class is over."

"I have no plans at the moment." Secretly, Cheryl had been hoping Terry might ask her out. As scared as she'd been on the back of his motorcycle, she actually wanted to go for another ride. Now that she knew what to expect, she hoped she could relax and enjoy it more the second time around.

"I'd like to take you out for lunch," Blaine said. "To someplace nice, out of town."

"You've piqued my curiosity. Where did you plan to go?"

"Winona Lake. Have you ever been there?"

"No, but I've heard it's beautiful," Cheryl responded. "And I understand there's a lot to do there."

"Should I go ahead and make reservations?"

"Yes, it sounds nice. I'll look forward to going."

"Great. And I forgot tell you that the restaurant we're going to overlooks the lake. See you Saturday morning at Emma's then."

Cheryl smiled when she hung up the phone. This would be a pleasant change over her boring plans to clean the apartment. She wasn't sure yet what type of relationship Blaine was seeking from her. Did he simply want to be friends, or was he hoping for something more serious? Deep down, she hoped he saw her only as a friend. When she was with Blaine, even though she'd never had any siblings, it felt more like hanging out with a brother rather than being on a date. In any event, eating lunch at a restaurant with a view of the lake would give her a chance to get to know Blaine better. Maybe she would discover that she liked him more than she realized.

Chapter 25

Elkhart

"Thank you for inviting me to join you for supper," Carmen told Paul's sister, Maria, when she entered her kitchen Wednesday evening.

Maria smiled. "We're happy to have you, and we're so glad you could join us."

"Is there anything I can do to help?" Carmen asked, looking around the homey room, and feeling a twinge of envy. She'd never realized how much she longed for a house of her own until she'd come to Indiana. Thanks to her job, Carmen was on the road so much she sometimes felt like she didn't have a place to call home.

"You can finish the green salad I started, while I take the enchiladas out of the oven," Maria replied.

"Sure, no problem." Carmen placed a tomato on the cutting board and cut it into small pieces.

"How are you enjoying your quilting class?" Maria questioned.

"It's interesting. I've learned a lot about quilts, and the wall hanging

I'm making is turning out better than I expected," Carmen replied. "At first I was a little nervous about quilting, but now I'm really liking it."

"Paul liked the class when he took it, too." Maria set the dish of enchiladas on the table. "It's been good for him and Sophia having you here. Paul said Sophia lights up when you're in the room."

Carmen felt the heat of a blush. "I've enjoyed spending time with them, too."

"Have you ever considered moving to Elkhart so you could be closer to your niece?" Maria questioned.

"My job's in Los Angeles," Carmen replied.

"I know, but maybe you could get a job as a reporter with one of the newspapers in our area."

"The idea of moving here does have some appeal," Carmen admitted, "but I'm not sure I could find another job I like as well as the one I have now. Besides, I enjoy the warmth of the California sun, and it's only October here, and already I had to buy a warmer coat."

"I know what you mean," Maria said, going to the refrigerator to get the salad dressing. "Of course, some people go south for the winter, but for those of us who have jobs, that's not an option."

"Is supper about ready?" Maria's husband, Hosea, asked, poking his head into the kitchen. "The girls are getting hungry, and Paul and I are having a hard time keeping them under control."

Maria gestured to the table. "We're just about ready, so bring in the crew."

As Carmen helped to get the rest of the things set on the table, she couldn't help wondering what she'd be doing if she were in Los Angeles right now. At first, having her own apartment had been exciting—especially after getting a job at the newspaper. But now, she'd begun to question whether she really wanted to go back to California. Sure, the warm weather was great, but everything that had once been so appealing was slowly losing its zest.

As Paul watched Carmen from across the table, a lump formed in his throat. She reminded him of Lorinda—same dark hair and eyes, and a nose that turned up slightly on the end. It was almost painful to look at her. Even though Carmen was a few years younger than Lorinda, she seemed mature and possessed an air of confidence. She had a special way with Sophia, too, and Paul knew his daughter would miss her aunt Carmen when she returned to California in a few weeks.

I'll miss Carmen, too, Paul admitted to himself. *If only we had more time to spend with her.*

"Are the enchiladas okay?" Maria asked, bumping Paul's arm. "You haven't eaten much on your plate."

"Uh, yes, they're fine." Paul stabbed a piece with his fork.

"Just fine?" Hosea asked, raising his eyebrows. "Usually you can't get enough of my *esposa*'s enchiladas."

Paul smiled at Maria. "They're very good. Guess I'm just a slow eater tonight."

"Paul's right," Carmen agreed. "This meal is delicious."

"The girls must think so, too." Maria motioned to Sophia and her two girls sitting near Carmen, eagerly eating their enchiladas.

As the meal continued, the adults talked about the chilly weather that had hit northeastern Indiana, and then the conversation moved to how things were going at the school where Paul taught. After that, Maria asked Carmen what it was like to be a newspaper reporter.

"It's interesting," Carmen said. "There's always something different to report."

"I imagine there's a lot more happening in Los Angeles than here," Paul said.

"There can be," Carmen responded, "but I'm often asked to travel to other places to cover news stories. My favorite ones to write about are human-interest stories, where I get to meet different people."

Paul listened with interest as Carmen explained more about her job. He could see that she was passionate about her work, and it made him doubt that she would ever give up her life in Los Angeles.

"I don't know about anyone else, but I'm so full I couldn't eat another bite," Hosea said, pushing away from the table. "Paul, would you like to join me in the living room to watch the evening news?"

Paul shook his head, snapping out of his thoughts. "You go ahead. Think I'll help Maria with the dishes. It'll be like old times when we were kids."

"I'd be happy to help Maria," Carmen was quick to say.

"That's okay," Paul said. "Why don't you spend some time with Sophia and the girls? Maria and I used to make a good team when we did the dishes together." He stood and started clearing away the dishes. Truth was, he'd hoped for a little one-on-one time with his sister this evening.

When Carmen, Hosea, and the girls left the kitchen, Maria filled the sink with warm water and added some liquid detergent. "You know," she said, smiling at Paul, "some people might think it's strange that a busy woman like me doesn't own a dishwasher, but I actually enjoy washing the dishes by hand."

Paul chuckled and reached for a clean towel, in readiness to dry. "I guess you take after our mother. I can't remember how many times I've heard Mom say over the years, 'I'll never own a dishwasher; they're just not for me.'"

"Like mother, like daughter," Maria said with a laugh. She glanced over at Paul as she placed some clean dishes in the drainer. "I sense you have something you'd like to talk about."

He nodded slowly. "You know me so well."

"What's on your mind?"

"Carmen." Paul lowered his voice. "Ever since she came here, she's been on my mind."

"I'm not surprised," Maria said, handing him another dish to dry. "She looks a lot like Lorinda."

"You're right, but it's more than that. I really enjoy being with her, and. . ." Paul's voice trailed off as he swiped the dish towel over the clean plate.

"Are you falling for her? Is that what you're saying?"

Paul shrugged his shoulders. "I–I'm not sure. I just know that being with Carmen makes me feel happier than I've been in a long time. Do you think it could be just because I miss Lorinda so much? Or could I actually be falling in love again?"

"Only you know that," Maria said in a big-sister tone of voice. "But if you'd like my opinion, I think you should spend as much time with Carmen as you can—maybe take her out a few times, just the two of you. If there is something brewing between you, you'll know soon enough."

"If Carmen and I go out by ourselves, would you be willing to watch Sophia?" he asked.

"Of course. The girls love spending time with their cousin."

Paul knew he didn't have much time since Carmen would be leaving in a few weeks. "All right then," he said. "I'm going to ask her out."

Goshen

Think I'll call Mom and see how Grandma's doing, Cheryl thought, glancing at the clock on her kitchen wall. It was almost ten, which meant it would be seven in Portland, so maybe she could catch her folks at home.

Cheryl reached for the phone and punched in her folks' number. Her father answered on the third ring.

"Hi, Dad. How are you doing?"

"I'm fine, Cheryl. How about you?"

"Doing good and keeping busy as usual." Cheryl switched the phone to her other ear. "Is Mom there?"

"No, she's at her garden club meeting. Should I ask her to call when she gets home?"

"No, that's okay. I'm just calling to see how Grandma's doing, and I'm sure you can tell me that."

"She's about the same. Doesn't say much when we go to the nursing home to see her, and she seems to be getting weaker."

"I'm sorry to hear that. As soon as Emma finishes Grandma's quilt and I'm done with the quilt classes, I'll be coming there to see Grandma. Maybe seeing that her quilt has been repaired will perk her up."

"I wouldn't count on it, Cheryl. I'm not even sure she'll know who you are."

"Why wouldn't she? Grandma knew me when I went to see her before I moved here."

"Some days she's fine, but other times she doesn't seem to know your mother. That's one reason we don't go as often to see her."

"I think Grandma needs people around here—people she knows and loves." Cheryl fought the urge to go see Grandma right away, but she wanted to wait until she could take the quilt for her birthday. She felt sure it would make a difference.

"If there's nothing else, I'd better hang up," Dad said. "There's a game show coming on TV that I want to watch."

"Okay, Dad. Have a nice evening." *I can't believe Mom doesn't visit Grandma very often. How can she be so selfish and unfeeling?*

When Cheryl hung up, she decided to check her e-mails before going to bed. She found one from April, with an invitation to her and Lance's wedding the first week of December. To add insult to injury, April had asked Cheryl to be one of her bridesmaids.

Cheryl grimaced. *The nerve of some people. If they think I'm about to go to their wedding, after what they did to me. . . What I should do is e-mail them back and give them a piece of my mind!*

"Be angry and sin not." The verse of scripture Ruby Lee had quoted to Cheryl a few weeks ago, came to mind. *Okay, I won't give them a piece of mind. But I'm not going to the wedding. It would be too painful. I'll send them an RSVP that I won't be attending.*

Middlebury

Anna slipped out of bed and tiptoed down the hall toward her sister Susan's bedroom. She should be asleep by now, and this was the perfect chance for Anna to search for her bracelet. She'd already looked in Arie's and Becky's rooms while they were helping Mom do the supper dishes. She would have checked Susan's room during that time, too, but Susan had been in there playing.

Holding a flashlight in one hand, Anna quietly opened the door. She shined the beam of light toward the bed, and when she saw that her sister was sleeping, she padded across the floor to Susan's dresser. The first drawer squeaked when she opened it, and she held her breath, hoping she hadn't awakened Susan. Hearing nothing, she pulled it the rest of the way out and rummaged through Susan's clothes. No bracelet there.

Anna continued to pull out drawers and look through each one, but there was no sign of her bracelet. *Let me think—where else could I look?*

Being as quiet as possible, she made her way to the closet and opened the door. Several of Susan's toys were on the floor, along with some shoes, a pair of rubber boots, and a jar of marbles. Anna thought it was strange that a young girl would collect marbles, but then Susan was a bit of a tomboy.

Anna knelt on the floor, where she discovered a stack of shoe boxes near the back of the closet. She opened the first one and saw that it was full of feathers. The second box held a collection of dried flowers, and the third box was full of pictures Susan had drawn of horses, cows, and chickens. Anna frowned. *Maybe Susan didn't take my bracelet after all.*

There was one more shoe box, and when Anna opened it, she gasped. Hidden under several pieces of paper, she found her bracelet. *So Susan must have gone through my purse, discovered the piece of jewelry, and hidden it here. Should I wake her and ask about it right now, or wait till morning? Or would it be better if I just took the bracelet and said nothing?*

Anna remained on her knees, contemplating things a bit longer. Then she snatched the bracelet and hurried out of Susan's room. She would decide what to do about this in the morning.

CHAPTER 26

Anna studied her youngest sister from across the breakfast table, wondering what she was thinking. Did Susan know the bracelet she'd taken from Anna's purse was no longer in her possession? Her face revealed no telltale sign of guilt or unease as she ate a slice of toast and giggled with their sister Becky about hiding from Arie earlier this morning.

Anna had planned to confront Susan about the bracelet on Thursday, but due to her work schedule and Susan being in school all week, she wasn't given the opportunity. If she didn't do it soon, however, it would be time to leave for the quilting class, so she was determined to speak to Susan after breakfast. Since it was Arie's and Becky's turn to do the dishes, and Susan would probably go outside to play after their meal, Anna decided that would be the best time to catch her. She was sure Susan hadn't told Mom about the bracelet, because if she had, Mom would surely have said something. Not only that, but if Susan had mentioned the jewelry to Mom, she would have had to admit that she'd snuck into Anna's room, gone through her purse, and taken the bracelet.

Anna ate her ham and eggs in silence, and as soon as breakfast was over, she cleared her dishes, grabbed her sweater, and followed Susan out the back door. Anna waited until her sister was a safe distance from the house. Then she hurried across the yard to where Susan knelt on the grass, petting a black-and-white kitten.

When Susan saw Anna approaching, she jumped up and started to move away. "Wait a minute. I need to talk to you," Anna said, placing her hand firmly on her sister's shoulder.

Susan looked up at Anna with a wary expression. "About what?"

"I think you know," Anna said sternly. "You took something of mine, and you had no right. You shouldn't have been in my purse."

Susan dropped her gaze as the kitten pawed at the hem of her dress. "I–I'm sorry, Anna. I was looking for some gum, and when I found the bracelet, I thought it was pretty, so I put it in a shoebox where I keep some special things." Her lower lip trembled. "You're not gonna tell Mom and Dad are you? I'd be in big trouble if they knew what I did."

Anna shook her head. "I won't say a thing, but you must promise never to do anything like that again. It's not right to take something that doesn't belong to you."

"I—I know. I'll go up to my room and get the bracelet right now."

"You don't have to do that," Anna said. "I already found it and took it back."

Susan's eyes widened. "You snuck into my room?"

Anna wasn't sure what to say. She'd just given her sister a lecture about sneaking into her own room and messing with her belongings, yet she'd done the same thing. "I suspected you had taken the bracelet," she said, carefully choosing her words. "So on Wednesday night after I was sure you were asleep, I went to your room to look around and found the bracelet in the shoe box in your closet."

"Guess we're even now," Susan said. "I took your bracelet, and you snuck into my room." Picking up the kitten, she skipped off toward the barn.

Anna sucked in a deep breath. *That went well enough. Now I'll either need to find a safe hiding place for the bracelet or give it back to Carmen.*

Shipshewana

Cheryl had just stepped out of her car when she heard the familiar roar of an engine. Turning, she saw Terry pull into Emma's yard on his motorcycle. When he turned off the engine and removed his helmet, he waved. She felt her face flush, which seemed to be happening a lot lately, especially whenever Terry was around.

"How you doing?" he called, swinging his leg over the cycle and pushing it toward the big tree to park it.

Cheryl waited until he'd put the kickstand down and caught up to her, then she smiled and said, "I'm fine. How about you?"

"Doing good, but I'll be better if you'll agree to go riding with me after class today," he said with a lopsided grin.

"I'm sorry, Terry," Cheryl said with regret, "but Blaine and I made plans for this afternoon."

Terry's smile faded. "Oh, I see. Guess that's what I get for waiting till the last minute to ask." He kicked a small stone with the toe of his boot and sent it skittering up the driveway. When they reached Emma's front porch, Terry stopped and turned to face Cheryl. "How about tomorrow afternoon? Would you want to get something to eat after church and then go for another ride on my Harley?" When Cheryl hesitated, he quickly added, "Or did the first ride freak you out too much?"

"I was scared at first," Cheryl admitted, "but once I got used to being on the bike, it was kind of fun." She hesitated, biting her lip. "Actually,

I was hoping you'd ask me out again." Her eyes widened, and she stepped back, regretting what she'd just said. Cheryl had never been that forward before—not even with her former boyfriend.

Cheryl held her breath and waited for Terry's response, knowing if she tried to explain, it could be even more embarrassing.

"You were?" Terry's smile returned. "Does that mean you'll go out with me tomorrow?"

Cheryl nodded and quickly stepped into the house. For a twenty-eight-year-old woman who was normally quite confident, she felt shy all of a sudden and needed to put a little space between herself and Terry. Aside from her reservations, Cheryl had enjoyed Terry's company last Sunday and figured she probably would again. Besides it was fun to be dating again—especially when she had two very different men taking an interest in her.

Following Cheryl, Terry was about to enter Emma's house, when Selma showed up. He waited, holding the door for her.

"I'm not late, am I?" Selma asked as she stepped onto the porch, panting as though short of breath.

"Well, if you are, then I must be, too," Terry responded with a teasing grin.

Selma's forehead wrinkled. "I slept longer than I'd planned this morning, and then—" She stopped talking and brushed a hand across her beige-colored slacks, where a glob of gray fur was stuck. Picking the hair off her pants and blowing it from her fingers, she watched as the air took the fluff and floated it into Emma's yard.

"Is that cat hair?" Terry questioned, remembering Selma's comment about not wanting any pets. He hadn't forgotten that Selma thought four-legged creatures were a nuisance.

Selma sheepishly nodded. "Yes, it is cat hair."

"Is that from the same stray cat you were telling our quilting class about? Scruffy, was it?"

Her cheeks reddened. "Yes, that's the cat that's been hanging around my place, and he's been getting into the house through the vent in my bedroom floor. To make matters worse, for the last several days I haven't had any heat coming up from that vent."

"Did you call the furnace company?" Terry asked as he and Selma entered the house.

She nodded. "But they haven't made it out to my house yet."

"Want me to take a look?" Terry offered. "I could follow you home after class."

"I don't have a basement, so you'd have to crawl under the house and you'd probably get dirty."

Terry shrugged. "That's no big deal. Being a roofer, I get dirty almost every day."

Selma's thin lips formed a smile. "Thanks, I'd appreciate that."

Crawling under Selma's house sure wouldn't be as much fun as going out with Cheryl, but at least Terry would be doing a good deed. He'd learned from Jan how good it felt to do something helpful for the older generation. He figured, too, that keeping busy today would take his mind off Cheryl and her date with Blaine.

CHAPTER 27

Good morning," Emma said after everyone had taken their seats around the sewing table. "Today we'll begin the quilting process, and if anyone has a question as we go along, please don't hesitate to ask."

Terry's hand shot up.

"What's your question, Terry?" Emma asked.

"Will we be using the sewing machines again? I had a hard time holding the material straight while I tried to sew last week."

Emma shook her head. "The quilting is done by hand with a needle and thread. Now, will everyone please place your work on the table?"

After the students did as Emma asked, she explained that the quilting process was stitching three layers of material together. "But before we begin the actual process, you'll need to cut a piece of cotton batting approximately two inches larger than your quilt top on all sides," Emma said. "The excess batting and backing will be trimmed even with the quilt top after all the quilting stitches have been completed."

Everyone watched as she and Lamar demonstrated.

"Now, in order to create a smooth, even quilting surface, all three layers of the quilt need to be put in a frame," Emma continued. "For a larger quilt you would need a quilting frame that could stretch and hold the entire quilt at one time. But since your wall hangings are much smaller than a full-sized quilt, you can use a frame that's similar to a large embroidery hoop." She held up one of the small frames she'd placed on the table. "It's important when using this type of hoop to baste the entire quilt together through all three layers. This will keep the layers evenly stretched while you're quilting. Just be sure you don't quilt over the basting, or it will be difficult to remove later on."

Emma waited patiently until each person had cut out their batting. Then Lamar stepped forward and said, "The next step will be to mark the design you want on your quilt top. But if you only want to outline the patches you've sewn with quilting, then no marking is necessary. You'll just need to quilt close to the seam so the patch will be emphasized."

Emma went on to explain about needle size, saying that it was best to try several and see which one seemed the most comfortable to handle. She also stated that the use of a snugly fitting thimble worn on the middle finger of the hand used for pushing the quilting needle was necessary, since the needle would have to be poked through three layers of fabric repeatedly. She then demonstrated on a quilt patch, showing how to pull the needle and thread through the material to create the quilting pattern. "The stitches should be tiny and even," Emma said. "They need to be snug, but not so tight that they'll cause the material to pucker."

Terry groaned. "That sounds hard, and look—I've already stitched my shirtsleeve to a piece of the material," he said, lifting his arm. "Guess I shouldn't have gone ahead of the others." Wanting to look a little nicer today, he'd worn a pale green shirt with long sleeves, but now he wished he'd worn a T-shirt. "At the rate I'm going, I'll probably mess my whole wall hanging up. Since this is the fourth class, I thought I'd be doing better by now."

"Don't worry, it takes time, and that's why Lamar and I are here to help you," Emma said. "For now, rather than worrying about the size of the stitches, just try to concentrate on making them straight."

"Better let me take a look at that shirtsleeve," Lamar spoke up, walking to Terry's side of the table. "I'll just cut the material off for you, and it's nothing to get riled about. At one time or another we've all had an unforgettable moment when trying something new. I'll bet someday you'll look back at this and laugh."

Terry held his wrist out to Lamar and watched as he quickly detached the material and loose threads. When Lamar was finished, Terry glanced over at Cheryl, who sat across the table from him. She was already pinning her batting to the patterned pieces of material she'd sewn last week, and from the smile on her face, he figured she was enjoying the whole process.

Quilting ain't for me, Terry thought as he fumbled with his pieces of material, trying to get them placed and stitched on the batting he'd cut. *I doubt I'll be looking back and laughing at anything that has to do with quilting. If it hadn't been for wanting to ask Cheryl out, I'd never have taken this class.*

Terry studied Cheryl's pretty face and golden-blond hair. She was a real looker, all right; but it was more than Cheryl's looks that had made Terry decide to ask her out again. Having spent last Sunday afternoon with her, Terry quickly realized that he was drawn to her personality. He liked hearing her laugh when he said something funny and was impressed with her caring attitude. Cheryl had also been such a good sport about riding on the back of his Harley. He appreciated that she didn't judge him because of the way he dressed or wore his hair, either.

Terry glanced over at Blaine, sitting beside Cheryl with a Cheshire cat grin on his face. *I'll bet he loved it when I stitched my shirtsleeve to that piece of cloth. Well, I guess it was pretty funny. Blaine's probably better for Cheryl,* Terry thought with regret. *If I had a lick of sense I'd back off, but if I did that, I'd never get the chance to really know her. Nope. I'm going out with her again tomorrow and see where it goes from there.*

Carmen glanced at Selma, who sat beside her. She was smiling and appeared much happier this morning. Up until today, she'd been so sullen. *I wonder what happened to bring on the change? Guess it wouldn't be right to ask, but it's sure an improvement.* Watching Selma as she sewed and hummed to herself, made Carmen feel happy, too.

Carmen turned her attention to Anna, sitting on the other side of the table. Even though she was doing a good job of quilting, her droopy eyelids and slumped shoulders made her appear to be sad. Had something happened at home? Did she have an argument with her parents or one of her siblings? Carmen hoped she could talk to Anna after class. Whatever was bothering the girl, Carmen was sure she wouldn't want to discuss it in front of the others. Maybe Anna would open up to her. After all, she had told Carmen some things about her parents and shared her feelings about them. But knowing Anna trusted her bothered Carmen, too, because she'd begun to question her motives in writing the negative article about the Amish.

"How are you doing?" Emma asked, placing her hands on Carmen's shoulders. "Are you getting the feel for quilting yet?"

Glad for the interruption, Carmen smiled up at Emma. "It's not as hard as I thought it would be, but it is slow and tedious."

Emma nodded. "It's good to go slow at first, though. That way you'll be able to get more even stitches. But remember, the more you do it, the easier it will get."

"I'm glad I signed up for this class," Carmen said. "Not just to learn to quilt, but to get to know you, Emma."

"My wife's easy to get to know, because she cares so much about people," Lamar spoke up from across the room, where he'd gone to get more pins for Blaine.

"And so do you," Emma said, smiling at Lamar when he returned to the table.

He grinned back at her. "Guess that's why we make such a good team."

Carmen couldn't help feeling a bit envious. It was obvious that Emma and Lamar were deeply in love. What she wouldn't give to find that kind of happiness with a man. *Lorinda and Paul had a special relationship,* she thought. *If she hadn't been killed, they might have had another child by now, and I'd be an auntie again.*

Carmen thought about the phone call she'd had from Paul last night, asking if she would join him for dinner tonight. He'd said Maria would watch Sophia, so it would just be the two of them. Carmen looked forward to spending some time alone with Paul. He was easygoing, kind, and quite good-looking. It was no wonder Lorinda had fallen in love with him. Given the chance, Carmen thought she could fall in love with Paul; although she doubted he'd ever feel that way about her. Besides the fact that Carmen was Lorinda's sister, her home and job were clear across the country. It was just a silly dream to think that anything romantic could develop between her and Paul, yet she couldn't stop thinking about it. In fact, the more Carmen tried to talk herself out of those possibilities, the more her mind kept going in that direction. Once more, Carmen wondered how Paul would feel if he knew the real reason she was here. What would he think of her then?

Blaine fidgeted in his chair, anxious for today's class to be over. Even though he was finally getting the hang of it, he was bored with quilting.

"How's it going?" Lamar asked, taking a seat beside Blaine.

"Okay, I guess, but sewing's not really my thing." He glanced around to see if anyone was listening.

"What is your thing?"

"That's easy; it's fishing."

"I enjoy fishing, too," Lamar said. "In fact, when the weather is nice I go to Lake Shipshewana every chance I get."

"Same here. It's a wonder we've never bumped into each other there." Blaine smiled, wondering why the two of them had never struck up a conversation about fishing before. The class would have been less boring if they had. "No matter what time of day, I can't think of anything I'd rather be doing than sitting at the lake with my fishing pole in the water."

"How about the two of us going fishing this afternoon?" Lamar suggested.

"As nice as that sounds, I've made other arrangements for today," Blaine said, with a feeling of regret. "If the weather's decent, maybe we could go next week after class."

Lamar gave a nod. "That sounds like a plan."

When class was over, Anna hurried out the door behind Carmen. "I need to tell you something," she said as they stepped into the yard.

"What is it?" Carmen asked, halting her footsteps.

"It's about that bracelet you gave me." Anna dropped her gaze to the ground. This was harder than she thought it would be. "As much as I'd like to, I—I just can't keep it."

"How come?"

"One of my sisters found it in my purse, and I'm afraid if I keep it my folks will find out." Anna shifted nervously from one foot to the other. "I appreciate that you bought it for me, and I hope you'll understand, but I need to give the bracelet back to you."

"I'll take it back on one condition," Carmen said as Anna handed her the bracelet.

"What's that?"

"If you'll allow me to buy you something else."

Anna shook her head. "That's okay; I don't really need anything."

"Oh please. I'd really like to get you something," Carmen insisted. "Is there anything special you'd like?"

Anna shook her head. "I'm fine, really."

Carmen looked disappointed, but she smiled and said, "Let me know if you change your mind."

Terry grimaced as he watched Cheryl leave her car parked in Emma's driveway and get into Blaine's SUV. It was hard to see her go off with Blaine when he wished she was leaving with him. He consoled himself with the thought that he'd see Cheryl tomorrow at church and then they'd spend the afternoon together. Right now he needed to head over to Selma's and take a look under her house. After that, he was anxious to take a ride on his Harley. He'd been struggling with an urge to smoke all morning and hoped that getting out on the open road might clear his head. Some days, Terry wondered if he'd ever lick his smoking habit, but because of Cheryl, he had a reason to conquer his addiction. She was a positive influence on his life in more ways than one. He actually found himself saying a little prayer that it would all work out.

CHAPTER 28

After Emma and Lamar finished eating their lunch, she returned to her quilting room to work on the quilt for Cheryl's grandma. Taking a seat in front of her quilting frame, she studied the colorful quilt. A lump formed in her throat as she thought about the gift of love Cheryl wanted to bestow on her ailing grandmother. Emma hoped she could get it done in time for Cheryl to take to Oregon for her grandmother's birthday. *I wish I could be there to see the look of surprise on the old woman's face when Cheryl presents her with the quilt,* she thought. *If Oregon wasn't so far away, I'd ask if I could accompany Cheryl to the nursing home where her grandmother lives.*

"Are you sure you should be working on that quilt right now?" Lamar asked when he entered the room.

Emma peered at him over the top of her glasses. "What do you mean?"

"You look tired. I think you've been doing too much lately." Lamar grabbed a chair, pulled it close to Emma, and took a seat. "I don't want you to get sick or end up with a case of the shingles like you had a year ago in the spring."

"I appreciate your concern," Emma said sweetly, "but I'm just fine. If I get tired, I'll go take a nap."

"I have a better idea," Lamar said. "Why don't the two of us take a ride to Lake Shipshewana? We can either walk around for a bit or just sit on a bench and watch people fish. It's a bit chilly outside, but not too cold yet, so it should be just right for a little relaxation together and a chance for some fresh air."

"Wouldn't you rather go alone, so you can fish?" she asked, knowing how much her husband enjoyed his time at the lake and the opportunity to bring home his catch for supper.

"That'd be nice, but I've made plans to go fishing with Blaine after class next week, so I can wait till then." Lamar leaned over and kissed Emma's cheek. "I'd like to spend this afternoon with you. It's a good day to be out among nature."

Emma smiled. "A trip to the lake does sound nice. I'll set the quilt aside for now, and return to it after we get back. Why don't I fix a thermos of hot chocolate and take along some of those kichlin I baked yesterday?"

Lamar smacked his lips. "That sounds *wunderbaar*."

As Terry lay on his back under Selma's house, he noticed a large rip in the foil-wrapped ductwork. He shined his flashlight around, wondering how the ductwork had gotten torn. Then he noticed several paw prints on the ground. They didn't look like those made by a cat, so he figured a family of raccoons might have been under the house and torn the ductwork open for warmth. Of course, Selma's cat had probably taken advantage of it, too, and found a way to get inside.

Terry crawled back out, went into Selma's house, and told her what he'd found.

"Can it be fixed?" she asked, scrunching up her face with a look of despair.

"Yeah, but I'll have to run to the hardware store to get some duct tape and aluminum wrap."

"I hate to put you to all that trouble," she said.

He shook his head. "It's no trouble, and it won't take me long. I'll just hop on my cycle and be back in a flash."

Selma opened her purse and handed Terry a fifty-dollar bill. "Will this be enough?"

"Yeah, that's plenty. I'll bring back the change."

"While you're gone, I'll fix some lunch," Selma offered.

"There's no need to do that," Terry said, shaking his head. "Don't want to put you to any trouble."

"It won't be any trouble at all, and it's the least I can do to repay your kindness," she insisted.

Terry shrugged. "Okay, if you insist."

When Terry returned from the hardware store, he went back under the house and fixed the torn ductwork while Selma scurried around the kitchen, setting the table and putting things out to make ham-and-cheese sandwiches. It wasn't often she had anyone to share a meal with in her home, so she looked forward to visiting with Terry as they ate lunch together.

When Terry returned to the house a short time later, she motioned to the table. "Like I promised, I have everything ready."

Terry grabbed the end of his ponytail and twisted it around his fingers a few times as he leaned against the counter in her kitchen. "I really don't need any payment for doing a good deed, but since I am kinda hungry, I'll be glad to take you up on that offer."

Selma smiled and gestured to the hallway outside of the kitchen. "You can wash up in the bathroom at the end of the hall."

Terry gave a nod and hurried down the hall.

Selma went to the refrigerator and took out mustard, mayonnaise, and pickles. By the time she'd placed them on the table and added a bag of potato chips, Terry was back.

"That's a nice picture of you I saw sitting on the bookshelf just inside the living room," Terry said. "How long ago was it taken?"

"That's actually my daughter, Cora, and the photo was taken some time ago," Selma said. "Would you like a bowl of soup to go with the sandwiches? I have some leftover chicken noodle soup in the refrigerator I can heat up."

"Thanks anyway, but a sandwich will be plenty for me." He grinned and pointed to the chips. "I might have some of those, too."

"Take all the chips you want." Selma gestured to the chair at the head of the table. "Have a seat, and I'll get you something to drink. Would you like coffee, milk, or apple cider? I don't have any soda pop."

"A glass of milk would be great," Terry replied, taking a seat at the table.

Selma poured Terry's milk and a glass of cider for herself. Then she took a seat across from him and opened the bag of chips. While they ate, they discussed the quilting class.

"I think everyone's wall hanging but mine will turn out good." Terry moaned. "I stink at sewing."

"It takes practice and patience," Selma said.

"Yeah, well, I probably won't sew another thing after the classes are done." Terry reached for his glass of milk and took a drink. "Don't even know what I'm gonna do with the wall hanging."

"Maybe you could give it to someone—your parents, perhaps?"

Terry shook his head. "Nope. My folks split up a few months ago, and I doubt either of 'em would want the wall hanging."

"I'm sorry to hear that. I'm glad my husband stayed true to me right up till the day he died." Selma sighed. "I wish I could say the same for my daughter, though."

"Did she separate from her husband?" Terry asked.

"Cora's not married. She left home several years ago, and I haven't seen her since my husband died."

"That really stinks." Terry took a bite of sandwich. "I can sorta relate to what you said, though. I have two sisters—Faye and Jenny—but rarely see 'em."

"Do they live out of state?" Selma questioned, adding a few chips to the inside of her sandwich. It was the way she'd been eating them since she was a girl.

"Naw. Faye lives in LaGrange, and Jenny lives in Goshen. They're too busy with their own lives to pay much attention to me." Terry's forehead wrinkled. "'Course they don't care for the way I look, so that might be part of the reason they don't come around much."

"Maybe it's your long hair your sisters don't appreciate."

"My hair ain't that long." Terry gave his ponytail a flip. "It's only shoulder-length when I'm wearing it down."

"Have you ever considered cutting it?"

"Never gave it much thought." Terry grabbed a few more chips. "Why, do you think I should?"

Selma shrugged. "I don't know; maybe." Truthfully, she'd never been fond of long hair on a man. Anything past the ears seemed too long to her. But then she was a bit old-fashioned. At least that was what Cora had always said.

"Maybe I will cut my hair someday," Terry said, reaching for another piece of bread, "but right now I like it this way."

"What about Cheryl? Does she like the way you wear your hair?"

Terry blinked a couple of times. "Uh—I'm not sure. What made you ask?"

Selma lifted her gaze toward the ceiling. "It's fairly obvious that you're smitten with her."

"So tell me about your daughter," Terry said. He obviously didn't want to talk about Cheryl. "How come she doesn't make contact with you?"

"We don't see things the same way." Selma's voice dropped to a near whisper. Whenever she looked at Cora's picture, her beautiful brown eyes seemed to bore right through her. But Selma couldn't get rid of the photo. It was all she had to remind her of the little girl who used to live here, whom she still loved but couldn't reach. "Cora has never liked me telling her what to do," she explained. "So she takes the easy road and avoids me."

"Guess we have something in common then," Terry said. "We both have family members who want nothing to do with us."

Winona Lake, Indiana

"This seems like a nice enough place," Cheryl told Blaine as they entered the BoatHouse Restaurant. Looking around, she noticed right away the welcoming décor.

"Yeah, my boss, Stuart, told me about it. Said the restaurant has great year-round lakeside dining, not to mention some pretty good food." Blaine patted his stomach. "Since it's way past lunchtime, I'm more than ready to eat."

Cheryl smiled as the hostess seated them in a booth near a window with a gorgeous view of the lake. Sliding into their seats, she felt like they had the whole place to themselves, with the high-backed booths separating them from the rest of the patrons. "It was worth the drive down here, don't you think?" she asked Blaine.

He nodded and perused the menu the hostess had given them before leaving their table. "Would you like some fried calamari, mozzarella wedges, or a battered veggie platter as a starter?"

"If I had an appetizer, I'd probably be too full to eat anything else." Cheryl studied the soups and salads on the menu. "The oriental chicken salad sounds good."

"What else would you like?" Blaine asked.

"Just the salad will be enough."

He studied her from across the table. "If you eat like that all the time, no wonder you're so thin."

Cheryl laughed lightly, feeling the heat of a blush.

Blaine tapped the menu with his index finger. "Think I'll have a shrimp cocktail and the Asian cashew chicken. I'll probably get a side order of sweet potato fries, too."

When their waitress returned, they gave her their orders; then Blaine started talking about the lake again. "From what Stuart's said, Winona Lake is a great shopping spot for anyone looking for unusual things like pottery, jewelry, wood carvings, and handmade silverware. After we finish eating, maybe you'd like to browse some of the shops while I check out the lake for the best fishing spots."

"Are you planning to fish today?" Cheryl questioned. She wondered if he hadn't brought her here just so he could spend the afternoon fishing.

"No, not today, but if I decide this is a good place to fish for bass, I might try it out sometime. Do you like to fish?" he asked.

"No, not really."

"Oh, I see." Blaine's frown revealed his disappointment. "So is it okay with you if I check out some fishing spots while you shop?"

She nodded. "Sure, that's fine." Truthfully, Cheryl didn't think this was much of a date if they went their separate ways after lunch, but she chose not to make a big deal out of it. Besides, it would give her a chance to look for some things she hadn't been able to find anywhere else. She might find something nice to give Grandma for her birthday, in case Emma didn't get the quilt done on time.

As they ate, Blaine talked about fishing, while Cheryl stared out the window. She tried to act interested at first, but it was obvious that Blaine's mind was on fishing, not her. Cheryl found herself drawn to the beauty of the lake and the cottages dotting the shoreline. She wondered what it would be like to wake up every morning and watch the sun rise as it reflected across the lake.

"Look at this." Cheryl motioned to the pamphlet she'd found propped up with the dessert specials, explaining the history of the restaurant. "It says here that this restaurant was built on the same foundation as the cafeteria that was constructed here in the 1940s, when the original boathouse was removed."

"Hmm. . . That's interesting."

Cheryl kept reading as Blaine finished eating his fries. "And get this. The original boathouse was built way back in 1895. It also says that in the 1960s, the cafeteria was converted to a roller skating rink."

"Is that so?" Blaine reached for his glass of orange soda and took a drink.

"I'll bet it was fun to roller skate here by the lake." Cheryl looked up from the brochure and realized that Blaine, now gazing out the window, was no more interested in the history of the restaurant than she was with his fishing stories. She couldn't help wondering why he never asked anything about her. Their conversation today, as well as the other times they'd talked, seemed pretty one-sided. Maybe she'd made a mistake agreeing to go out with him again.

When the meal was over, Blaine said he would meet Cheryl where his SUV was parked, in two hours.

"That's fine. I'll see you then." Cheryl hurried off toward one of the stores.

She felt guilty for feeling this way, but she actually looked forward to being alone for a while. It wasn't that Blaine was unpleasant; they just didn't have much in common. *Maybe I haven't given Blaine a fair chance,* Cheryl thought. *Guess I could try fishing with him sometime; although sitting in a boat with a fishing pole really isn't my thing.*

Chapter 29

Shipshewana

Despite the chill in the air, the lake is beautiful today," Emma said, looking at the pristine waters as Lamar helped her out of the buggy. "I'm glad you suggested we come here this afternoon."

Lamar's eyes twinkled. "I thought we both needed a little break, and there's nothing like fresh lake air to make one feel energized. Look there, toward the center of the lake," he said with the excitement of a young boy.

Emma turned her attention to the geese Lamar was pointing at.

"Good thing we brought some bread along. Maybe we can entice them over to the shoreline so we can feed 'em."

Breathing deeply of the fresh air, Emma watched as the majestic-looking birds glided quietly over the surface, making small ripples in the lake's calm waters. Lamar had been right—the air was crisp and clean smelling. As always, Lamar looked at the positive side of things. She thought back to when she'd first met him and how in the beginning, she had avoided spending time with him. It didn't take long for Lamar to worm his way into her heart, however, and she was glad she'd agreed to become his wife. Others, including their families, said they complemented each other.

I think it's true, Emma mused, glancing at Lamar as he secured their horse to a nearby tree. *I certainly enjoy his company, and we work well together at home and teaching the quilting classes.*

As they walked down the path, Emma's thoughts shifted, reflecting on all the times she'd come to the lake with her first husband and how Ivan had carved their initials in a tree that stood in this very spot until a storm took it down. As difficult as it had been losing Ivan, Emma knew that she'd been blessed in both of her marriages. That special old tree was gone, but thanks to Lamar cutting out the piece of wood with the initials in it, Emma had a beautiful table that would someday become a cherished heirloom for her children and grandchildren.

Emma knew the importance of passing things on to the next generation. That's why she'd taught her daughters and granddaughters how to sew and quilt. Since Mary lived close to Emma, she often came over so she and Emma could do some quilting together. It was fun having someone to quilt with while getting caught up on one another's lives.

"How did you think things went with the class today?" Lamar asked, bringing Emma's thoughts to a halt.

Emma sighed. "Okay, I guess, but I wish Anna would open up to me. She seemed even more sullen than usual this morning."

"She does seem to be catching on to quilting, though," Lamar observed.

"Jah, but I'm concerned because Anna doesn't say much to anyone except Carmen." Emma stopped walking and turned to face Lamar. "I have a hunch that young woman is not going to join the Amish church."

"What makes you think that?"

"She has a chip on her shoulder and seems to be dissatisfied with the Amish way of life. I recognize it because when I was a young girl that's how I felt."

Lamar's mouth gaped open. "Oh Emma, I find it hard to believe that you ever had a chip on your shoulder or were dissatisfied being Amish."

"It's true. I was restless and rebellious and almost ran off with my boyfriend, but I came to my senses in time." Emma's face heated just thinking about it. Even after all these years she felt shame for what she'd put her parents through.

"Maybe you should share this with Anna," Lamar suggested. "Let her know that you understand what she's going through."

"I would if she'd open up to me, but I can hardly bring up the subject for no reason at all."

Lamar took Emma's hand and gave it a gentle squeeze. "I think we should pray about this, don't you?"

Emma nodded. She'd been praying for Anna, as well as her other five students, and would continue to do so.

Winona Lake

Blaine left the Lakehouse store, where he'd spent the last half hour looking at various items involving water sports, and headed for his SUV to wait for Cheryl. After talking to a fisherman he'd met in the store, he'd learned that Winona Lake was known as one of the better bass fisheries in northern Indiana. He'd also been told that it was best to fish during the early morning hours before any power boats hit the water. The thing that made him want to come back the most was learning that in addition to largemouth bass, there were also walleye and bluegills. The man had said the shallower water of the lake was best fished from a kayak with a flat bottom because the thick vegetation that grew there could create a problem for motor boats.

Blaine glanced around the parking lot, then over toward one of the shops. *Where is she, anyway?* he wondered, looking at his watch. *Cheryl should have been here by now. What could be keeping her?* Blaine pulled out his cell phone to call her and frowned. *That's great; my battery's dead. Think I'd better drive past some of the shops and see if I can spot her.*

Cheryl stepped out of the Whetstone Woodenware shop and headed for the parking lot where Blaine's vehicle was parked. She'd spent a little more time in the shop than she'd planned, but at least she'd found a nice hand-carved soup ladle to give her mother for Christmas. She'd also purchased a set of wooden salad tongs for herself. Since Cheryl's dad loved coffee, she'd bought him a wooden scoop for measuring out coffee grounds. She wished she'd been able to spend a little more time in that shop, but she was already late.

As Cheryl switched her bag of purchases to the other hand, she looked for the spot where Blaine had parked his SUV before they'd gone to eat. *What's going on? Blaine's vehicle isn't there. Did he move it? Could I be mistaken about where he parked it?*

Feeling a sense of panic, Cheryl dashed up and down the aisles of parked cars, searching for Blaine's rig, but to no avail. Out of breath, she halted and looked at her watch. She'd gotten here fifteen minutes later than when they'd agreed to meet, so at least she wasn't too far off the mark. But then, she started blaming herself. *This is my fault. I should have been paying attention to what time it was and spent less time shopping.* Was it possible that Blain had become impatient and left without her?

Was he capable of doing such a thing?

Why didn't he call me? Cheryl fretted, reaching into her purse to retrieve her cell phone. When she didn't find it there, she remembered having set it on her dresser this morning to charge the battery. "That's just great; I left home without it," she mumbled, looking both ways and wondering what direction to take.

As Terry approached Winona Lake on his Harley, he lowered his speed. The resort town looked busy today, with many cars lining the streets. Even the parking lots were full. He saw several boats on the lake and people walking from shop to shop.

Terry hadn't planned on coming to the area today, but after he'd left Selma's and taken to the road, he'd just kept going, enjoying the ride. Winona Lake was where he ended up.

Think I'll look for a spot to park my cycle and then head into one of the restaurants for something to eat, Terry thought. The sandwiches he'd eaten at Selma's had filled him for a time, but he'd worked up an appetite riding down here from Shipshewana.

When Terry turned onto the next street, he spotted a blond-haired woman coming out of a parking lot. She looked kind of like Cheryl. After doing a double-take, he realized it *was* Cheryl!

Terry pulled his cycle next to her and stopped. She gave him a blank look at first, but then her mouth formed an O. "Terry, wh–what are you doing here?" she stammered.

"After I finished helping Selma with a little problem she had, I decided to take a ride, and this is where I ended up. It's a nice fall day for a road trip, fresh air and all. I've been here before, but not for some time." He studied Cheryl a bit and noticed that her face was red and her forehead glistened with sweat. "What are you doing here?

And where's Mr. Clean? I thought the two of you had a date this afternoon."

"We did, but we went our separate ways after lunch and were supposed to meet back at his car. But when I got there, Blaine's SUV was gone." Cheryl's forehead wrinkled. "And I wish you wouldn't call him 'Mr. Clean.'"

Ignoring her last comment, Terry said, "Where'd the guy go? Don't tell me he went home without you."

"I—I don't know. I'm worried that he might have, because if Blaine was still here, I'm sure his vehicle would be in the lot. Why else would he have moved it?"

Terry shook his head and muttered, "Some date he turned out to be. I've done a lot of things I'm not proud of in my life, but I've never left a date stranded."

"Do you have a cell phone?" she asked. "I need to call him."

Terry shook his head. "No cell phone for me today. I forgot and left it home this morning. Where's your cell phone?"

She frowned. "I left it at home."

"Well, if you need a ride, I'd be happy to give you a lift," Terry offered. "I always carry an extra helmet with me."

Cheryl hesitated, but finally nodded. "Thanks, I appreciate that, but what about my package? How am I supposed to carry it if I'm holding on to you?"

"That's not a problem." Terry pointed to the saddlebags on the back of his cycle. "Just stick it in there."

"Okay, but if you don't mind, I'd like to ride around town once or twice and see if we can spot Blaine's vehicle. Before we head home, I just want to be sure he's not still here someplace, looking for me."

"Sure, we can do that. But if we don't see the guy, then I say we head outta here. We can stop on the way back to Emma's, where you left your car, for a bite to eat. I was gonna eat here, but I can wait."

Blaine had driven past all the shops in town several times, but there was no sign of Cheryl. Since his cell phone was dead, he'd gone to a pay phone and tried to call her, but all he'd gotten was Cheryl's voice mail. This was frustrating, and he wasn't sure what to do. Cheryl had to be somewhere in town, and he sure couldn't leave without her, so he decided to go back to the parking lot where they were supposed to meet and check one more time. If Cheryl wasn't there, he'd leave the SUV parked and walk into every single shop until he found her.

A few minutes later, Blaine pulled into the parking lot. The spot he'd been in before was taken, but there was another slot a few cars away. He didn't see any sign of Cheryl, however. Pulling into the empty spot, he turned off the ignition and got out. *Guess I'd better head for the shops*, he told himself.

Blaine had only walked a short distance when he heard the roar of a motorcycle. Looking to his right, he spotted a guy on a Harley, and a woman with blond hair on the back. She held on to the biker's waist as they headed out, in the opposite direction. Blaine blinked a couple of times and stared in disbelief as realization set it in. Even with his helmet on, he could see it was the redheaded roofer from the quilting class driving the bike, and Cheryl, with wisps of blond hair sticking out from under her blue helmet, was his passenger on the back!

CHAPTER 30

Blaine's hands shook as he stood on the sidewalk and watched Terry's bike disappear out of town. *The nerve of that guy, running off with my date! I'll bet he had it planned all along. For all I know, Cheryl might have been in on it, too. I wonder if she told him we were coming here today?*

If Blaine hadn't been so far from his vehicle, he would have gone after them. But trying to catch up to the fast-moving motorcycle would be a challenge, and with his luck, he'd probably end up with a speeding ticket.

Stuffing both hands into his jacket pockets, Blaine walked back to the place where he'd left his rig and continued to mull things over. *Should I try calling Cheryl when I get home and demand to know why she rode off with Terry, or do I just let it go and forget about her?*

Blaine wished now that he hadn't taken Stuart's advice and asked Cheryl out in the first place. Terry had shown up on their first date at the bowling alley, and now again today! *Strange coincidence, if you ask me. Or is it?* Blaine hated feeling this way, but what else could he think?

"Maybe I should give up on women," Blaine mumbled as he approached his car. His track record wasn't good. First Sue walked out of his life, and now it appeared as if Cheryl had done the same without even giving them a chance to get to know each other.

Of course, Blaine thought as he opened the vehicle door and slid in behind the wheel, *I haven't really tried to get to know Cheryl.*

He remembered that back at the restaurant most of their conversation during lunch had been about him. He'd barely listened when Cheryl read the history of the BoatHouse Restaurant. Since it didn't have anything to do with fishing, he hadn't been that interested. Still, he should have at least made some effort to be involved in the conversation.

Blaine decided he would give Cheryl a call when he got home. Perhaps he'd jumped to conclusions, and she'd been looking for him while he'd gone looking for her and thought he'd left. He hoped that was the case and that she hadn't planned to meet Terry the whole time.

Shipshewana

When Anna left Emma's after the quilt class, she pedaled her bike around Shipshewana for a while, feeling sorry for herself. It wasn't just that she'd been forced to give up the beautiful bracelet. She felt sad because there were only two weeks left of the quilting classes, which meant Carmen would be going back to California. Anna would miss the talks they'd had, although she really didn't know a lot about Carmen. During the times they'd spent together, Anna had mostly talked about herself. Of course, that was partly due to Carmen asking so many questions about the Amish way of life. Anna wondered why Carmen was so curious. Of course, Anna was curious about things concerning the English life, and more times than not, she found herself wishing she could wear beautiful garments like Carmen's instead of her plain clothes.

Knowing she should be getting home before Dad came looking for her, Anna turned her bicycle in the direction of Middlebury. She'd have to offer an excuse for being late, and the only thing she could think to say was that she'd been hungry after class and had gone to a restaurant in Shipshewana for something to eat. It wouldn't really be a lie, since she had eaten a hamburger and chocolate shake at one of the restaurants.

As Anna continued to pedal toward home, she thought about her decision to move to Sarasota. If she'd kept the bracelet Carmen had given her, she could have taken it with her. Oh well, it was too late for regrets.

Anna thought once again about the best way to tell her folks that she'd be leaving the first week of December. She knew they wouldn't be in favor of her going to Florida with Mandy, but she was old enough now to make her own decisions.

When Lamar turned their horse and buggy onto the driveway, he handed Emma the reins and said, "Think I'll hop out and check the mail. It'll save me a trip walking out after I put the horse and buggy away."

"Would you rather I get the mail?" Emma asked.

He shook his head. "That's okay, I'll do it. No need for you to get out."

Emma smiled as she watched Lamar climb down from the buggy and walk to the mailbox by the side of the road. He was always so thoughtful and considerate.

When Lamar returned to the buggy, he handed Emma a stack of mail and took up the reins.

As they headed up the driveway toward the barn, Emma thumbed through the mail. She smiled when she saw a letter from her sister Rachel, who lived in Middlefield, Ohio. Tearing open the envelope and quickly reading Rachel's note, Emma's smile widened.

"What's that big grin about?" Lamar asked. "I'm guessing whatever you opened is not a bill."

"No, it's not. It's a letter from my sister Rachel, and she's coming for a visit."

"How nice. When will she arrive?"

"In two weeks. It's been almost a year since I've seen her, so I'm looking forward to her visit." Emma placed Rachel's letter in with the rest of the mail and sighed. "The only thing that concerns me is that there are still two more quilting classes to go, and the quilt for Cheryl's grandmother isn't done yet. So I may not have enough time to clean house and get things ready for Rachel's visit."

Lamar reached over and patted Emma's hand. "Not to worry; I'll help as much as I can. I'm sure Mary and your granddaughters will, too."

Selma stood at the door, looking out and calling for Scruffy. She hadn't seen any sign of the cat since early this morning and was beginning to worry. *Could he have returned to wherever he came from?* she wondered. *Maybe he wasn't really looking for a new home. It could be that he was lost and just needed someplace to get in out of the cold.* Selma hated to admit it, but she missed the pesky cat. His gray-colored coat had looked better after she'd combed out the mats, and she had even given him a collar with a small bell so she could tell where he was in the house.

"Guess that's what I get for letting the critter worm his way into my house and heart," Selma muttered, closing the door. It seemed like she was destined to lose everyone she cared about—even a pet. It was as if the cat had deliberately forced his way into Selma's life, only to desert her once she'd begun to care.

"Just like Cora," Selma grumbled, shuffling into the living room and collapsing on the sofa. She remembered how Terry had mentioned Cora's picture today and how just talking about her had been painful. Yet in some ways, telling Terry about Cora had given Selma a small measure of peace, because he seemed to understand.

Selma picked up the remote and turned on the TV. She scanned the list of shows that were on but didn't see anything that really interested her as she continued to hit the CHANNEL button. She glanced toward the bookcase where the framed photo of Cora always sat. No wonder Terry thought it was her in the photo. It was like looking at herself when she was sixteen years old. Selma and her husband, John, had all but given up hope of ever having any children, but then, when Selma was in her late thirties, they were blessed with a beautiful baby girl.

The photo had been taken more than fifteen years ago, but Selma remembered it as if it were yesterday. John, Cora, and Selma had gone on a picnic, and after they'd eaten their lunch, Cora had sat on a fallen tree, gazing at a field of wildflowers.

Selma closed her eyes to relish the memory. She and John had cleaned up everything and were discussing some colleges Cora might attend in the not-too-distant future. Suddenly, John nudged Selma's arm and pointed at their daughter sitting on the log as though in deep thought. Wanting to capture the moment, Selma picked up her camera, zoomed in on Cora, and snapped the look of contentment on the young woman's face. Of all the pictures Selma had of her daughter, this one was her favorite. Everything about that special day had been perfect, even the glow on Cora's face. Looking back, it was hard to think that Cora was now thirty years old. Since Cora had not married,

Selma was sure she'd never be a grandmother.

Not wanting to get depressed like she normally did when thinking too deeply about the past, Selma picked an old rerun she'd seen many times before, but at least it was a humorous show and one she wouldn't have to think too hard about. "Mindless entertainment" was what Selma called it.

After a few minutes, when a commercial came on, Selma got up to make a cup of hot tea. Walking past the bookcase, she glanced once more at Cora's photo.

When Selma stepped into the kitchen, she looked out the window, but there was no sign of Scruffy. *Guess the cat hasn't been gone all that long. Maybe I'm overreacting. He'll probably be back, meowing at my door before it's time for bed.*

"I don't know about you, but I'm sure hungry," Paul said to Carmen as they entered the Blue Gate Restaurant in Shipshewana.

"I'm hungry, too," she admitted. "And anxious to try some of the Amish-style meals they serve at this restaurant."

"Have you eaten here before?" Paul questioned as they approached the hostess to request a table for two.

Carmen shook her head. "No, but I've heard about it. Judging by all the people I see, I'm guessing the food here must be good."

Paul placed his hand in the small of Carmen's back as they followed the hostess to their table. Once they were seated and had placed their orders, he smiled at Carmen and said, "You look nice tonight. I like the pretty turquoise barrette in your hair."

Carmen smiled. "Thank you, Paul. It was a birthday present from my dad."

Paul cleared his throat a couple of times. "I've been wondering about something."

"What's that?"

"Are you seeing anyone? I—I mean, do you have a steady boyfriend?"

She shook her head. "Why do you ask?"

"Oh, just curious. I figured a beautiful woman like you would have at least one guy who was serious about her."

"No, not really," she said.

Paul couldn't explain it, but he felt relieved knowing Carmen wasn't dating anyone.

His thoughts were interrupted when their waitress returned with two plates of turkey, mashed potatoes, and green beans. *I wonder how Carmen would respond if I asked her to stay in Indiana?* Shaking the notion aside, Paul picked up his fork and started eating. No matter how much he wished it wasn't so, Carmen's job and her home were in California. He needed to keep his focus on something else and quit wishing for the impossible.

CHAPTER 31

Goshen

For the beginning of a workweek, traffic was light. In Cheryl's eyes this was always a good thing, aside from the fact that her job was only a fifteen-minute drive from where she lived. Following two days off, Monday mornings were hard enough, especially when it had been a good weekend, like the past one was.

As Cheryl headed to work, all she could think about was how the weekend had gone, and how much she'd enjoyed being with Terry again. They'd stopped at a café on the way back from Winona Lake, but since Cheryl was still full from the lunch she'd had earlier, she'd sipped iced tea and visited with Terry while he ate a burger and fries. She'd enjoyed listening as he told her about some of his biking trips and was pleased when he asked her some questions about growing up near the Oregon coast. Not like Blaine, who hadn't asked Cheryl anything about her past or personal life. In fact, her conversations with Blaine in no way compared to her time spent with Terry. The two men were as different as day and night.

Cheryl was fairly sure Mom and Dad wouldn't approve of Terry because he was such a free spirit, but that was what intrigued her the most. She knew, too, that Dad wouldn't like Terry's long hair. Cheryl couldn't really explain it, but she felt more comfortable with Terry than any other man she'd dated. When she'd first met him, a few things about him irritated her, but the more time she spent with Terry, the more he seemed to be growing on her.

On Sunday, Terry had come to church again. This time, he'd seemed more relaxed and had even taken part in the singing. Ruby Lee had led the music and chosen several lively choruses. Cheryl had snuck a peek at Terry during the praise-and-worship time and was happy to see him clapping along and grinning as they worshiped the Lord. After church, Cheryl and Terry had gone out for lunch and ended the day with another ride on his Harley. Only this time, Jan and his daughter, Star, joined them—for church, as well as lunch and the three-hour road trip. Cheryl had been exhausted when she went home that evening but had felt exhilarated at the same time. She'd never imagined riding on the back of a motorcycle could be so much fun.

Having Star along had put Cheryl more at ease on the bike, but she didn't think she'd ever want to ride a motorcycle by herself the way Star did—not even if it had a fancy custom paint job. Cheryl had to admit, the starbursts in bright neon colors fit Star's personality, as well as her name.

The only downside of the weekend had been the misunderstanding with Blaine. After she'd arrived home that evening, she'd received a phone call from Blaine, asking why she hadn't waited for him and saying he'd seen her ride off with Terry. He'd sounded upset, but once Cheryl explained what had happened and said she thought he'd left town without her, Blaine seemed to understand.

I probably shouldn't compare Terry and Blaine, Cheryl told herself as she pulled into her parking space behind the attorney's office. *But Terry has a sense of humor, and he makes me laugh. In comparison, Blaine seems kind of boring.*

Mishawaka

"How was your weekend?" Stuart asked when he met up with Blaine in the parking lot of the sporting goods store.

Blaine frowned. "Let's just say it wasn't the best."

"What happened?"

"I took Cheryl to lunch at that restaurant in Winona Lake on Saturday, like you suggested, and it didn't turn out so well."

"Was it the service or the food?" Stuart questioned.

"Neither. What ruined the day was when Cheryl left with Terry."

Stuart's eyebrows shot up. "Terry Cooley?"

"Yeah. They rode out of town on his motorcycle."

"I don't get it. If Cheryl went to Winona Lake with you, how'd she end up with Terry?"

"At first I thought they'd pre-planned the whole thing," Blaine said as they started walking toward the store. "But then I called Cheryl Saturday night, and she said when she'd gone back to the parking lot to meet me and discovered that my rig was gone, she panicked and thought I'd left town without her."

Stuart rubbed his chin. "Why would she have to meet you? I thought you were together."

"We were during lunch, but afterwards Cheryl went shopping while I checked on some fishing spots in the area."

Stuart stopped walking and squinted his eyes. "You're kidding, right?"

"No, I'm not. I've never fished in that area and wanted to know what the lake has to offer."

Stuart thumped Blaine's back. "If you want my opinion, you should have gone shopping with Cheryl and done fish scouting on your own time. Women like it when men go shopping with them. Pam sure does."

Blaine shook his head. "Sue never wanted me to go shopping with her."

"Sue. . .Sue. . .Sue. You've got to quit thinking about her, my friend. That relationship's over, and you need to move on."

"I know that, but I'm not sure Cheryl's the right woman for me," Blaine said as they entered the building. "She seems to like Terry better anyhow, so I think I'm gonna back off."

Shipshewana

Emma had just taken a seat at her sewing machine to begin working on the binding of the quilt for Cheryl's grandmother when her daughter Mary entered the room.

"I see you're still busy with that old quilt," Mary said, moving to stand beside Emma's chair.

Emma nodded. "I need to get it done before the final class so Cheryl can take it to Oregon for her grandma's birthday." She drew in a deep breath and blew it out quickly. "But I need to get busy cleaning the house so everything will be ready when Rachel arrives. At times like this, it seems there just aren't enough hours in the day."

Mary placed her hand on Emma's shoulder. "Listen, Mom, I've been thinking about this ever since yesterday when you told me about Aunt Rachel coming. I want to reassure you that I'll do all I can to help get the house ready in time. In fact, I don't think you need to do anything. Just concentrate on teaching your last two classes and getting that quilt done on time, and leave the cleaning to me and the girls."

Emma stood and gave her daughter a hug. "Danki, Mary. I don't know what I'd do without you. I know you have your hands full at your home, too."

Mary smiled. "You're welcome, Mom. And don't worry about me. Remember, helping each other when there's a need is what family is for."

"You're sure wearing a big grin today," Jan said as he and Terry headed down the road in his truck toward the small town of Emma to bid on a roofing job. "Are you still flying high from your date with Cheryl yesterday?"

Terry nodded, popping a piece of bubble gum in his mouth. "I can't help it, man. There's something special about Cheryl. I feel like a different person since I met her."

Jan looked over at Terry and grinned. "You act like a different person, too. Never seen you so happy and eager to please any woman before. You've got it bad, don't you?"

Terry shrugged. "I don't know. Maybe. I just really like being with her, and she makes me feel. . .well. . .special—like she really cares about me."

Jan gave the steering wheel a rap. "The question is, do you care for her?"

Terry clenched his fingers. "Just said I do, didn't I?"

"But do you care enough for Cheryl to set your fears about marriage aside?"

"Who said anything about marriage?"

"I did, and I said it 'cause if you really like Cheryl and you keep going out with her, eventually she's gonna expect some sort of commitment."

Terry winced and tried to change the subject. "Hey, I wonder if

Emma Miller has ever been to the town of Emma." He slapped his knee, watching Jan roll his eyes. "All kidding aside, let's stop at the little Emma Café for lunch today. I hear they have some really good pizza and home-cooked meals."

"Sounds good, but I'm not letting you off the hook that easy, pal," Jan said. "Seriously now, friend-to-friend, think about what I said, and don't make the same mistakes I have in the past."

Terry didn't want to think about making a serious commitment right now. He was just getting to know Cheryl and really hadn't thought much beyond that. Could he set his fears about marriage aside and continue to pursue a relationship with Cheryl that might lead to commitment, or would it better if he broke things off now before one or both of them got hurt?

Selma had just finished the breakfast dishes when she heard the tinkling of a bell, followed by a distinctive *meow!*

She dried her hands on a dish towel and hurried to open the back door. Scruffy sat on her porch, but her heart gave a lurch when she saw blood and realized that the poor cat was bleeding.

"Oh my!" Selma gasped, scooping the cat up and taking him inside. "What happened to you, Scruffy?"

Without so much as a second thought, Selma placed the cat on the kitchen counter so she could see how badly he was hurt. All sorts of things went through her mind. Did Scruffy get hit by a car? Had he been in a fight with another cat, or maybe a dog? Was it possible that some wild animal had attacked the cat?

Meow! The cat looked up at her as if to say, "Please help me."

After a quick examination, Selma discovered several lacerations and knew Scruffy needed to see the vet. Stitches might be needed, so there was no time to waste. Dr. Benson would know what to do. While she was there, Selma would ask about preventive shots the cat might need, even though she had no idea if Scruffy had received any before.

She hurried to the utility room, where she grabbed a cardboard box and an old towel. Wrapping the towel around Scruffy, she lifted him from the countertop and carefully placed him in the box. Then, after calling the vet and saying it was an emergency, Selma grabbed her car keys and purse, while mentally figuring out the quickest route to the animal clinic. Hoisting the box and looking down at poor Scruffy, she closed the door behind her. Selma wasn't sure how the cat would react when she put him in the box, but so far, so good. She sighed with relief when Scruffy curled into a ball and purred as if he understood that she was taking him to a place where he would be helped.

Dear Lord, Selma silently prayed as she hurried across the yard to get her car, *please let this poor cat be okay.* From that moment on, Selma knew for sure that Scruffy was here to stay.

CHAPTER 32

Shipshewana

Selma sat in her rocking chair, looking down at Scruffy, who was sound asleep in the wicker bed she'd prepared for him after returning from the vet's yesterday. The poor cat had several gashes that needed to be stitched, but Selma was thankful his injuries weren't any worse. Dr. Benson had said it looked like Scruffy might have tangled with another cat, which made Selma wonder how that other cat had fared.

Dr. Benson had given Selma some pills to mix in Scruffy's food that would help with infection. He'd also given Scruffy a shot and suggested that Selma get the cat neutered as soon as he'd recovered from his injuries, as it might make him less apt to fight. The doctor said he thought Scruffy was about six months old. When Selma went back with the cat for his follow-up appointment in two weeks, he would get the needed shots, and Selma would set up another appointment for his surgery.

Selma reached down, and when she stroked Scruffy's silky head, his left ear twitched, but he didn't open his eyes. The cat hadn't done much more than sleep since she'd brought him home. At least early this morning she'd been able to get him to drink some water and eat a little food. The vet said not to worry if Scruffy didn't have much of an appetite and seemed to sleep a lot. Those were some of the side effects from the medication he'd been given. Plus, the cat was sore from the sutures, which was another good reason to keep him calm and quiet.

As Selma continued to look at the slumbering cat, she wished she could take away his pain. "You'll be okay, boy," she whispered, petting Scruffy's head. "You have a home with me for as long as you like."

The cat emitted a soft purr, and Selma sighed contentedly. It felt kind of nice to know that someone needed her, even though it was an animal. She hadn't experienced that in a long time.

Topeka, Indiana

Carmen had been driving around Amish Country all afternoon, stopping to talk to a few Amish people and watching them interact with each other in the various Amish-run stores. She needed to start writing her article soon but had been procrastinating.

As she parked in front of another Amish store, she thought about the good time she'd had with Paul last Saturday evening. In fact, she found herself daydreaming about him a lot lately. If she closed her eyes, she could almost see his smiling face, hear the laughter in his voice, and smell his musky aftershave.

She also thought about precious little Sophia and how every time the little girl saw Carmen, she would reach out her arms to her. Until she'd gotten to know her niece, Carmen had never desired to be a mother. Now, the idea of having a child of her own would be like a dream come true.

Carmen's cell phone rang, interrupting her musings. She glanced at the caller ID and grimaced. It was her boss—probably calling to check up on her again. She thought about letting it go into voice mail but knew she'd be prolonging the inevitable. Mr. Lawrence was a persistent man and would no doubt keep calling until she finally answered.

"Hello, Mr. Lawrence," Carmen said, holding the phone up to her ear.

"Hey, Carmen. I'm calling to see how things are going. Have you got that article finished yet?"

"No, I'm still working on it, and I thought you said I could have the full six weeks."

"I did say that, but there was another TV show on about the Amish last night, and I thought this would be a good time to publish the article on wild Amish teenagers and their parents who look the other way while the kids do whatever they want."

"It's not like that, Mr. Lawrence. From what I've found out—"

"So how soon can you have the article done?" he asked, cutting her off.

"I—I don't know. I'm going to need a little more time to gather information."

"Well, good grief, you've been there for four and a half weeks. I'd think by now you ought to know something."

"I have learned a lot," Carmen said, "but not enough to write the story yet. I promise I'll have something written up soon."

"How soon?"

Doesn't he ever let up? Carmen pressed her hands together until her veins protruded. "I need another week and a half. Can you give me that long to complete the story?" she asked, trying her best to sound cheerful.

Silence. Then he said, "Okay. A week and a half, that's all. I expect a story on my desk by then, and it had better be a good one, Carmen, or you'll be back to writing news about the freeway traffic." Mr. Lawrence hung up without even saying good-bye.

Carmen let her head fall forward onto the steering wheel and groaned. *I need to write that article, no matter how much I don't want to. If I don't, I may lose my job. But how can I in good conscience write the negative article he wants me to when it's not even true that all Amish kids go wild into drinking, drugs, and sex during their running-around years?*

Middlebury

"Mom, Dad, there's something I need to tell you," Anna said after her family sat down to eat supper.

"Can it wait till we're done eating?" Dad asked. "I've been working hard all day and am really tired, so I'd like to eat without a bunch of noisy conversation."

Anna nodded. "Sure, Dad, it can wait." *Maybe it's better this way,* she decided. *It would probably be best to talk to Mom and Dad privately, rather than in front of my sisters and brothers. I'm just anxious to get this over with.*

Earlier that day while working at the window shop, Anna had decided to tell her folks that she planned to go to Florida with Mandy in December. She was tired of keeping her plans bottled up inside and knew the longer she waited, the harder it would be. She hoped that for once they would understand her feelings and accept her decision to leave home and strike out on her own.

As Anna began eating, her stomach tightened. She wasn't sure she'd be able to finish her meal. The longer she waited to say what was on her mind, the more she questioned her decision to tell Mom and Dad tonight. Would it hurt to wait awhile longer—maybe until after the last quilting class? By then, she'd have her wall hanging done and could give it to Mom as a sort of peace offering.

When the meal was over and her siblings had left the kitchen, Anna began helping Mom clear the table. She'd just placed the first stack of dishes in the sink, when Dad spoke up. "Anna, what was it you wanted to talk to me and your mamm about?"

Anna swallowed hard and turned to face him. "It was nothing important. It can wait till another time," she said, hoping the trembling she felt in her body didn't show in her voice.

"Now's a good time for me." Dad leaned back in his chair and clasped his hands behind his head. "Take a seat, Anna, and tell us what's on your mind."

Anna hesitated, and then looked at Mom, hoping she'd come to her rescue and say she didn't need to talk about anything tonight. But Mom took a seat at the table and motioned for Anna to do the same.

"Is this about the bracelet that young woman from the quilting class gave you?" Mom asked after Anna had seated herself in the chair next to her.

Anna gasped. "H–how do you know about that?"

"Susan told us," Dad announced. "She also admitted that she took the bracelet from your purse and put it in a shoe box in her closet, but that you found it there and took it back." He released his hands from behind his head, leaned forward slightly, and stared hard at Anna. "Why would you feel the need to have a fancy bracelet?"

"I—I didn't feel the need," Anna stammered. "Carmen gave it to me as a gift, and I—"

"And you just couldn't say no?"

Dad's piercing gaze made Anna shiver, and she quickly looked away.

"So was the bracelet what you wanted to tell us about?" Mom asked, reaching over to touch Anna's arm.

Anna knew bringing up Florida right now would cause a rift, and she wasn't prepared to deal with an uproar. As she tried to think of something to say, a cry from her youngest sister arose from the next room.

"Mom, Susan knocked your pretty vase on the floor!" Becky shouted.

Anna watched with relief as both her parents jumped up from their chairs and headed for the living room.

While Mom and Dad were gone, Anna got up and quickly finished washing the dishes. When that chore was done, she went up to her room and shut the door. A headache had been coming on all afternoon, and now her head was thumping so hard she could hardly think.

I'm going to bed, she told herself. All she wanted was to get rid of the pain in her head and blot out what she knew would be coming when she finally found the nerve to tell Mom and Dad she was leaving.

CHAPTER 33

Shipshewana

Today was Emma's fifth quilting class, and Terry looked forward to going. Not because he liked to quilt, but he was anxious to see Cheryl again and hopefully go to lunch with her after the class. He hoped by getting there early he'd be able to sit beside her while they worked at the sewing table. It wouldn't set well with him if Blaine got there first and nabbed that chair. As far as Terry was concerned, after what Blaine had pulled last Saturday, leaving Cheryl without a ride home, she shouldn't give him the time of day.

Terry had just parked his truck and gotten out, when "Mr. Clean's" SUV pulled in. As soon as Blaine hopped out, Terry marched up to him and said, "I can't believe you'd have the nerve to show your face here this morning."

Blaine blinked, taking a step back. "Wh–what do you mean?"

"You left Cheryl alone without a ride home last Saturday, remember?"

Blaine's eyes narrowed as he came forward, poking his finger into Terry's chest. "As I recall, you stole my date."

Keeping a lid on his temper, Terry looked Blaine right in the eye and calmly said, "You were nowhere around, so what was I supposed to do, leave her stranded?"

Blaine shook his head. "Do you really think I'd leave her alone like that, without transportation? I can't believe you'd confront me with a statement like that."

"Look," Terry said, trying to smooth things over and not wanting to provoke a fight, "I was only trying to help by giving her a lift."

"Well, you could have helped a lot more if you hadn't shown up and whisked Cheryl away. Eventually, we'd have found each other, and then I would have taken her home."

Cheryl joined them on the porch just then. Terry was surprised; he'd been so intent on his discussion with Blaine, he hadn't heard her car pull in.

"Do you really need to rehash this again? I thought I'd explained all this to you on the phone last weekend," she said, looking at Blaine.

"Whatever," he said with a brief shrug before heading into the house.

Cheryl looked at Terry with questioning eyes. "I just got in on the end of your conversation with Blaine. Was he giving you a hard time about last Saturday?"

Avoiding the fact that he'd been the one who'd confronted Blaine, Terry nodded. "Yeah, but it's okay. We didn't come to blows or anything, so no harm was done."

"Well, you don't have to worry about Blaine. I'm not going out with him again."

"You're not?"

She shook her head. "We really don't have anything in common, and I don't enjoy being with him the way I do you. For some reason, Blaine and I couldn't seem to connect." Cheryl lowered her gaze, while Terry watched a blush appear on her beautiful face. "With you, I feel like I have a connection," she said in a voice barely above a whisper.

Terry felt ten feet tall. Yet he was uncomfortable about expressing to Cheryl how he felt about her. "So does that mean you'll go out to lunch with me after class this afternoon?" he asked, trying to sound casual.

"That would be nice. I'd be happy to go."

Carmen entered Emma's quilting room, feeling a bit nervous and distracted. All she could think about was how she felt forced to write a story that wasn't true about the precious Amish friends she had made. *I don't think I can do it,* she told herself. *I need to write the truth, not something that will please my editor. For now, though, I have to quit thinking about this and focus on something else.* Carmen took a seat on one side of the table. Paul would be coming by after class with his daughter, because they'd made plans to take Sophia for a carousel ride at the Davis Mercantile in Shipshewana, so that was something to look forward to.

From what Carmen had read in a brochure she'd picked up, the carousel had been fully restored and featured hand-carved farm animals. Later they'd be going to the Red Wagon, a toy store also in the Davis Mercantile. She was sure Sophia would be excited about that. Paul had mentioned that he would treat them to lunch at the Daily Bread, where several Amish-style dishes were served. Carmen hoped if there was time that they could stop by the Scrapyard, where a variety of scrapbooking supplies were sold. With all the pictures she'd taken here in Amish Country, not to mention the ones of Paul and

Sophia, Carmen had decided to begin a scrapbook, as a remembrance of this special trip.

As Emma stood at the head of the table, ready to teach the class, she felt concern. Terry and Cheryl were the only ones smiling, and she figured that was because they were sitting together. It was interesting to see how their attitudes had changed toward one another from the first quilting class until now. They'd obviously set whatever differences they had aside and found some things they enjoyed about each other.

Sort of like how it was with Lamar and me, Emma mused.

She turned her attention to the others. Blaine's shoulders sagged, as if in defeat; Carmen appeared agitated as she twisted her finger around the ends of her hair. Anna, whose eyes were red and puffy, appeared to have been recently crying. Selma hadn't arrived yet, and Emma hoped that when she came in today, she'd be in a good mood.

Emma was about to begin the class, when Selma finally showed up. Instead of the usual lime-green attire, Selma wore a pretty fall sweatshirt with light brown slacks. Her sweatshirt wasn't plain, either. It had a delicate white collar and on the front was an image of a maple tree in vivid colors with a hay-filled wagon underneath. Nestled on top of the bales of hay was a cat, much like the one Selma had described that she'd taken in.

"You look nice and fallish today," Emma complimented. "That's a pretty top you're wearing."

"Thank you," Selma answered. "Sorry I'm a little late, but my cat got into a fight with another cat, and I spent some extra time this morning getting him to eat his food."

"I'm sorry to hear that," Emma said with concern. "Is the cat going to be okay?"

Selma nodded. "The vet stitched his wounds and gave him an antibiotic, so as long as I keep him inside and quiet until he heals, Scruffy should be fine."

"That's good to hear," Terry spoke up. "That little critter's a mighty nice cat."

Selma smiled, looking perkier than Emma had seen her before. "I didn't think so at first, but he's sort of grown on me." Selma turned her attention to Emma again. "Did I miss anything by being late?"

Emma shook her head. "I was about to tell the others what we'd be doing today."

"I hope we're going to continue quilting," Cheryl said, "because I'm not finished with that part of mine yet."

"Neither am I," Terry agreed. "And I'm all thumbs, so I'm not sure I'll ever get it done."

"I'll help you with it," Lamar volunteered. "You, too, Blaine," he quickly added.

Blaine perked up a bit. "Thanks, Lamar, I appreciate that. And I'm really looking forward to going fishing with you after class today."

"Same here," Lamar said. "Let's hope the fish will be biting this afternoon. Oh, and by the way, Emma made us some sandwiches to take along."

Blaine smiled at Emma. "Thanks, that was nice of you."

"I was happy to do it," Emma responded. She was glad to see that Blaine's attitude had improved. She'd noticed that he still seemed a bit withdrawn around everyone and hoped going fishing with Lamar might loosen Blaine up a bit. Now if she could just see a smile from Carmen and Anna.

"Today we'll finish the quilting part of your wall hangings and then get the bindings pinned in place," Emma said. "Next week we will sew the bindings, and your wall hangings will be completed."

With Lamar's help, Emma handed everyone's project to them, along with pins, needles, thread, thimbles, and large embroidery hoops. While everyone worked, she went around to make sure the women were doing okay, while Lamar supervised the men. After each of them finished quilting, Emma showed how to cut and pin the binding. Following that, she suggested they take a break for refreshments.

"That sounds good to me," Terry said, rubbing his hands together. "What have you got for us this time, Emma?"

She smiled. "I made some apple crumb bread. And if any of you want the recipe for it, I'll gladly share."

Cheryl and Selma's hands shot up, but the others just sat there. Well, maybe after they tasted it, they would change their minds.

During their refreshment break, Emma told Cheryl that she was making progress on her grandmother's quilt. "I'm sure I'll have it done for you by next week," Emma said.

Cheryl smiled. "I'm looking forward to seeing the quilt and anxious to give it to Grandma when I go there for her birthday."

"How long will you be gone?" Terry asked.

"Probably just a few days," Cheryl responded. "Unless my boss gives me some extra time off, I can't be away from work too long, so I'll fly to Portland on a Friday morning, and return to Indiana Monday or Tuesday of the following week. I don't have my plane tickets bought yet, though. I'm waiting to hear from my mother about the date for Grandma's party. We may have it on a different day than her actual birthday in order to work around my parents' busy schedules."

"I hope your grandmother appreciates you coming for her birthday," Selma spoke up. "I didn't even get a phone call or a card from my daughter on my last birthday." She sniffed and blinked a couple of times, as though trying to hold back tears. "Cora hates me, and it's probably my own fault."

The room got deathly quiet. Emma glanced at Lamar to get his reaction, but he said nothing. Since everyone looked so uncomfortable, Emma felt she had to say something. Placing her hand on Selma's trembling shoulder, she quietly said, "Would you like to talk about it?"

Selma drew in a quick breath and released it with a shuddering sigh. "Cora left home after she graduated from high school, and the only time's she's been back was for her father's funeral. She never calls or writes, and whenever I've called her, she's always cut me off, saying she's too busy to talk."

"Why'd your daughter leave home?" Lamar asked.

Selma's voice quavered. "For years, my husband and I didn't think we could have any children, but then in my late thirties, we were blessed with a daughter." She dabbed at her tears. "Everything was wonderful when Cora was little. We did lots of fun things together. But as time went by, we started to disagree about things. Cora excelled in the business courses she took during high school, and John and I thought she should go to college to better her skills, so that one day she might get a job in management. I managed a flower shop during that time, and I loved my job, but Cora was satisfied with just doing office work." Selma paused again and blotted her tears with the tissue Emma handed her. "Cora said I was hard on her and expected too much and that I wanted her to be just like me. All I really wanted was for my daughter to reach her full potential." Selma drew in a deep breath and continued. "I'm afraid Cora was right. I didn't listen to what she wanted, and there were other issues, too. Even with my husband, I looked for the negative instead of the positive. I've wished so many times that I could go back and change things."

"That's what my folks do with me, too," Anna interjected. She pursed her lips. "They don't really listen to my feelings or hopes for the future. I talk, but they don't listen, if you know what I mean. That's why I'm planning to. . ." Her voice trailed off.

"What are you planning to do?" Emma questioned.

Anna shook her head. "Nothing. I shouldn't have said anything."

Standing at the head of the table, Emma looked at each of her students. "In 1 John 4:12, it says: 'If we love one another, God dwelleth in us, and his love is perfected in us.'"

"That's a good verse," Lamar added. "It reminds us of the importance of loving others—and that includes our families, whom we often take for granted. Just because we don't always see things the same way doesn't mean we should give up on someone in our family or shut them out of our lives." He smiled at Selma. "In hindsight, I think we all wish we could go back and do things differently. But then, if we've learned something from the experience, that's important, don't you think?"

Selma nodded slowly.

"Would you like a piece of advice?" he asked.

Selma nodded once more.

"Get in touch with your daughter as soon as possible and let her know how much you love her. If you've done something to offend her, apologize and ask if you can start over."

"That's excellent advice," Emma agreed. She turned to face Anna. "You might need to think about that as well, where your parents are concerned."

"You don't understand," Anna said, choking on a sob. "Nothing I do pleases Mom and Dad. They want to keep me a little girl forever, never letting me make my own choices. Well, I have made my choice, and today I'm going to start doing what will make me happy!" She jumped up, grabbed her sweater and purse, and raced out of the house, leaving everyone in the room with their mouths hanging open.

Chapter 34

Why don't we take your car when we go out to lunch?" Terry suggested as he and Cheryl left Emma's house. "You probably wouldn't want to ride in my truck."

"Don't worry about me," Cheryl said with a shake of her head. "I don't mind riding in a truck."

"Okay, but I've gotta warn ya, my truck's kinda noisy."

"Then I guess I'll just have to talk a little louder," she said with a chuckle.

Terry grinned and opened the door on the passenger side for her to get in.

"Your truck's not so bad," Cheryl said as she climbed in and looked around. "In fact, you keep it pretty nice inside compared to some I've seen." She ran her hand over the leather seat.

"Well, you haven't heard the engine yet. And to be honest, the inside of my truck doesn't always look this good," Terry admitted.

"You could have fooled me. Even this bench seat looks brand new."

"Actually, it is. I had it replaced a few weeks ago, which is what prompted me to clean out the truck." Terry chuckled. "Couldn't have a cluttered truck with a brand-new seat."

Cheryl smiled. "I know what you mean. When I get something new for my apartment, it almost always triggers me into buying something else. Guess I get that from my mom. She used to drive Dad crazy every time he did some kind of improvement or repairs to the house. I remember the time she asked him to paint the living room. After it was done, Mom wanted all new furniture and pictures for the room because the walls looked so clean and nice." Cheryl giggled, as she reminisced. "She said the old stuff just wouldn't do."

As they drove out of Emma's yard, Terry glanced at Cheryl and said, "Speaking of nice—I think you're pretty nice, and easy to please."

She smiled, feeling the heat of a blush erupt on her cheeks. "I try to be, but I'm sure my parents might say otherwise. When I was a little girl, my dad said I was spoiled."

"How come? Did your folks give you everything you wanted?"

Cheryl shook her head. "Far from it. But my grandma sort of spoiled me. Not with gifts so much, but by giving me lots of attention—something I didn't get much of from Mom or Dad."

"I'm surprised at that. Didn't you mention when we went out to lunch last week that you're an only child?"

Cheryl nodded.

"Everyone I know who grew up without brothers and sisters pretty much had their parents all to themselves."

"Well, that wasn't the case for me. Dad kept busy at work, and so did Mom. And when they weren't working, they were involved in some activity that took them away from home. If they could work it into their schedule, which wasn't very often, they'd try to spend some time with me. But even then, I never felt special. I think they were just trying to fulfill their parental duty." Cheryl sighed. "That's why I spent a lot of my childhood with Grandma, and it's how we became so close."

"Is this the same grandma who owns the quilt you're having Emma fix?" Terry questioned.

"Yes, it is. Grandma Donelson is my mother's mom, and when my grandpa passed away ten years ago, Grandma moved in with us. We became even closer after that. She's in a nursing home in Portland now, not far from where my parents live."

"What about your dad's parents? Are they both still living?"

"Yes, but they live in Idaho, so I don't get to see them much." Cheryl nodded at Terry. "What about you? Are your grandparents alive, and if so, do they live nearby?"

"My dad's folks are both dead, and my mom's parents live in Oklahoma. I know I should, but I don't keep in touch with them much." Terry pulled into a gas station. "I hope your stomach can hold out for lunch a while longer, 'cause this old truck needs some gas."

She smiled. "I think I'll make it."

Terry turned off the ignition and hopped out of the truck. While he pumped the gas, Cheryl reached into her purse, pulled out her cell phone, and turned up the volume. She'd had it muted during the quilting class, not wishing to disturb anyone should it go off. As she was putting the phone back into her purse, a package of mints fell out. When she leaned over to pick it up, she discovered a pack of cigarettes on the floor of the truck.

"That's just great," Cheryl mumbled. "Terry's obviously started smoking again." *Or maybe he never quit and just managed to hide it well. I can't date a guy who smokes, not with my allergies.*

When Terry got back in the truck, Cheryl held the cigarettes out to him. "What's this? I thought you said you'd quit smoking."

His eyebrows shot up. "I did. Those ain't mine. They're not even the brand I used to smoke."

"Oh really? Whose cigarettes are they, then?"

"I picked up a hitchhiker on the way to class this morning, and the guy tried to light up, but I told him, 'Not in my truck.' I'm guessing he must have left his cigarettes when I dropped him off. You do believe me, don't you?" he asked, looking anxiously at Cheryl. "By the way, I didn't explain this before, but that's why I had to put a new seat in this truck. Because of my smoking, I burned a hole in the old seat. That bad habit was a costly one, and I found out the hard way that it's expensive in more ways than one."

Cheryl sat trying to process all of this. She wanted to believe Terry and hoped he was telling the truth, because she would never get involved with another man who wasn't honest with her.

Terry reached for her hand. "I'm not lying, honest."

"Okay," she said, relaxing a bit. "I'll take you at your word."

"Sure is a nice day to be at the lake," Lamar remarked as he and Blaine sat at a picnic table, eating the lunch Emma had prepared for them.

Blaine nodded eagerly as he bit into his roast beef sandwich. "Like I said before, for me, there's nothing like being in the fresh air near a body of water, where the fish are just waiting to be caught. Even if I don't catch any fish, there's nothing I enjoy more than being out here like this. It sort of helps clear my head and allows me to put aside any problems I have."

Lamar chuckled. "I like to fish, too. It's very relaxing, but I'd give it up if Emma asked me to."

Blaine's forehead wrinkled. "You're kidding, right?"

"Nope. Nothing and no one is as special to me as my dear wife."

"Does Emma ever go fishing with you?" Blaine asked.

"She has a few times, but she usually keeps busy making the quilts she sells to one of our local quilt shops. When I go fishing, it's most often with my son-in-law or one of his boys."

Blaine was about to comment, when his cell phone rang. "Drat! I forgot to turn that stupid thing off." He glanced at the caller ID and blinked when he realized it was Sue calling. *I wonder what she wants. Guess I'd better answer it and find out.*

Flipping his phone open, Blaine said, "Hello."

"Hi, Blaine, it's Sue."

"Yeah, I knew that when I saw your name on my caller ID."

"Are you busy right now?" she asked.

"I'm eating lunch with a friend."

There was a pause. "Are you on a date?"

"What? No. I'm with Lamar Miller, and we're at Lake Shipshewana." *Not that it's any of your business,* Blaine thought with irritation.

"Oh, I see. Well, I won't keep you, but there's something I wanted to say."

"What's that?"

"I ran into Stuart and Pam at the mall last night. They were shopping with their kids, and Stuart mentioned that you'd been taking some quilting classes. I never pictured you doing something like that."

"It's true. Stuart got me into it with a bet we stupidly made."

"Yes, he mentioned that. Stuart also said you've been seeing a woman you met there, and I. . .I was wondering if you're getting serious about her."

"At this point, I can't really say. Cheryl and I have only gone out a few times." Blaine wasn't about to admit to Sue that he wasn't planning to see Cheryl anymore. No point in giving her the satisfaction. Besides, why did she care? Their relationship was over.

"Oh, I see."

Blaine wasn't sure how to read Sue's tone of voice. Was she jealous? Did she wish that she and Blaine were still dating? Did he dare to ask? No, that would be setting himself up to get hurt again.

"Look, Sue, I really can't talk anymore."

"Okay, sure. I'll let you get back to your lunch. Good-bye, Blaine."

"Bye, Sue." *Please don't call again; it hurts too much.* Blaine turned off his cell phone and stuffed it in his shirt pocket. Then he grabbed his can of soda pop and took a drink.

"Sorry for the interruption," he said, setting his empty can down. "That was my ex-girlfriend, Sue."

"You still care for her, don't you?" Lamar asked.

"What makes you think that?"

"I can see it on your face."

Blaine didn't know why, but he ended up telling Lamar all about Sue and how she'd turned down his marriage proposal, and they'd broken up.

"Would you like a piece of advice?" Lamar asked.

Blaine shrugged. "I guess so." With the eager expression on Lamar's face, he figured the elderly man was just waiting to give his opinion.

"Sue must still have some feelings for you, or she wouldn't have questioned you about Cheryl."

"You really think so?"

Lamar gave a nod. "If you love this woman, then maybe you shouldn't give up on her." Lamar reached into the picnic basket for another sandwich and handed it to Blaine. "You know, when I first started caring for Emma, she wouldn't give me the time of day."

"So what'd you do?" Blaine asked, his interest piqued.

"I kept pursuing her—did nice things for her and hung around till she couldn't say no." Lamar snickered. "It was a challenge at first, but well worth the wait. Now Emma and I are quite happy together."

Blaine smiled. "That's obvious. You two seem like you were made for each other—as some might say, you're soul mates."

Lamar bobbed his head. "But we wouldn't be married today if I hadn't made an effort to win Emma's heart. So I'm thinking maybe you gave up too soon on winning the hand of the woman you love."

"Maybe so, but I don't think pursing Sue is a good idea because she might turn me away, and I don't want to be hurt again."

"Well, you'll never know unless you try, and since Sue called, my guess is she misses you."

"I'll give it some thought," Blaine said. "But we came here to do some fishing today, so why don't we get to it?"

"Hey, Anna, come with me to the women's restroom," Mandy said when Anna met her at the 5 & 20 Restaurant after she'd left Emma's quilting class. She held up a paper sack. "I want to show you something."

Curious to know what her friend had in the bag, Anna followed Mandy into the restroom.

Once inside, Mandy opened the sack and pulled out two pairs of jeans, two knit tops, and a pair of lightweight jackets. She gave one set of clothes to Anna. "Put these on, and take down your hair. We're gonna spend the rest of the day as English girls."

"Doing what?" Anna asked, her heart beating with excitement. Here was a chance to see what it felt like to look English, but even so, she was apprehensive.

"Let's start by having a couple of burgers for lunch, and then we'll go shopping for some makeup and jewelry."

Anna's eyes widened. "What if someone sees us? As much as I'd like to do what you suggested, I don't want my folks to find out. It was bad enough they found out about the bracelet Carmen gave me. It would be a hundred times worse if they learned that I was walking around Shipshe wearing makeup and dressed in English clothes."

Mandy laughed and poked Anna's arm. "You worry too much. With our hair down and wearing these clothes and some makeup, no one's gonna know who we are."

"They might, and I'm not willing to take that chance. Especially when we're so close to home."

"No problem. We'll go to Elkhart or Goshen and have a fun day there."

"How are we supposed to get there, Mandy? Either of those towns are a long ways for us to ride on our bikes."

Her friend nodded. "You're right, which is why I thought we could hitchhike."

Anna shook her head vigorously. "No way! Hitchhiking could be dangerous."

Mandy pulled a cell phone out of her purse. "Okay, worrywart, if you don't want to hitchhike, then I'll call my brother, James, and ask him to give us a ride."

James, still going through his running-around years, had bought a car. And Mandy, being the free spirit she was, had a cell phone her folks knew nothing about.

"Well, what do you say?" Mandy nudged Anna's arm again. "Should I give James a call or what?"

Anna nodded. She'd wanted to experience the English world, so she'd take a chance and go with Mandy today.

Chapter 35

Goshen

While sitting in a booth beside Mandy, at a burger place in town, Anna stared down at her English clothes. It felt strange to be wearing them, and the jeans felt a bit tight, but it was kind of fun and exciting; especially once she'd looked in the mirror and realized how cute the clothes looked on her. Since Anna had never worn makeup before, Mandy had shown her how to apply it. Anna was amazed at how the eyeliner and mascara made her eyes look bigger.

It had worked out well that Mandy's brother had been able to give them a ride to Goshen, where they were less apt to be seen by anyone they knew. Of course, as Mandy pointed out, with the makeup and jewelry they wore, even if they were seen by someone they knew, they might not be recognized.

"Look over there," Mandy whispered, leaning close to Anna's ear. "See those cute guys at the table near the door? They're watching us."

Anna glanced in that direction. Two young men, one with blond hair and the other with coal-black hair, stared at them with big grins. Before Anna could comment, the one with blond hair left his seat and strolled across the room, stopping in front of Anna and Mandy's table. The other fellow followed, and they both plunked down on the other side of the booth.

"You girls live in Goshen?" the dark-haired boy asked. "Don't think I've seen you around this burger joint before."

Mandy rolled her eyes. "Goshen's a big town, and there are lots of fast-food restaurants, so what are the odds that you'd have seen us before?"

The boy leaned his head back and laughed. "Guess you're right about that." He looked at Anna and winked. "I'm Bill. What's your name, sweetie?"

Anna's cheeks warmed, but before she could reply, Mandy quickly said, "She's Anna, and I'm Mandy."

Bill motioned to his blond-haired friend. "This is my buddy, Tony, and we've been watching you two ever since you came in."

Tony grinned and winked at Mandy. "How'd you like to spend the rest of the day with us? We promise to show you a good time."

Anna held her breath and waited to hear how Mandy would respond. She hoped she wouldn't say yes, because the way these two guys looked at them—like hungry animals—made Anna nervous. She also noticed the outline of a pack of cigarettes stuffed inside the sleeve of Tony's T-shirt. She shuddered to think how she and Mandy would react if these boys insisted that they smoke with them. Anna had never smoked a cigarette before; she had no desire to, either. Just the smell of cigarette smoke made her head feel stuffed up.

"We appreciate the offer," Mandy said smoothly, "but my friend and I have other plans for the day."

"What kind of plans?" Bill asked.

"We're going shopping," Anna interjected.

Tony smiled. "Shopping, is it? Well, maybe we'll just tag along then."

Oh no, Anna thought. *How are we going to get away from these two? I really don't want to go anywhere with them.*

Mandy smiled, tipping her head. "Feel free to go with us if you want, but you might get bored."

"I don't think so," Tony said with a quick shake of his head. "Who could be bored hanging around two girls as hot-looking as you?"

Anna cringed. All of a sudden, she didn't feel so cute. This day wasn't turning out the way she'd hoped. She had merely wanted to have a little fun wearing English clothes, and she wished she could make Tony and Bill go away. She feared that if she and Mandy went anywhere with these two, things could turn out badly.

"Aren't we supposed to meet James soon?" Anna asked, looking at her friend.

Mandy nodded. "Oh, that's right. I'd almost forgot." She smiled at Tony and sweetly added, "Maybe we'll see you some other time."

Bill frowned, but Tony merely shrugged and said, "Well, if you've got another date, you should have just said so."

Anna was about to say that James wasn't her date, but changed her mind. If the guys thought she or Mandy had a boyfriend, they'd probably leave them alone.

Tony stood and stuffed his hands in his jean's pocket. "We'll be sitting over there, in case you change your mind."

As Tony and Bill sauntered off, Anna blew out her breath in relief. "I'm glad they went back to their table. I didn't like the way those two looked at us, and I didn't want to go anywhere with them, did you?"

Mandy shrugged her slim shoulders. "It might have been kinda fun, but with James coming to pick us up in a few hours, it wouldn't have worked out so well."

"I hope they don't come back over here," Anna said, feeling kind of shaky inside. "Worse yet, what if they follow us when we do our shopping?"

Mandy leaned close to Anna and whispered, "I think I know a way we can sneak out of here without them knowing."

"Really? How?"

Mandy smiled. "Come with me to the ladies' room, and I'll show you." Moments later, two young women in Plain clothes slipped unnoticed out of the restaurant.

Elkhart

"This has been such a nice day," Paul told Carmen as he lifted Sophia off the carousel.

She nodded enthusiastically. "I'm going to miss all the fun times I've had with you and Sophia when I go back to California."

Then don't go, Paul thought, but he didn't voice the words.

"Why don't you and Sophia come out to see me during your spring break next year?" Carmen suggested. She bent down and gave Paul's daughter a kiss on the cheek. "You'd like that, wouldn't you, little one?"

Sophia giggled, and the look of adoration Paul saw on her face as she lifted her hands up to Carmen, put a lump in his throat. "Sophia's going to miss you, and so am I," he said, making eye contact with Carmen.

"I'll miss you both, as well." Carmen took one of Sophia's hands and Paul clasped the other one as they walked past several shops in the Davis Mercantile. When they came to the scrapbooking store, Carmen suggested that Paul take Sophia to the toy store while she bought a few scrapbooking supplies.

"That's probably a good idea," Paul said. "If we all go in, Sophia will get restless."

Carmen smiled. "We can either meet outside the scrapbook store, or if I get done before you do, I'll join you in the toy store in twenty minutes or so."

"Sounds good." Paul bent down and scooped his daughter into his arms. "Off we go, little one. Let's find you a new toy."

Carmen had been looking at scrapbooking supplies about twenty minutes, when her cell phone rang. When she saw that it was her boss, she reluctantly answered the phone. *He doesn't give up,* she couldn't help thinking.

"How's it going, Carmen?" Mr. Lawrence asked. "Have you got that story wrapped up yet?"

"Not quite, but by the time I get back to the office, I'll have that story about the Amish and how they let their young people go wild during their time of rumschpringe."

"Okay, but I may not be here when you do," he said. "I have to take my wife to see her niece who just had a baby, so if I'm not here, just give your story to the assistant editor, Mike, and he can look it over before it goes to press."

"Okay. Have a good trip, Mr. Lawrence."

Carmen had no more than hung up, when out of nowhere, Paul, with Sophia perched on his shoulders, stepped up to her. "Who were you talking to, and what's this about writing a story on the Amish?"

Caught off guard, and realizing that Paul had obviously heard her conversation with Mr. Lawrence, Carmen swallowed hard and moistened her lips with the tip of her tongue. "Umm. . .I thought you took Sophia to the toy store."

"Never mind that. What's this about?" Paul asked again, pointing to Carmen's cell phone.

Unsure of where to begin, Carmen drew a deep breath. "Let me explain."

"Yes, please do. I'm all ears."

Quickly, Carmen told Paul that she'd been sent to Indiana to write a story for the newspaper in Los Angeles that would shed some light on the topic of rumschpringe and why the parents of Amish young people allowed them to run wild during that time.

Paul frowned, while shaking his head. "So the whole time you've been taking Emma's quilting classes, and spending time on your own with Anna Lambright, you've been gleaning information for your story?"

Carmen nodded, hoping to explain a little more. "But it's turned out to be more than that, Paul. During the time I've been here, I've come to—"

Paul held up his hand. "You don't need to say anything more; I get the picture. You've used my Amish friends to get the story you want, and now you're going to shed a bad light on the Amish way of life."

"It's not like that. I really—"

"I don't want to talk about this," Paul said. "If you're done shopping, I'll drop you off at your hotel and you can say good-bye to Sophia, because we won't be seeing you again before you return to California." Paul lifted Sophia from his shoulders and held her in his arms.

Carmen cringed at the way he looked at her and recoiled at his next verbal blow.

"I'm really disappointed in you, Carmen. I never thought you'd stoop so low. And all those months I had to live with you thinking the accident that killed my beloved wife was my fault. . .well, I should have known from that what kind of a person you really are."

Paul's icy stare and the tone of his voice was enough to make Carmen know that she'd lost his respect. No matter what she said, he wouldn't listen.

I should not have agreed to do that story, she thought with regret. *No matter what I say or do, Paul will never trust me.*

Middlebury

James picked up Anna and Mandy later than expected, and by the time they got back to Shipshewana, Anna really had to hustle to get home, riding her bike, which she'd left locked to the bike rack outside the 5 & 20 restaurant.

When Anna walked into her house, flushed from the hard ride, she found Mom and Dad in the living room. Dad was reading the newspaper, while Mom knitted on the prayer shawl she'd started a few weeks ago.

"You've been gone most of the day, Anna," Mom said, setting her paper aside. "Where have you been?"

"I went to lunch and then did some shopping with Mandy." Anna plopped down in the empty chair across from her parents.

"You know we don't approve of you hanging around that girl," Dad said, looking at Anna over the top of his reading glasses.

"Mandy's a good friend," Annie defended, grasping the arms of her chair. Then throwing caution to the wind, she leaned forward and blurted, "I'm going to Sarasota, Florida, with Mandy in December." There, it was out, and she felt a sense of relief for finding the courage to finally say it—that is until she saw her parents' reactions.

Dad's face turned beet red, and he slapped his hand down on the end table next to the sofa so hard that Mom's knitting yarn fell off and unraveled as it rolled across the floor.

"Anna Lambright, I forbid you to go!" he shouted. "And if you leave here against our wishes, you may as well stay in Sarasota and never come back!"

"I'm an adult now, and I have a right to make my own decisions," Anna argued. "I need some time to decide whether I want to join the Amish church or not." Tears stung Anna's eyes as she abruptly stood. What was the point in trying to explain? "I'm sorry you feel that way, Dad, but there was no good time to tell you this. I figured you'd react this way, but my mind is made up." Unable to say anything more, Anna ran up the stairs to her room, slamming the door behind her.

CHAPTER 36

As the week went by, Emma became more excited. Her sister was supposed to arrive on Friday but had called and said that due to a few extra stops her driver had made, she'd be a day late, and that Emma should expect her to arrive sometime Saturday.

"I hope Rachel gets here after the quilting class today," Emma told Lamar as they sat at the kitchen table Saturday morning, drinking coffee. "I want to give her my undivided attention, and if she comes in the middle of class, I won't be able to do that."

Lamar placed his hand on Emma's arm and gave it a tender squeeze. "Try not to fret. Rachel will get here when she's supposed to get here, and if happens to be when in you're in the middle of teaching your class, then you can introduce her to everyone."

Emma smiled. "That's true, and since she's also a quilter, she might enjoy seeing what my students have been doing."

"Speaking of which," Lamar said, rising from his chair, "I hear the roar of a motorcycle, so I'm guessing Terry must be here."

When Terry pulled his cycle into Emma's yard, he noticed that no other vehicles were there. He figured he was probably early, but that was okay because if the class went longer than normal today, he'd have to leave early. He'd be heading out for a three-day fund-raiser bike trip this afternoon and didn't want to be late meeting up with Jan and Star, along with the rest of the people who'd be riding with them. This fund-raiser was to help a family who'd recently lost everything when their house burned down. Since Terry had gone to school with the man, he wanted to help out in any way he could. In fact, he and Jan had offered to help rebuild the family's house, as had many of their biker buddies.

Terry stood on the porch a few minutes, watching for Cheryl's car. He hoped she would get here soon, so he could tell her about his plans. If she didn't, he'd try to sneak in a few words with her during class.

After waiting several more minutes and seeing Selma, Blaine, Anna, and Carmen show up, Terry finally gave up and went inside, too.

Emma smiled as everyone took a seat around the table. "Today we'll finish the binding on your wall hangings," she said. "But I think we should wait until Cheryl gets here."

Terry glanced at his cell phone to check the time. "I'm in a hurry, so if you don't mind, I'd like to start sewing right away."

"Go right ahead. Lamar can help you finish up," Emma responded. "The rest of you are free to do the same. Cheryl's wall hanging is almost done, so when she gets here I'm sure it won't take her long to finish it."

Goshen

Cheryl had forgotten to set her alarm, so she was already running late, but just as she climbed into her car, her cell phone rang. Seeing that it was her mother, she quickly answered the phone. "Hi, Mom. How's Grandma doing?"

"I was there the other day, and she didn't know who I was. I'm not sure it'll do any good to have a party for her."

"With or without a party, I'm still coming for her birthday," Cheryl said.

"Have you booked your flight yet?"

"No, but I'm going to do that as soon as I get home from the quilting class today. I should have done it sooner, but I've been watching for a cheaper rate, and there hasn't been any." Cheryl took a deep breath. "Do you think she'll recognize me?"

Mom sighed. "I don't know."

"I'll give you a call as soon as I get my tickets booked so you or Dad will know when to pick me up."

"All right, Cheryl. We'll talk to you soon."

Cheryl's heart was heavy as she clicked off the phone. She was tempted to skip Emma's class today, but it was the last one, and she really wanted to finish her wall hanging. She'd also planned to have lunch with Terry. If those weren't reasons enough, Emma had promised she'd have Grandma's quilt done today, so Cheryl needed to pick it up. Maybe once Grandma saw her old quilt again, she would regain some memories.

"Thanks for helping me get this done so fast, Lamar," Terry said, looking at the clock on the far wall and knowing he had to leave soon. Cheryl still hadn't arrived, and he hoped he would have time to explain why he had to cancel their lunch date today. Lately, Terry had been so wrapped up in wanting to be with Cheryl, it had taken him by surprise when Jan reminded him that the charity ride was this weekend.

"Are you doing something special this afternoon?" Lamar asked, placing Terry's finished wall hanging in a cardboard box.

"Yeah, I have plans with a few of my biker friends. We're going on a road trip for a few days to help a friend in need, and I just found out this morning that we're supposed to leave this afternoon."

"Are you finished up?" Emma asked, walking over as Lamar handed Terry the box.

Terry nodded. "I hate to do this, but as I was telling Lamar, I've got a trip to take and need to get going. Is it okay if I leave my wall hanging here till I get back?"

"Certainly," Emma said.

He smiled at her. "Just want you to know that I appreciate all you and Lamar have done in helping me make the wall hanging." He rubbed his forehead. "This sure isn't the way I wanted to leave on our last day of class, and I didn't even get to see Cheryl and explain why I have to postpone our lunch plans."

"Don't worry about it." Lamar put his hand on Terry's shoulder. "When she gets here, we'll explain things to her. Just be safe on that trip, and have fun."

"I'll ask Lamar to fill me in on this trip you're taking," Emma said. "But while you're still here, I need to tell everyone something."

When Emma had the class's attention, she began to explain. "I know this is the last day of class, but with my sister arriving today, I want to spend as much time with her as possible, so I was thinking of setting another time when we can all get together and visit awhile. Would two weeks from today work for all of you? I'll make a dessert, of course," she quickly added.

Everyone agreed, except Carmen, who said she had to return to California.

"I hate to run off like this," Terry said, looking at Emma, "but I'll catch up with you when we get back together here." With that, Terry hollered, "See you all soon," and headed out the door.

Terry hopped on his cycle and started the engine. Revving up the engine and knocking the kickstand back with his foot, he headed out. He thought this road trip might serve a twofold purpose. Besides raising money for a needy family, it would give him some time to clear his head so he could deal with all the things he'd been thinking about concerning Cheryl and where their relationship might be headed.

As Emma and Lamar supervised the students, Emma began to worry. Not only was Cheryl late for class, but Rachel wasn't here yet, either. She hoped Rachel's driver hadn't run into bad weather or experienced any problems with her vehicle.

Lord, please bring my sister and Cheryl here safely, Emma silently prayed, *and help me not to worry so much.*

Needing to focus on something else, Emma moved across the room to help Carmen, who'd just dropped a package of pins. As she approached the sewing machine where Carmen sat, she noticed that the young woman's hands were shaking, and her eyes were rimmed with tears.

"Oh dear, what's wrong?" Emma asked. "There's no reason to be upset about dropping those pins."

"It. . .it's not the pins," Carmen said, sniffing. "I've done something I'm not proud of, and I think I've ruined my relationship with Paul."

Emma placed her hands on Carmen's trembling shoulders. "I'm sure whatever you did can't be that bad."

Carmen bobbed her head, while swiping at the tears running down her cheeks. "Yes, it is."

Emma didn't want to pry, but she thought it might help if Carmen talked about it. She was on the verge of asking, when a knock sounded on the door. Lamar said he would get it, and he returned moments later holding a suitcase, with Rachel at his side.

Emma hurried across the room and gave her sister a hug. "Oh Rachel! It's so good to see you!"

Rachel nodded, her pale blue eyes sparkling with the joy she obviously felt. Then she looked around the room and said, "I can see that you're busy right now, so I won't interrupt. Lamar can show me to my room."

"Nonsense," Emma said with a shake of her head. "I want you to meet my quilting students." She took Rachel's arm and led her around the room, introducing her to each one. By this time, Carmen had dried her eyes and looked a little perkier. When Rachel reached out and shook Carmen's hand, Carmen smiled and said, "It's nice to meet you."

Thinking this might be a good time to take a break, Emma announced that she was going to the kitchen to get some refreshments.

"I'll help you," Rachel said, following Emma into the other room.

When they returned with a tray of cookies, coffee, and iced tea, Emma was pleased to see that Cheryl had finally arrived, after being over an hour late. The young woman's face looked drawn, and Emma suspected that she, too, might be upset about something.

"Sorry I'm so late," Cheryl said, turning to Emma. "I forgot to set my alarm last night, and then I got a call from my mother." She paused a moment and drew in a sharp breath. "My grandma's not doing well, so I'm anxious to go home to see her." Cheryl's voice trailed off and she dropped her gaze to the floor.

"I'm so sorry to hear that," Emma said, gently touching Cheryl's arm. "I have the quilt ready for you, so you'll be able to take it when you go. In fact, I'll get it right now."

While Emma went after the quilt, Cheryl glanced at the empty seat, then noticed Lamar heading her way.

"Are you looking for Terry?" he asked.

"Yes. How'd you know? Didn't he make it to class today?"

"He was here, and you missed him by about fifteen minutes," Lamar explained. "He had to leave early because he was meeting his friends. Seems like they're going on some sort of bike ride for a couple of days. He said he'd call you when he gets back."

Just then Emma returned with the quilt. She asked Lamar to hold one corner, while she held the other, so Cheryl could see how it had turned out.

"Oh, it's beautiful," Cheryl murmured. "I think Grandma's going to be pleased."

Rachel, who stood off to one side, moved forward. She stared at the quilt and gasped. "Ach, my! This isn't *meechlich*!" she said, lifting her eyebrows in obvious surprise as she brought her hand up to her mouth.

"What isn't possible?" Emma questioned, watching as her sister drew closer to the quilt and examined every detail.

"The *gwilt*. It belonged to our sister Betty."

"Why would you think that?" Emma asked.

"See here," Rachel said, touching the underneath side on one corner of the quilt. "Those are Betty's initials. I remember when she embroidered them there."

"Betty?" Cheryl said, her eyes opening wide.

Rachel nodded. "She's our oldest sister, but she left the faith and moved away when she was eighteen years old."

Emma's lips pursed as she stared at the quilt. "I've never met Betty. She left home shortly before I was born. I'd only heard my family talk about Betty a few times, but I know from what little had been said that it hurt our parents deeply when Betty left. And in all those years, she never returned or made any contact with our family. I can't imagine how I would have felt if one of my children had done that."

Emma turned to Cheryl. "I wonder how your grandmother ended up with our sister's quilt. Do you know where or from whom she bought it?"

Cheryl stood motionless, as though in a daze. In a barely audible voice, she squeaked, "Betty is my grandmother's name. I don't know how it's possible, Emma, but I think Grandma might be your sister."

CHAPTER 37

Portland, Oregon

Emma's excitement rose as she followed Cheryl and Rachel off the train. Needing to find out if Cheryl's grandmother was their sister Betty, Cheryl had booked train tickets for all three of them, since Emma and Rachel weren't allowed to fly. Spending two days on the train gave them time to visit and let all that they'd learned sink in. Cheryl seemed especially thrilled to find out that Emma might actually be her great-aunt.

The train trip had been pleasant for Emma, except for the worry she felt about the health of Cheryl's grandmother. The scenery had been beautiful as they'd headed west, zipping through the central states, then the mountainous areas, until they'd ended up here in Portland.

"Oh, there's my folks." Cheryl motioned to the middle-aged couple walking toward them. After she'd hugged her parents, she introduced Emma and Rachel.

"So if what Cheryl told me on the phone is true, then you two would be my aunts," Cheryl's mother, Katherine, said, giving Emma and Rachel a hug. "I wasn't aware that my mother had any sisters. She's never said much about her past, and when I asked about her childhood, I was told that she had no family. I figured that meant no siblings."

"I was only seven years old when Betty left home, but I remember that she was upset about something," Rachel said as they headed toward the baggage claim area. "Later on, our folks explained that Betty wanted to live in the modern world and thought our ways were old-fashioned. Betty and Dad had words, and he said if she left home she shouldn't come back." Rachel sighed deeply. "I suppose she took him at his word, because we never heard from her again. I remember Mama crying many times over losing Betty."

Reflecting on all of this, Emma thought of Anna and how dissatisfied she seemed with her life. She hoped for Anna's sake, as well as her parents', that she wouldn't decide to leave the Amish faith. *When I get home, I'll talk to Anna and her parents,* she decided. *They need to have more understanding where Anna is concerned, and Anna needs to appreciate her family. Maybe our story will open their eyes.*

"Let's get your luggage put in my van, and we'll be on our way to the nursing home," Cheryl's father said. "I'm sure you ladies are as anxious as Cheryl is to see Betty."

Shipshewana

"Have you talked to Cheryl since we got back from our road trip?" Jan asked as he and Terry pulled into a gas station to fill up Jan's truck.

Terry shook his head. "I've tried leaving several messages, but she doesn't respond. I even drove over to her apartment last night, but she wasn't there." He gripped the edge of his seat, fighting the sudden urge for a cigarette, which he hadn't felt for several weeks. "Man,

I hope Cheryl's not mad at me."

"Why would she be mad?"

"'Cause I left Emma's early last Saturday without telling her why. I had hoped I could explain to her in person that I'd totally forgotten about the charity ride we'd planned. All I could think about was going to lunch with Cheryl again." Terry heaved a sigh as he rubbed the bridge of his nose. "My heart must be clogging my brain these days."

Jan opened the truck door. "Didn't you say that Lamar told you Cheryl had gone to see her grandmother, whose health isn't good?"

"Yeah, that's right."

"Cheryl's probably busy with things and hasn't checked her messages."

"Maybe so.

"Well, I'd better get the gas pumped or we'll never get to our next job."

While Jan filled the gas tank, Terry pulled out his cell phone and tried calling Cheryl. All he got was her voice mail again. He left a message: "Hi, Cheryl, it's Terry. I've been trying to get a hold of you for the last three days. Could you please call me back as soon as you get this message?"

Los Angeles

"What is this?" Mr. Lawrence asked, slamming the morning's newspaper down on Carmen's desk.

"If you're referring to my article, then it is what it is," she said, meeting his steely gaze. Carmen wondered why she worked for this harsh, demanding man.

"Of course I'm referring to your article!" He pointed a bony finger at the newspaper. "This was not written the way it was supposed to be, Ms. Lopez, and I can't believe Mike let it be published in my absence."

"I wrote the truth as I saw it. Isn't that what a good reporter is supposed to do?"

His face reddened. "Humph! Just how much digging did you really do?"

"I spoke to several Amish people while I was in Indiana and got to know some personally."

"You made those people sound like a bunch of saints."

Carmen shook her head vigorously. "I did not. I made them sound as they are—a kind, gentle people, who deal with their problems by relying on each other for support, while maintaining their strong moral values. They put God first in all things and hold their family members in high regard." Carmen paused for a breath. "They live life simply and by their own choice, not because they're forced to. Do they have problems? Certainly. But then don't we all?"

"That's all fine, well, and good," he said, leaning on the desk, "but an article like this isn't sensational enough. I was hoping for something juicy and shocking, like the things we've heard on the news, where some Amish have gone bad."

Carmen's jaw clenched. "So what you're saying is, if one person, no matter what his nationality or faith, does something wrong, that makes all people of that group bad?"

He shifted his stance. "Well, no, but—"

"But you're unhappy with me because I made this a positive article and not a negative one, is that right?"

He nodded.

Carmen took another deep breath. "I know a lot of readers out there want nothing more than to read about bad things happening to people. But with the way the world is these days, I believe many more people want to read about the good things that happen."

He opened his mouth, but Carmen rushed on. "Everyone has things going on in their own lives, and I know, at least for me, that I'd rather hear about pleasant things and noble situations. You know—something noteworthy. There are a lot of decent folks in the world, but for some reason, the majority of things we see on TV and read about in the paper dwell on the bad stuff that happens. If that's what sells, then I'm not sure I want to be a part of it anymore."

"This newspaper is about selling papers, Carmen," Mr. Lawrence reminded. "And my reporters will do whatever it takes to get good stories."

"I'm sorry you feel that way." She rose from her desk. "As of this moment, I'm turning in my resignation."

"Well, that's good, because if you hadn't quit, I would have fired you."

Breathing deeply to calm her nerves, Carmen forced a smile and said, "I'll clean out my desk and be gone before the end of the day."

Chapter 38

Portland

A lump formed in Cheryl's throat as she and her mother stood next to Grandma's bed. Grandma's eyes were closed, and she seemed unaware of their presence. It was quite warm in the room, but Grandma was covered with a blanket. Even so, Cheryl could see the outline of her body, which looked small and fragile. It was upsetting to see how frail Grandma had gotten since the last time they'd been together. Was it only a few years ago that she'd been so perky?

"Mom, wake up," Cheryl's mother said, gently shaking Grandma's shoulder.

Grandma's eyes opened, and she blinked a couple of times. "Katherine?

"Yes, Mom. I'm here with Cheryl, and we've brought some guests along." Cheryl's mother motioned to Emma and Rachel, who stood off to one side.

Grandma gave no indication that she saw them, as she stared at

Cheryl with a blank expression.

"Grandma, do you know how I am?" Cheryl asked, leaning in close to be sure Grandma could see her face.

Grandma studied Cheryl a few more seconds, then gave a slow nod. "You're my granddaughter."

Cheryl breathed a sigh of relief. She glanced at Mom and saw tears in her eyes. Did she feel guilty for being too busy to spend time with her own mother?

"Grandma, I want to introduce you to some very special people," Cheryl said, motioning for Emma and Rachel to move closer to the bed. "I think you might already know them. They're sisters, and their names are Emma and Rachel."

"When you were young, was your name Betty Bontrager?" Rachel asked, leaning close to Grandma's bed.

Grandma's eyelids fluttered.

"Did you grow up in Middlebury, Indiana? Were your parents named Homer and Doris?" Emma softly questioned, standing next to Rachel.

Grandma released a shuddering breath and coughed, while trying to sit up.

With Cheryl on one side, and her mother on the other, they eased two pillows behind Grandma's back and helped her get into a sitting position.

"There, Grandma, is that better?" Cheryl asked, holding her grandmother's hand.

Grandma nodded as tears filled her eyes. "Do I know you?" she asked, looking at Emma and then Rachel.

"Our parents were Homer and Doris Bontrager," Rachel repeated. "Our oldest sister's name was Betty."

Grandma covered her mouth as a heart-wrenching sob tore from her throat. "I. . .I'm that Betty. I never thought I'd see any of my family again." She looked at Cheryl and her mother. "I. . .I mean, the family I was born into," she said, lifting a shaky hand to swipe at the tears dripping onto her weathered cheeks.

Concerned for her grandmother, Cheryl stepped between Emma and Rachel. "I think this might be a bit too much for her. Maybe we should slow down and let her process things."

Cheryl was amazed that Grandma, whose memory was failing, seemed to remember these details now. Perhaps she'd longed to see her family so badly that it had been ever present on her mind.

Before Emma or Rachel could respond to Cheryl's request to slow down, Grandma shook her head and said, "No, let them go on."

"Whatever happened? Why'd you stay away all those years?" Rachel asked, tears dribbling down her own wrinkled cheeks. "Our mother's heart was broken, you know."

Even with Cheryl's comforting touch, Grandma continued to sob as she rocked back and forth. "I didn't want to stay away. I. . .I was scared. I prayed that we'd all be together someday, but Papa said he never wanted to see me again. I was afraid if I came back I wouldn't be welcome, and I couldn't handle the rejection." Grandma drew in a shuddering breath. "Staying away and having no contact with my family seemed easier, but I never forgot them."

Emma took Grandma's other hand. "It's too late to change the past, but we've been given a second chance. The Lord led us to you, and for that I'm so thankful." She took a seat in one of the chairs near Grandma's bed, and motioned for Rachel to do the same. "Now let's not waste a minute. I want to get better acquainted with the sister I never knew."

Cheryl placed the box with the quilt in it at the foot of Grandma's bed. "I have something I'd like to give you." She lifted the lid, removed the quilt, and gently covered Grandma with it. "Happy birthday, Grandma."

"It's my old quilt!" More tears fell as Grandma stroked the edge of her quilt with loving hands. "But it's not tattered anymore. It's even more beautiful than when my mother gave it to me. How did this happen?"

Cheryl explained that she'd taken the quilt to Emma to be repaired, and then told Grandma the details of how Rachel had recognized the quilt and they'd figured out that Grandma must be their long-lost sister.

Tears were shed all around, as two happy sisters, a mother, and her daughter, gathered around Grandma's bed. Cheryl knew that for the rest of her life she would cherish this special moment and the story of how the once-tattered quilt had brought them all together.

Mishawaka

After fixing himself a microwave dinner of macaroni and cheese, Blaine decided to relax in his recliner the rest of the evening. This was the night he usually watched a program about fishing.

Tonight's show featured rainbow trout and had been filmed in the Finger Lakes region of New York. Any other time, Blaine would have quickly become engrossed in a program like this, but unfortunately, all he could think about was the conversation he'd had with Lamar, concerning Sue.

Why did Sue call me like that? he wondered for the umpteenth time. *And why did she want to know about me going out with Cheryl?*

"Women," Blaine muttered as he stared at the TV. "They sure can be hard to figure out."

The phone rang, startling him out of his thoughts. Caller ID told him it was his brother Darin.

"Hello," Blaine answered, wondering what his brother wanted.

"Hey, Blaine. How ya doing?" Darin's voice sounded full of excitement. "It's been awhile since we talked. Hope things are going good for you."

"I'm doing fine. How about you?"

"I have some great news. I'm a dad!" Darin shouted.

Had nine months gone by already? Blaine wondered, holding the phone away from his ear.

"Michelle went into labor this morning, and at 4:35 this afternoon, our baby boy was born. Can you believe it? I'm officially a dad!"

"That's great, Darin. How are Michelle and the baby doing? Oh, and what'd you name your son?"

"They're both doing great. We named him Caleb Vickers, and he weighs a little under seven pounds."

Blaine listened as his brother told how great it had been to be there when the baby was born. He was happy for Darin and Michelle but felt envious. He could almost foresee the next visit when his family got together. It would most likely be at Thanksgiving or Christmas, which wasn't too far off. There would be more questions about him, of course. Had he met anyone yet? Did he ever plan to settle down and have a family of his own?

Blaine would love to have a family someday, but it didn't just happen out of the blue—although at times he wished his soul mate would suddenly appear.

Blaine listened awhile longer as his brother nearly talked his ear off. Finally Darin said he'd better hang up because he had several other calls to make.

When Blaine hung up, he grabbed the remote and clicked off the TV. *Man, my life is the pits!*

Elkhart

Carmen had been gone less than a week, but it felt much longer to Paul. He hadn't said it out loud, but he really missed her.

Why did she have to betray my trust? Paul fumed as he sat at his desk, prepared to boot up his computer. If only she hadn't come here to write a negative story about the Amish. They got enough negative press coverage—much of it exaggerated or based on untruths. The majority of Amish people were humble, hardworking, and living their lives as their ancestors had done. As was so often the case, when one of their kind did something wrong and it made the news, many people began to think that all Amish were bad.

Think I'll go online and see if I can find the story Carmen wrote for the newspaper she works for, Paul decided. *I'd like to see how damaging it was.*

After finding the Los Angeles newspaper's website, he did a search for Carmen's story. Sure enough, there it was, in the News section: "Amish Values" by Carmen Lopez.

Oh boy, here it comes. She's going to start bashing the Amish values. Paul read the story out loud: "There are many myths about rumschpringe, which is a time for Amish young people to decide whether they want to join the Amish church. Most Amish youth don't leave home during this time. Amish parents do not encourage their children to break the church rules, but to behave morally during their running-around years. Some stories about rumschpringe portray it as a time of wild parties and experimentation with drugs and alcohol. This kind of behavior is an exception rather than the norm. Some groups of Amish young people may meet in town and change into 'English' clothes. The girls may even wear makeup or try on jewelry, and Amish boys may buy a car during this time. But many own horses and buggies, which they use to court a young woman. Dating among the Amish typically involves attending Sunday night 'singings,' participating in games and activities with others their age, and having the young man visit in the young woman's home. The key purpose for rumschpringe is for Amish young people to decide if they want to join the Amish church."

Paul leaned in closer and murmured, "She got that right."

Dropping to the next paragraph, he continued to read: "Although some young people choose to separate themselves from the Amish way of life, almost ninety percent of Amish teenagers eventually choose to be baptized and join the Amish church. Those who choose to leave are not shunned unless they have already joined the church and then choose to break away. Amish communities and individual families vary in their views of the best response to offer during rumschpringe. Some parents allow certain behaviors, while others hold a tighter rein."

Paul nodded as he continued to read. "During my recent six-week stay in northeastern Indiana, I got to know several Amish people quite well and observed their customs. It's the opinion of this reporter that Amish parents do not condone wild or immoral behavior, and they do try to monitor their young people's actions. The Amish I came to know and respect put God first in their lives and have strong family values. Most of us 'Englishers,' as the Amish often refer to those who are not Amish, could learn a lot from the Amish way of life, where simplicity and a devotion to God are the foundation of their faith."

"Well, what do you know?" Feeling as though all the air had been sucked out of his lungs, Paul leaned back in his chair with a groan. He sat running his fingers through his hair, then stood and began to pace, wrestling with what he should do. He'd misjudged Carmen. She hadn't written a negative story, after all. It was quite the opposite.

Paul returned to his chair and bowed his head, asking for God's guidance in all of this. A still, small voice seemed to be saying, "Call her!"

With no hesitation, Paul reached for the phone and quickly punched in Carmen's number. He just hoped it wasn't too late and that she would accept his apology.

Chapter 39

Shipshewana

It's sure nice to have you back. How was your trip?" Lamar asked after he'd helped Emma's driver carry hers and Rachel's luggage to the house.

"It was good, but we're both exhausted," Emma said, squeezing Lamar's hand.

Rachel nodded. "It was a worthwhile trip, however."

"Two weeks is a long time to be gone from home, but I'm glad it worked out for you to spend time there and get to know your long-lost *schweschder*," Lamar said.

"I know," Emma agreed, "and what a joy it was to discover that one of my special quilting students is actually my great-niece. It's no wonder Cheryl and I felt a connection. I keep thinking if we had gone to Florida instead of staying here and holding another quilting class, I may have never met my sister Betty or discovered that I had a niece and a great-niece I knew nothing about."

"Did you connect with Cheryl's mother, as well?" Lamar asked.

Emma sighed. "Not like I did with Cheryl, but Katherine, who was equally surprised to learn that she had Amish relatives, did seem to appreciate getting to know me and Rachel, and I look forward to corresponding with her in the days ahead."

"Same here," Rachel agreed.

"And how is your sister doing?" Lamar questioned.

"Not well, but better than when we arrived in Portland," Rachel interjected. "I think our reunion gave her a lift, and we promised to keep in touch through letters and phone calls. I just hope her memory doesn't go."

"Maybe we can plan a trip there sometime," Lamar said, placing Emma's suitcase in the entryway.

"I wouldn't want to travel that far during the winter months, but if Betty's up to company in the spring, we might think about going then." Emma smiled at Lamar and then turned to Rachel. "Lamar and I are planning to spend the winter months in Sarasota, Florida."

Rachel's blue eyes brightened. "Will you be staying in Pinecraft?"

Emma nodded. "Lamar has a cousin who owns a house there, and he said we could rent it for a reasonable price."

"That will be nice," Rachel said. "Maybe I'll drop down and visit sometime during your stay."

Emma smiled. "We'd welcome that, wouldn't we, Lamar?"

He bobbed his head. "Emma and I are always open to having company."

"What will you do while you're in Florida?" Rachel questioned.

"Oh, I don't know," Emma replied. "We'll probably do some sightseeing and get to know the area and the people. We have several friends who've relocated to that area and some who go there for the winter months, so it'll be nice to visit with them as well. And of course it will be wunderbaar to spend some time on the beach, soaking up the sun and looking for shells."

"That's right," Lamar agreed, "and I'm looking forward to doing some fishing."

Rachel touched Emma's arm. "Do you think you might teach a quilting class while you're there?"

"Oh, I don't know about that," Emma said. "I'd really planned on just taking it easy all winter."

"Well, I certainly don't blame you. We all need that from time to time." Rachel yawned. "Now, if you'll excuse me, I think I need to take it easy for a spell. If you don't mind, I'm going upstairs to rest for a bit."

"No problem," Emma said. "I'd do the same if my students weren't coming over today, but I did promise them that we would all get together one last time to share how everyone's doing."

As Rachel left the room to head upstairs, a knock sounded on the door. "I'll see who it is," Lamar said as Emma took a seat. A few seconds later, he was back with Carmen at his side.

"Now this is a pleasant surprise," Emma said, smiling. "I thought you'd gone back to California."

"I did, but I came back." Carmen dropped her gaze as she shifted her weight from one foot to the other.

"If you two will excuse me, I need to go feed the goats and then check for any phone messages that may have been left this morning," Lamar said, glancing at Emma. Did he sense that Carmen wanted to speak with her alone?

Carmen waited until he left the room, and then she leaned against the table as if needing a little support. "I need to tell you something, Emma."

"Oh, what's that?"

"Before you say anything, please hear me out. I came here to take your quilting classes under false pretenses."

Emma blinked. "I'm not sure what you mean."

"I came to Indiana to do a story on the Amish—a negative story that would shed a bad light on rumschpringe."

"Oh my!" Emma clasped her hand over her mouth. "I had no idea you came here for that. Is this the reason you were asking me so many questions about our young people and their running-around years?"

Carmen nodded, her eyes filling with tears. "After getting to know you and Anna, I came to realize that things weren't as I'd thought them to be, and I just couldn't write the story the way my boss wanted me to." She paused, reached into her purse, and pulled out a newspaper. Handing it to Emma, Carmen said, "Here's the story I ended up writing, and it's the one that went to print, although my boss wasn't happy about it."

Emma repositioned her reading glasses and read the article slowly, to be sure she didn't miss anything. When she was done, she looked up at Carmen and said, "That was a nice article. You didn't show us as being perfect, but neither did you shed a bad light on us, the way some reporters have done. That's not to say that some of the things written about certain Amish people haven't been true. Unfortunately, there are bad people in all walks of life."

"Not you, though, Emma," Carmen said, touching Emma's shoulder. "You're one of the kindest, most thoughtful women I've ever met."

"Does Paul know about this article?" Emma asked, pointing to the paper.

Carmen shook her head. "He knows I planned to write it, but as the negative article my boss wanted me to compose. Paul doesn't know anything about the one I actually wrote. When he found out I was sent here to write a damaging article, he was very upset and accused me of taking advantage of you." She sniffed and swiped at the tears running down her flushed cheeks. "I'm afraid he won't let me see Sophia anymore, and I was hoping that—"

"That something might develop between you and Paul?" Emma interrupted.

Carmen nodded. "I've come to care for them both so much, and if there was anything I could do to make things right, I surely would."

"You already have."

Carmen jumped at the sound of Paul's voice. "Paul, where did you come from?" she squeaked.

"I just got here—came to see Lamar and Emma," Paul said as he strode into the room, holding Sophia's hand.

As soon as the little girl saw Carmen, she squealed and ran toward her. Carmen opened her arms and gave Sophia a hug.

Emma smiled. It was obvious the child loved Carmen as much as Carmen did her. "You know," Emma said, "I think I'll go out to the kitchen and fix some refreshments. If you'll excuse me, I'll be back soon."

"Do you need some help?" Carmen asked.

"No, I can manage. Just stay and visit with Paul, and I'll take Sophia with me." Emma took the child's hand and ushered her out of the room.

Carmen turned to Paul, and was about to say something, but he spoke first. "Carmen, before you try to explain anything, I have a few things I'd like to say."

"Go ahead, Paul."

"I've been trying to call you, but all I ever got was your voice mail."

"That's because I'm not home; I'm here," she said, feeling a bit apprehensive. Was he going to chastise her again for her betrayal? What could he say to her that he hadn't said before?

"I'm surprised you're here," Paul said. "I thought you were still in California."

"I was, but I came back so I could take care of a few matters," she replied, her defenses rising.

"Well, believe me, I'm glad you're here, because I read your article online and need to apologize for the things I said before you left for California."

Blinking, Carmen could hardly believe her ears. "I accept your apology," she said, feeling a great weight lifting off her shoulders, "but I'm really the one who needs to apologize. When I came here on this assignment, I had no idea what to expect or that I'd meet such wonderful Amish people, like Emma, Lamar, and Anna." Carmen looked into Paul's eyes. "I wasn't thinking about how all this would hurt you and Sophia. I–I care for you both." She didn't dare say how much.

"We care for you, too," he said, taking her hand. "And if I had my way, you'd stay in Indiana and forgot about California."

Carmen smiled up at him. "That's good to hear, because I've quit my job at the newspaper there and have found one at the newspaper in Goshen."

Paul's eyes widened as a genuine smile stretched across his face. "Now that is good news!"

Sophia was seated in the high chair in Emma's kitchen, happily eating a cookie with a glass of milk, so Emma decided to take the rest of the cookies into the living room to share with Carmen and Paul. She'd just stepped into the hall when she saw the young couple holding hands and looking lovingly at each other. *Better not disturb them right now,* she decided. *Think I'll give them a little more time alone.*

Emma had no more than reentered the kitchen, when Lamar came in from outside. "Look who just arrived," he said, motioning to Anna, who followed close behind.

"Oh Anna, it's good that you came today. Carmen is in the living room with Paul." Emma gestured to Sophia, sitting in the high chair. "This is Paul's little girl, Sophia."

Just as Emma said her name, Sophia looked up and gave Anna a big grin.

"She's so cute," Anna exclaimed.

Emma smiled, watching as Anna walked over to Sophia and tickled her under the chin.

"I'm going back outside," Lamar said. "I plumb forgot about checking for phone messages."

When Lamar went out the door, Emma turned to Anna and said, "How have you been?"

Anna's cheeks colored. "It's hard to explain, because I'm still confused, but I think my eyes have been opened to some things."

"Oh? What kind of things?" Emma asked.

"Lately I've been feeling like I need to get away someplace on my own. And I've had an opportunity to go to Florida with my friend Mandy in December." Anna stopped talking, as if to regroup her thoughts; then she slowly shook her head. "I thought this would be my chance to get out on my own for a bit. I wanted a taste of something different—maybe even try out the English way of life. Then two weeks ago, after our last quilting class, Mandy and I went to Goshen and we dressed in English clothes, let our hair down, and even wore some makeup. It was fun until a couple of English fellows came into the restaurant and wouldn't leave us alone."

"Did anything happen?" Emma asked with concern.

"No, thank goodness," Anna replied. "Mandy and I slipped into the restroom, washed off the makeup, and changed back into our Amish clothes. Somehow we were able to slip back out without those guys even recognizing us."

"I'm glad to hear that," Emma said, placing a comforting hand on Anna's arm.

"When I got home that evening," Anna continued, "and told my folks who I was with, Dad yelled and Mom's face turned red. They never did approve of me hanging around with Mandy, but she's my best friend. Then I got angry and blurted out to Mom and Dad that I was going to Florida, and that my mind was made up."

Emma almost knew what was coming next. It sounded all too familiar after recently hearing her sister Betty's side of the story, but she let Anna go on telling her what had happened.

"So when I said that, Dad told me if I went to Florida, I could just stay there and never come back." Anna's chin quivered, and her eyes filled with tears. "How could Dad say something like that to me?"

"I'm sure he didn't mean it, Anna. He was only speaking out of anger and concern."

Anna sighed. "Well, ever since then, Dad and I are hardly talking, and Mom is so upset she keeps begging me not to go. I'm so confused and don't know how to fix things between us. If I don't go to Florida and get some experience on my own, I don't think things will ever change for me here at home."

"I understand," Emma said, giving Anna a hug. Then she quickly told her about meeting her oldest sister for the first time, and how and why Betty had left home. She then stated, "Betty's decision to leave home, and our parents' response to it, affected everyone. If you're going to leave home and think you'll want to come back, then you should tell your parents that. In fact, I think it would be good if you tell them everything you've told me just now, Anna. And if you like, I'd be happy to speak with your Mom and Dad, too."

"Would you really do that for me?" Anna asked.

Emma nodded. "I had it in my mind to do that anyway. Since Lamar and I have decided to spend our winter in Sarasota, I'll let your parents know that we'll be there in case you need anything. That might set their minds at ease."

Anna smiled as she dried her tears. "Danki, Emma. I think that would help, and I'll look forward to seeing you in Florida."

Emma motioned to the door leading to the living room. "As I mentioned, Carmen's here, and I'm sure she'll be happy to see you, so why don't you go in and say hello?"

"Okay, I will." Anna started out of the room but turned back around. "I'm glad I talked to you, and I appreciate your concern and support." She pivoted around and hurried down the hall.

Seeing that Sophia had smudges of cookie on her face, Emma went to the sink and wet a paper towel. She'd just finished cleaning the little girl up when Lamar entered the kitchen.

"I just checked our phone messages," he said, "and there was one from Blaine."

"Oh, what'd he say?" Emma asked, lifting Sophia down from the high chair.

"Well, first he wanted to let us know that he'd become an uncle again. Seems his brother Darin and his wife, just had their first *boppli*—a little boy."

"Isn't that nice?" Emma smiled. "I'll bet Blaine is excited.

"He was and said he'd be heading up to Canada around the holidays when all his family will be together." Lamar paused before continuing. "Guess what else?"

"There's more?" Emma asked.

Lamar gave a nod. "Blaine also said that he wouldn't be able to come here today because he's meeting Sue for coffee."

Emma quirked an eyebrow. "Isn't she Blaine's ex-girlfriend?"

Lamar nodded. "Guess she wants to get back together, and at my suggestion, Blaine's giving her a second chance."

Emma tweaked her husband's nose. "Is that so? And I thought I was the only matchmaker in this family."

"Oh really? Who, might I ask, have you been trying to get together?"

Emma gestured to Sophia. "Her daed's in our living room right now, talking to Carmen."

Lamar's eyes twinkled. "Ah, I see. And I'm guessing you had something to do with that?"

"Well, I didn't set it up, if that's what you mean, but after Carmen showed up, Paul and Sophia came by. When I saw that Paul had some things he wanted to say to Carmen, I brought Sophia in here so the two of them could talk in private." Emma's voice lowered to a whisper. "I peeked in on them a few minutes ago, and they were holding hands. Anna, in fact, just went to join them. And by the way, Anna opened up to me, and we had a good talk."

Lamar grinned. "That's *gut*, jah?"

"Yes, it's very good on both accounts."

A knock sounded on the back door, and Lamar called, "Come in, it's open!"

Selma stepped in, smiling from ear to ear. "I'm not late, am I?" she asked.

"No, Carmen and Anna are here, and they're in the living room with Paul," Emma replied.

"And Blaine's not going to be able to make it," Lamar added.

"Well, there's something I want to share with you," Selma said, clasping Emma's arm. "I called my daughter last night, and we had a long talk. I apologized to Cora for the things I've said in the past that hurt her, and she said she was sorry for leaving home and not keeping in touch with me."

"Oh, that's wonderful," Emma said, giving Selma a hug. "I'm happy to hear that things are working out between you and your daughter."

"It's because of you, Emma," Selma said, tears gathering in the corners of her eyes. "You taught me more than just how to quilt. You helped me realize the importance of loving and accepting others."

Emma smiled. "I think we all learned a lot from each other during our quilting classes."

The roar of an engine drew Emma's attention to the kitchen window.

"Sounds like Terry and Cheryl are here," Lamar said with a chuckle. "I'll let them in."

When Cheryl and Terry entered the kitchen, Emma knew immediately that they had worked things out, for they wore huge smiles on their faces.

"Cheryl told me the good news," Terry said, stepping up to Emma. "Special things seem to happen when folks take your quilting classes. Jan found his daughter during one of your classes, and now Cheryl's found her great-aunt and you've found your sister." Terry, looking into Cheryl's eyes, smiled and took her hand. "I found you, and it's almost too good to be true."

Emma was surprised to see that Terry had cut his hair and was dressed in nicer clothes. He obviously wanted to make a good impression on Cheryl.

Lamar winked at Emma, and she winked right back. She knew

beyond a shadow of a doubt that this would not be the last group of would-be quilters she would teach. Whether it was here in Indiana or in Florida during the winter, she knew that God would send the right people at just the right time.

Emma's Apple-Crumb Bread

Ingredients:

½ cup butter
1 cup sugar
2 eggs
1 teaspoon baking soda dissolved in 2 tablespoons milk
2 cups flour
½ teaspoon salt
1 teaspoon vanilla
1½ cups chopped apples

Topping:

1 teaspoon cinnamon
2 tablespoons butter
4 tablespoons flour
2 tablespoons brown sugar

Preheat oven to 325 degrees. Cream together in a bowl the butter, sugar, and eggs. Add the baking soda dissolved in 2 tablespoons milk. Finally, add in the flour, salt, vanilla, and chopped apples. Pour into a 9" x 5½" greased bread pan. Combine topping ingredients and sprinkle over top of bread batter. Bake for 1 hour.

Discussion Questions

1. In this story, Anna was dissatisfied with her life and wanted to leave home to try out the "English" way of life. Why do you think some teenagers (Amish or English) are anxious to leave home and strike out on their own?

2. Due to his parents' breakup, Terry feared marriage and commitment. How can a person whose life has been affected by a breakup learn to have a meaningful relationship without fear or worry that it will happen to them?

3. After Carmen was asked to write an article that would shed a negative light on the Amish, she came to realize that things weren't quite the way she thought they were. Have you ever been asked to do something you believed would please your boss or brighten your career and then realized what you'd been asked to do was wrong? How did you handle the situation?

4. Blaine felt uncomfortable in a group setting—especially when he was expected to do something unfamiliar to him, such as quilting. Have you ever been afraid to try something new for fear of saying or doing something foolish? How can we help ourselves or someone we know get over feeling self-conscious when trying something new?

5. Selma had been holding a grudge ever since her daughter left home. This compounded her fear of rejection and lowered her self-esteem, making it difficult to develop a relationship with others. Has a fear of rejection ever kept you from reaching out to others?

6. Cheryl was an only child and felt all alone growing up due to the lack of her parents' attention. Have you ever felt that way? What are some ways we can deal with painful childhood memories or feelings of rejection from our parents?

7. Was it fate or God's intervention that kept Emma and Lamar from going to Florida too soon? Has a reverse decision ever opened a door to something unexpected in your life?

8. Carmen felt that too much of the news was based on negative events. Would you rather read about tragedies and other people's problems, or do you prefer to read about the good things people do or that happen to them? Does hearing about other people's problems make ours seem any less?

9. Lamar tried to hide from Emma the fact that his arthritis was acting up. Do you think spouses should ever keep things about their health from each other?

10. At times Emma felt like she was not getting through to her students or helping them with their personal problems. She didn't want to pry, but she hoped they would feel free to share with her so she could help mentor them as she'd done with several other people who had previously come to her home to learn to quilt. What are some ways we can minister to others without prying into their personal lives?

About the Author

New York Times bestselling author **Wanda E. Brunstetter** became fascinated with the Amish way of life when she first visited her husband's Mennonite relatives living in Pennsylvania.

Wanda and her husband, Richard, live in Washington State but take every opportunity to visit Amish settlements throughout the States, where they have many Amish friends. Wanda and her husband have two grown children and six grandchildren. In her spare time, Wanda enjoys photography, ventriloquism, gardening, beachcombing, and having fun with her family. Visit Wanda's website at www.wandabrunstetter.com, where you can learn more about her books and contact her.

Other Books by Wanda E. Brunstetter:

Adult Fiction

The Half-Stitched Amish Quilting Club

The Discovery Saga

Goodbye to Yesterday

The Silence of Winter

The Hope of Spring

The Pieces of Summer

A Revelation in Autumn

A Vow for Always

Kentucky Brothers Series

The Journey

The Healing

The Struggle

Brides of Lehigh Canal Series

Kelly's Chance

Betsy's Return

Sarah's Choice

Indiana Cousins Series

A Cousin's Promise

A Cousin's Prayer

A Cousin's Challenge

Sisters of Holmes County Series

A Sister's Secret

A Sister's Test

A Sister's Hope

Brides of Webster County Series

Going Home

Dear to Me

On Her Own

Allison's Journey

Daughters of Lancaster County Series

The Storekeeper's Daughter

The Quilter's Daughter

The Bishop's Daughter

Brides of Lancaster County Series

A Merry Heart

Looking for a Miracle

Plain and Fancy

The Hope Chest

Amish White Christmas Pie

Lydia's Charm

Love Finds a Home

Love Finds a Way

Children's Fiction

Double Trouble

What a Pair!

Bumpy Ride Ahead

Bubble Troubles

Rachel Yoder—Always Trouble Somewhere
8-Book Series

The Wisdom of Solomon

Nonfiction

Wanda E. Brunstetter's Amish Friends Cookbook

Wanda E. Brunstetter's Amish Friends Cookbook Vol. 2

The Best of Amish Friends Cookbook Collection

The Simple Life

A Celebration of the Simple Life